•❖•

The Pinocchio
of C. Collodi

The
Pinocchio
of C. Collodi

Translated and Annotated by
James T. Teahan

Illustrated by Alexa Jaffurs

Schocken Books   New York

First published by Schocken Books 1985
10 9 8 7 6 5 4 3 2 1   85 86 87 88
Copyright © 1985 by James T. Teahan
Illustrations © 1985 by Alexa Jaffurs

Library of Congress Cataloging in Publication Data
Collodi, C., 1826–1890.
The Pinocchio of C. Collodi.
Translation of: Le avventure di Pinocchio.
Summary: A wooden puppet full of tricks and mischief,
with a talent for getting into and out of trouble, wants
more than anything else to become a real boy.
1. Children's stories, Italian. [1. Fairy tales.
2. Puppets—Fiction] I. Teahan, James T. II. Title.
PZ8.C7Pi 1985   [Fic]   84–22245

Designed by Ann Gold
Manufactured in the United States of America
ISBN 0–8052–3912–X

To the man Carlo Lorenzini (1826–1890), Italian patriot, frustrated journalist, and disillusioned public servant, this work is respectfully dedicated. It is also gratefully dedicated to his alter ego, C. Collodi, Pinocchio's amiable creator who understood children and who contributed so much to the entertainment and the education of so many with so pathetically little acknowledgment by those who most profited by his genius.

Contents

Contents

Contents

Contents

Contents

*lame and is sold to a man who wants to
use his skin to make a drumhead.*

Acknowledgment

My thanks to sister-in-law Isabella Bottini, niece Carla Bottini Feré, and nephew Giovanni Bottini for allowing me to use as my studio the wine cellar of their villa in the mountains overlooking Lago Maggiore. Also, my unbounded gratitude to Carla and Gigi for so skillfully helping me to know the real Pinocchio.

· ❖ ·

Introduction

*which you should certainly read even
if you have never in your life read an
"Introduction" to anything*

A very long time ago—an evening in the late autumn of 1922,
to be more exact—a forlorn young man sat in a fumed oak
Morris chair in the living room of number three Howard Court
on Staten Island. From an upstairs room came the petulant wails
of Freddie, his fourteen-month-old nephew. In his lap sprawled
another nephew, the chubby (perhaps fat?) five-year-old Jim.

The young man was Uncle Charlie Teahan, and he had been
charged with the task of minding the children—"baby-sitting"
was of much, much later coinage—while parents attended a concert in Manhattan. I, of course, was the fat kid on Uncle
Charlie's lap, and the ululating infant in the upstairs crib was
my little brother, and the reason that I can now assert that
Mother and Father had gone to a concert that night owes to the
fact that I clearly recall Uncle Charlie's wry remark the next
day: "Jimmie and I had our own little concert right here, didn't
we Jim?"

The point of this recollection is that Uncle Charlie was required, by clamorous demand, to read to me before I went to
bed. And it shouldn't be at all difficult to guess the text of
the evening: C. Collodi's *The Adventures of Pinocchio* in
English translation. Certainly this was not to be my first
acquaintance with Collodi's marvelous puppet for, despite my
tender years, I had already known Pinocchio for at least a
year and a half, having had it read to me at bedtime, chapter
by fascinating chapter by that patient young woman, my
mother, former teacher, alumna of Potsdam Normal School,

Class of '11, now ninety-six years old with perfect recollection of the pleasant, comfortable bedtime readings in that dream which is the long ago.

The fact is, *Pinocchio* was the story most beloved of my childhood, and Mother had read it to me so often and with such old-time teacher's devotion to diction and detail that, with my five-year-old mind still unencumbered by the intellectual rubbish it would accumulate later on, I had committed the whole thing to memory long before I learned to read. This, it seems, was just enough to shake Uncle Charlie's youthful faith in himself, however briefly, as a man of the world.

In June 1917, Charles John Teahan had graduated Clarkson College of Technology with a degree in chemical engineering and the mottoed assurance that he was "A Workman That Needeth Not to be Ashamed" (2 Timothy, II: 15). Within two weeks he was a conscript private in the United States Army with strong prospects of being sent to France to battle the Hun as well as to experience the delights of that cynosure of cultural refinement, Paris. He did indeed get to France, but happily he never met the Hun. Unhappily, he never saw the City of Light either, for he was laid low by a bout of influenza in a staging camp near the miserable village of Abbeville. But there he was five years later, fully recovered from the flu and the ravages of the Great War, a dashing, urbane bachelor of twenty-seven and a rising research chemist with Du Pont, reduced to reading silly kids' bedtime stories.

Before the evening ended, though, Uncle Charlie's attitude changed. He had begun the reading listlessly and not a little smugly, but he was brought up short when I found it necessary to correct his pronunciation of my hero's name (he had managed to make it sound like "Pinotchy-oh") and even the name of old Geppetto. Then I discovered that he was actually skipping phrases—and even whole sentences—here and there, thinking to fool me. But Mother had done her job far too well for me to be fooled by a mere college graduate, and Uncle Charlie was at last so firmly set straight in the matter that he began to read *The Adventures of Pinocchio* a bit more objectively. By the time he had finished the fifth chapter, I was in deep sleep on the couch, and he went on to finish the whole book before Mother and Father got home!

Young bachelor Charlie had made the extraordinary discovery of a fact that every child over the age of four and, indeed, every literate parent of the time, already knew: *Pinocchio* is not just another condescending collection of fairy stories scribbled out for little children! It is a *novel*, a novel for children to be sure, but nonetheless a remarkably imaginative and lively novel of the "apprenticeship" genre, as thematically developed as say, the best of the Horatio Alger stories. This is the quaintly heroic tale of the generally intractable, unruly, but ultimately golden-hearted wooden puppet, that Pinocchio with whom I, together with millions of other children of the nineteen-twenties and 'thirties grew up. This is the book that was read to us at bedtime by our parents, evening after cozy evening or in practically the same serial form as was Collodi's original, and read so many times that by the time we ourselves learned to read, we knew the thing by heart.

Later on, when kids learned to read and to think consecutively, they turned once again to the familiar and fondly remembered *Adventures of Pinocchio* and, even with having to wade through the cumbersome and often obtuse idiom to which early translators resorted, they managed to read it themselves, often as I did myself, again and again. What had become a classic of Italian literature nearly a half-century before had now become an American, as well as a British, classic by adoption. C. Collodi's willful puppet had managed to become childhood's first literary hero for legions of thinking kids, and the Pinocchio tradition not only flourished throughout the childhood and adolescence of my generation, but it infected the mothers and fathers of that generation. This is far more than can be said of such simon-pure heroes of juvenility as the Rover Boys, the ubiquitous Tom Swift, or the Boy Allies—properly pronounced *Boy-Alleys* in the dialect of Staten Island youth in those days.

Of course, Tom Sawyer and Huckleberry Finn, as well as Tarzan of the Apes (*Tozznyapes*) inevitably outmatched the Italian puppet as heroes. But, for Heaven's sake, they were Americans! (Tarzan's British origins were totally ignored), and they were real flesh-and-blood guys, weren't they? And anyway, we knew old Pinocchio the puppet intimately and fondly long, long before we'd even met these others. That intimacy and fondness endured, lurking in subconscious chinks and crannies of minds inevitably turned adult. To many children of my generation, Pinocchio was as much the picaresque adventurer as Lemuel Gulliver, Tom Jones, don Quixote or, for that matter, Tom Mix. For us the little Tuscan blockhead was the very first in a long train of fictional figures who came to epitomize the frailties and the vanities, as well as the occasional traces of dignity and nobility of the human character.

I must hasten to point out here, however, that not all of my generation knew the genuine Pinocchio, for scarcely had the first English translation of Collodi's wonderful little work been introduced than it was seized by opportunists in the form of well-meaning, and sometimes self-righteous pedagogues who emasculated the story by abridgement and euphemism in their efforts to adapt it more gently to the infant Anglo-American ear and eye. Then came the hurried, inept translations. I remember at an early age skimming through one of these and finding this howler: the Italian word *carabiniere* (policeman) incredibly was confused with *carbonaio* and translated as "charcoal burner" thus making no sense at all of the several episodes in which Pinocchio was persecuted by the Carabinieri.

Finally there were the pirates, the shirtsleeves printers fancying themselves publishers who churned out scores of inferior versions of the Collodi classic. These thieves not only pirated the adapted editions but often, for the sake of scrimping economy, they further truncated and mutilated the adaptations so that what was passed off on an unsuspecting audience as genuine often bore little resemblance to the original beyond the name *Pinocchio* and the fact that the story concerned itself with an animate puppet. Meanwhile, it is sad to think that the author of *The Adventures of Pinocchio* received little or nothing for his labors in his native Italy where the story is still read to small children by fond parents or grandparents.

It is even sadder to realize that C. Collodi received absolutely nothing from any other country, including our own, for his delightful little novel which has been translated, I am told, into more than ninety foreign languages and, in America at least, so prostituted and mistreated, the while bringing profit to its abusers.

You may well ask how such injustice could be countenanced in this age of copyright sanctity. The answer is simple and starkly despicable:

Pinocchio the puppet first saw the light of day in 1881 in the Italian city of Florence in a serialized story which was published in a children's periodical. The tale of the willful marionette so caught the fancy of the Florentine adults who read the serial to their young that in 1883 it was published as a book which enjoyed a certain but uncertifiable popularity until Collodi died in 1890 at the age of sixty-four. The shameful fact is that it was not until 1886 that a uniform international copyright system to protect authors from literary piracy was provided for by the Berne (Switzerland) Convention. Even then, as *The Oxford Companion to English Literature* puts it, "Most states with any pretensions to civilization and culture became parties to the Convention, but the United States . . . did not." It is easy then to understand—arithmetically if not morally—how Collodi's rights to his own work in anything but its Italian form could be blithely and cynically dismissed.

When *The Adventures of Pinocchio* was published as a book in 1883, by the reasoning of the Berne Convention, it had already been in the public domain three years. This, of course, allowed the first English translation by Mary Alice Murray to be published with impunity in England in 1892. Meanwhile, until 1891 there was no copyright law in the United States that afforded protection to foreign authors; printers and publishers theretofore dealt with such writers by rule of conscience, of which property there seems to have been precious little in the nineteenth century when one considers the cavalier treatment of no less a literary luminary than Charles Dickens by American publishing pirates.

For that matter, even the Chace Act of 1891 provided a foreign writer cold comfort. He could indeed enjoy copyright protection in America if he submitted two copies of his work to the Library of Congress and if those copies were printed from type which had been set within the borders of the United States. By the time the Chace Act was passed poor Collodi had been in his grave a year agone. At that, even had he lived, it is highly unlikely that he could have afforded the great expense of having his original work set in type in America on the doubtful gamble that it would sell here.

Besides, it was in Italian, he was Italian at the wrong time, and what did Italians know about writing or about children anyway?

But, of all people! it was Walt Disney who was responsible for the all but total destruction of the tradition of the genuine Pinocchio! In 1940, the Walt Disney Studio reduced Collodi's *Adventures of Pinocchio* to a mere cartoon absurdity—a fact bitterly resented by every literate adult at the time—by putting the finely drawn character of the good-for-nothing, knavish puppet into a cloyingly cute cartoon creature which was less a wooden puppet than a naughty-but-nice little boy. And what they did to the subordinate characters! That extraordinary company of human and animal creatures that Collodi had so cannily and skillfully designed to convey to his readers his expression of the social and political evils of his post-revolution Italy simply vanished in Disney's hands and were replaced with the hokey stereotypes so dear to the movie cartoonist.

In the Disney version of *Pinocchio*, only eight secondary characters survive, and those not very identifiably: Geppetto, the Fairy, Talking Cricket, the Fox and Cat, the Pigeon, Lampwick, and the Coachman. These are all that remain of the original enchanting cast of nearly fifty characters which included such marvelous creatures as the puppets, Punchinello and Harlequin; the ferocious puppet-master, Fire Eater; the fierce Green Fisherman; the Snake with the Smoking Tail; the Poodle Coachman; the Gorilla Judge, the Black Rabbit Pallbearers; the grateful police dog, Alidoro; the compassionate Marmot; the Snail Housekeeper; the preachy Firefly; the Owl and Crow consulting physicians; numerous donkeys and a clutch of thieving Polecats. With the very flesh of Collodi's little *romanzo buffo* stripped away and discarded by cinematic "adapters," *Pinocchio* becomes little better than a Bugs Bunny or a Woody Woodpecker cartoon except for its exquisite artwork, its beautifully articulate animation, and its charming musical score.

Of course now I shall be accused of heresy but, I protest, wrongly so. I know only too well that Walt Disney has been a god to generations, and I know too that to virtually all of those of you who read this, he was the very Zeus, the Creator and Prime Mover of such minor Olympians as Mickey Mouse, Donald and Daisy Duck, Pluto, Dumbo, and that ineffably beautiful Snow White and her coterie of little men. But Walt Disney was dear to my generation, too. My own adolescence was frequently illuminated, and sometimes in one way and another influenced, by his wonderful animated cartoons which in my day were only an occasional treat when they were shown in movie theaters as "short subjects" that came between the newsreels and the feature pictures.

However, I must make one point of this matter quite clear: such creatures as Mickey, Donald, Daisy, Pluto, a charming cow called Clarabelle, and numerous other animal characters were the delightfully amusing products of Disney's own particular genius. In passing, I must mention that it was this genius too that, because of preposterous objections raised by that mean-spirited little moral patrolman of the 1930s, Will Hays, head vigilante of Hollywood's censorial "Hays Office," designed a chic housewife's apron to be worn by Clarabelle Cow to conceal her udder from the view of evil-minded, ogling children, at the same time making her an even more amusingly endearing character. But once these figures had become well established in the mind of his public, Disney went on to produce other feature-length films in which his pictorial skill combined with the imaginative use of story, music, and color, brought the art of cartoon animation to perfection. And these films are, for the most part, liftings and borrowings from other stories and tales as, for example, *The Sleeping Beauty, Cinderella, Snow White and the Seven Dwarfs, The Three Little Pigs, The Ugly Duckling*, and *The Brave Little Tailor*. But these are adaptations of folktales and fairy stories which had their vague origins in times long beyond recall, and which have been passed down by word of mouth, each in as many as a dozen and more versions.

Meanwhile, *The Adventures of Pinocchio* can by no means be considered a folktale or a fairy tale. Nowhere in the literature of Tuscany, much less in the literature of Italy, could I find anything upon which Collodi might have based his concept of a wooden puppet as a storybook hero. Nor could I find anywhere in the vast Italian folkloric tradition a single story, tale, or anecdote from which Collodi might have borrowed material with which to flesh out episodes of his little novel. Just as certainly as Mickey Mouse was the brainchild of Walt Disney, Pinocchio was the exclusive product of C. Collodi's genius. Collodi first invented Pinocchio, and then invented Pinocchio's world which he went on to furnish with creatures of his own imagination. Pinocchio, then, belonged to Collodi as surely as Alice belonged to Lewis Carroll, as Gulliver belonged to Jonathan Swift, or as Huck Finn belonged to Samuel Clemens.

The truth of the matter is that in his decision to adapt the story of Pinocchio to cartoon purpose, Disney made an artistic mistake. As a matter of fact, the mistake was probably made by advisors on his staff which, by 1940, had grown to prodigious size. Walt Disney, in his eagerness to find a story as appealing as *Snow White* or *Sleeping Beauty* to put on film, no doubt enthusiastically accepted the advice of his staff to take a chance on *Pinocchio*—and, of course, it paid off!

However, while it paid Disney Studios off, it also did something else; it practically destroyed Collodi's fine work. Not for us, you must understand, for Collodi's Pinocchio had long since become an indelible part of the experience of our growing up, but for you, those who came along, let us say, after the fall of 1936. By 1940, when those kids were primed and ready for entertainment of the literary sort, they were most likely taken to the kiddie's matinee at the local movie house where, most of the time, they were treated to much the same sort of cinematic pabulum that children are still fed on Saturday morning television. Of course, the high point of those movie shows was the chance showing of a Disney cartoon—any Disney cartoon—and when it was introduced by a full-screen image of Mickey or Donald emblazoned against a brilliant sunburst, the very house would come down with the explosion of applause, cheers, and screams of delight that followed.

Disney Studios had long since demonstrated absolute superiority in the production of animated cartoons. Then, when the cartoon version of *Pinocchio* was made and released, this dominion over a broadcast medium so powerful and pervasive, and so simply accessible to hundreds of thousands of persons of all ages, made it seem to unsuspecting parents to be a waste of time and effort to read the story of Pinocchio to their young when it was so much easier just to take them to a theater and let them *watch* it!

Well, this actually was true of the Disney version of *Pinocchio*, but that Disney version was anything but what Collodi had intended. It was so simplistically far from the original as to make it altogether a different story, as you are now about to discover. It was reduced, as I have already observed, to a pretentious absurdity which, despite its entertaining qualities, went on to breed the ultimate in absurdity as demonstrated by this non sequitur from the motion picture *Close Encounters of the Third Kind* (produced, incidentally, some forty years later), as a young father says to his son,

> ". . . how old are ya?"
> "I'm eight . . . ?"
> "Ya wanna be nine? Tomorra night yer gonna see *Pinocchio*. I grew up with Pinocchio . . . ya'll see Pinocchio . . . and see a lotta furry animals . . . and magic . . . and ya'll have a grand time!"

This apparently is all that C. Collodi's labor of love, the lively biography of a blockheaded puppet, has come to mean to young Americans!

Now, if you have managed to get this far, I think I should tell you a thing or two about the real creator of the real Pinocchio. To begin with the customary triviality, he was born Carlo Lorenzini on November 24, 1826 in the Italian city of Florence, capital of the province of Tuscany where the scene of *Pinocchio* is generally laid. In 1860, for reasons best known to himself, he changed his surname to Collodi, which was the name of the village near Pescia where his mother had been born. He was known ever afterwards as C. Collodi—not Carlo Collodi, mind you, but simply C. Collodi.

Carlo Lorenzini was a born revolutionary which perhaps is

redundant when describing a twenty-two-year-old Italian of the mid-nineteenth century. In any case, the year 1848 found him among the legions of hot-eyed young Tuscans who fought intermittently on the side of King Carlo of Sardinia against the stifling rule of Austria. Meanwhile, in that same year he appears to have begun his career in journalism with the establishment of a journal of political satire called *Il Lampione* (The Street-lamp). In the following year, however, good King Carlo was dealt an ignominious defeat and, with the return of the Austrian hegemony, he was forced to abdicate his throne while the general suppression of the press which inevitably followed, forced Lorenzini to abdicate his own little office and *Il Lampione* was summarily shut down. However, despite the loss of his mischievous little newspaper, a few years later he was somehow able to supplant it with what we must assume to have been a less inflammatory journal called *La Scaramuccia* (Controversy).

It seems, though, that Lorenzini's enthusiasms and his loyalties were divided. Evidently he was what our own Thomas Paine, "Penman of the American Revolution," would have described as a "summer patriot" for, as is customary still among European espousers of rebel causes, he seems to have fought only now and then, as his spirit and time-to-spare permitted, with Garibaldi's ragtag, scrape-up army of the Risorgimento, as the Italian revolution was called. Meanwhile, there are now a few Italian scholars who from instinctive but pardonable pride would have us think that the author of *The Adventures of Pinocchio* had been a hero of the revolution who, for his services as soldier and political propagandist, was rewarded handsomely by appointment to various cushy civil offices where he continued serenely to write and to bask in the warmth of his literary successes.

I had rather, however, rely more upon the lean and objective run-down of Lorenzini's career which is provided by the *Italian Encyclopedia of Science, Literature, and the Arts* published in Milan in 1930 "under the noble patronage of His Majesty [Vittorio Emmanuele III], king of Italy." I discovered a complete set of this most dependable work at Naples in the library of my venerable brother-in-law, the equally dependable Tonio Parmiciano, himself no mean painter, historian, and student of Italian Arts and Letters. It was from these two sources that I gleaned the following information:

To be sure, after the resounding success of the Risorgimento, Lorenzini returned at last to Florence in 1860 where he triumphantly, if briefly, revived *Il Lampione* and forever afterwards, as a writer at least, he went by the name of C. Collodi. He did indeed enter civil service and he did continue to write articles and essays of some political significance, but things were not at all the way popular biographers have put it.

Most usually, revolutionary campaigns, and perhaps most notably those pursued in Italy and in other Mediterranean regions, are fought in the field by hot-headed middle-class idealists and a desperate, hollow-eyed peasantry, convinced that revolution and bloodshed are the only means to deliverance from oppression and wrenching poverty. The conviction persists, as it most certainly did among Garibaldi's magnificently miserable "Thousand," *i Mille*, as his army was called, until it is discovered that victory brings deliverance and ascendancy not to them, but to an unspeakably arrogant nobility, a corrupt judiciary, and a greedy, moneyed middle-class elite who have received all the benefits for which they fought and often shed blood.

Collodi, of course, was one of the intellectual idealists who returned from the wars to resume his career in a bright new society. He was soon to discover, though, that for the most part, this new society offered him and his former comrades-in-arms little more freedom of expression or prosperity than they were afforded by the alien regime they had routed. So it was that the disillusioned young man seems to have settled finally for a thoroughly mundane career which did involve journalistic activity to one degree and another. However, his principal occupation was that of civil servant, and he appears to have been a rather subdued and generally unenthusiastic employee of the state from 1860 until 1881, first in the Commission of Theatrical Censorship, and later in the Prefecture of Florence. It was in the latter office, no doubt, that Collodi developed and nursed his abiding distrust of, and contempt for, the Carabinieri, the Italian national constabulary that he persistently mocked and caricatured in *Pinocchio*. The articles that he wrote during this period continued much in the vein of those of the old *Lampione*—petulantly critical of the prevailing social and political condition—but there was little in them of enduring interest although, between 1881 and 1892, significantly after the success of *Pinocchio*, they were collected and published in volumes which were variously entitled *Macchiette* (Caricatures), *Occhi e Nasi* (Eyes and Noses), *Storie allegre* (Cheerful Tales), and, ponderously, *Divagazione criticoumoristiche* which translates much more comfortably to "Satirical Ramblings."

It was not really until his mature years that Collodi turned to writing for children, and he began modestly in 1875 at the age of fifty by translating the famous French fairy tales of the eighteenth century French poet, Charles Perrault, whose *Contes de ma mère l'Oye* translates to something hauntingly like "Stories of My Mother the Goose." He followed this with a product of his own genius, the story called *Giannettino* (Little Johnnie), which gave impetus to a series of books which included such titles as "Little Johnnie's Travels Through Italy," "Little Johnnie's Geography," "Little Johnnie's Grammar Book," and so on. The *Giannettino* series was ostensibly written for the education of children, to be read by them or to be read *to* them by adults. They seemed also, however, to have served a somewhat sly secondary purpose, one which Collodi more nearly achieved in what was to be his unwitting tour de force, *The Adventures of Pinocchio*. That purpose was to propagate among the largest possible audience his own often extreme ideology beneath the gentle cloak of the entertaining tale.

The "Little Johnnie" books, however, while they appear to have fulfilled modest local purposes, fell far short of classical substance. But, if *Giannettino* failed to bring fame and riches to his creator, he did him another service and, ill-defined as it was, it was a most valuable service indeed, for here and there in the "Little Johnnie" books there were fleeting glimpses of a real, growing boy, not the traditional stock figure of total wickedness or of total virtue, but an urchin whose nature was more a balance of puerile meanness bordering on viciousness and, in the end, deep-seated feelings of human compassion and contrition. And whether or not Collodi had the purpose in mind when he chose to make a crude wooden puppet the titular hero of his masterwork, the choice was providential, for he was thereby rescued from the enmity and wrath of those whose prideful parental blindness was sure to have prevented their seeing the potential for wickedness in their own children, particularly in their sons.

In a very tentative way, then, Giannettino was the immediate antecedent of Pinocchio whose history first appeared as a serial in a little weekly periodical called *Giornale dei bambini*, "The Children's Newspaper," with the title *The Adventures of Pinocchio: the Story of a Puppet.* Then in 1883, *The Adventures of Pinocchio* was published in a single volume of modest size and presented to the Italian public as a children's novel—without hint of Collodi's subliminal design. It came thereafter, and deservedly, to be considered the finest work of its kind in Italian literature.

Since 1881, the adventures of old Geppetto's "marvelous marionette" with which, as he wistfully proposes to Mastro Cherry, "I could travel all over and make him perform . . ." so that ". . . this way I could earn enough money for my little bit of bread and my little glass of wine" has appeared in literally countless editions and almost from the very beginning, its reading has been required of nearly every Italian elementary school pupil.

I must point out, however, that for all the remarkable durability of *The Adventures of Pinocchio*, its author cannot, even with the advantages afforded him by the vigorous and colorful idiom of his native language, be thought of as a great writer or even, by any rigid literary measure, a *good* writer. This tale of a puppet fails even to approach the structural consistency and fluency of action of its near-contemporary *Alice's Adventures in Wonderland*, yet in its own madcap way it is no less delightfully entertaining than Carroll's more finely wrought English delirium.

As is ever the case with an author who has produced a classic, a body of criticism has developed around C. Collodi. And, as is ever the case, there is here a disparity of criticism that ranges from mature insight to sophomoric speculation. Some critical observations of *Pinocchio* are truly thoughtful and scholarly and reflect real appreciation of Collodi's attainments and failures as a writer. Others are laughable in their graduate-school-bred determination to uncover hidden meaning where no meaning is hidden, and to interpret inconsistency, ambiguity, and downright sloppy composition as depth of thought and subtlety of expression.

I have read one scholarly paper which is almost entirely devoted to one of Collodi's widely noted discrepancies: the fact that, while Pinocchio has never had any schooling, and in early chapters was demonstrated to be quite illiterate, in chapter 23 he is readily able to read the sad inscription on the Fairy's tombstone. The author of the treatise loyally refuses to believe that a writer of such stature and reputation who, if this was indeed a careless error which he had every opportunity to discover and correct later, could in good conscience allow it to stand. Thus, he concludes, there is some subtle, arcane logic behind it all.

Much the same critical attitude has been taken toward other Collodi textual inconsistencies. For example, there was the matter in chapter 5 of his referring to the "omelet" flying out the window and, later in the same chapter, referring to the same as a poached egg. And there was the instance in which Collodi forgot in later chapters that Pinocchio had not been equipped with ears at his creation, and the case in which he had old Geppetto carve his Pinocchio for the purpose of having him perform as a marionette in order to keep the old man in relative comfort, only later to turn things about so that the puppet must go to school to learn a trade by which he could support his old Daddy.

The fact that seems to be overlooked by many critics is that Collodi was *not* a writer of stature and reputation in his own time. He was a part-time journalist of hack grade, and like most hack journalists, he didn't care a rap about correcting errors after a piece had been published. He seems to have kept his editing to a comfortable minimum, and whatever polish appears upon the rhetoric of *Pinocchio* is no doubt imparted by an eloquence bred of Collodi's own enthusiasm for his subject.

Yet another overlooked fact is that *Pinocchio* first appeared as a serial in a children's weekly "newspaper" to be read by children themselves or to be read to them much as the modern "funny papers" are read to small children by their parents. Since the writing of the story was avocational to Collodi, he most surely had other matters of livelihood to occupy his mind as he struggled to bat out weekly episodes. In some instances, then, it looks as if he had been so harried and crowded by printing deadlines that he sometimes lost minor threads of his own tale and then, if they ever were recovered, he seems simply to have neglected to correct the resulting inconsistencies.

To make a successful book out of the fragmented chapters of the original *Pinocchio* should really have been as unlikely as trying to do the same thing nowadays by combining, say, a year's accumulation of weekly episodes of "Little Orphan Annie" or "Mary Worth" without special editing. But whoever it was that managed to make not only a readable children's novel, but a charming literary classic as well, out of the double-handful of the weekly chapters of the pulp *Pinocchio* performed a small editorial miracle.

At last, then, it must be realized that what most nearly established C. Collodi as an "author of stature" was not the fluent magic of his pen, or his mastery of syntax, style, and structure, but rather his liking for, and understanding of, children. He knew that children love to hear the adventures of other children recounted. And, too, he also seemed uncannily aware of the fact that a child's mind is so uncluttered by niggling details of logic and order that he doesn't really give a hoot about the kind of ambiguity and inconsistency which seems so to bother the adult critics who insist upon considering Collodi's astute nonsense from an adult point of view.

Collodi's true talent, then, lay not so much in his facility of rhetoric, but rather more in the vigor of his imagination. In addition to the stroke of genius in his selecting as his theme the painful metamorphosis from willful wooden puppet to upstanding flesh-and-blood boy, this remarkable Tuscan scribbler invented his own situations and story incident, his own imagery, and his own satirical analogies and parallels. As a matter of fact, as Tolkien was to do years afterwards with *The Hobbits*, Collodi even devised his own highly credible mythology and folklore with which to bring greater color to his charming tale.

Le avventure di Pinocchio: storia di un burattino was literally the creation and the property of C. Collodi. It owed nothing to any source but the inventive intellect of a man who despised the political institutions of his time, and who, because he happened to like kids, tried through them and their parents in a small and entertaining way to change things around for the better. If Collodi was truly a man of no great literary pretensions, it is just as well, for what was his very own seems to have been taken out of his hands to bring profit to others of his own country, and to suffer mutilation and debasement at the hands of foreign opportunists.

It was in Naples in the summer of 1980, when I was confined to the house because of a hip-fracturing accident which was for me just one more end-of-the-world, that my wife gave me a copy of *Le avventure di Pinocchio* which I had never read in Italian. It all came back! Again I loved the story and it thrilled me even more than it had in those lovingly recalled autumn evenings at number three Howard Court. It pleased me to read it again and to discover in it the same sort of humorous innuendo that I had discovered in *The Adventures of Huckleberry Finn* when I read it again at a mature age.

I decided then and there that it was time for me to set matters right with not only a new, more readable translation of *Pinocchio* which would introduce the present generation of children and their parents, and even grandparents, to the real story of which they were unknowingly cheated in 1940. I decided, too, to annotate my new translation for children so they might better understand Pinocchio's nineteenth-century Italian background. I have annotated it as well for those grownups who may be reading *Pinocchio* to their children and would like to be prepared to answer the sort of searching questions that Uncle Charlie couldn't answer.

You have been very patient to have come with me this far into the sort of thing that people generally avoid reading entirely, but I hope that after all the effort it will have been worth your while.

You grownups who are now about to have a new experience of this endearing tale of Pinocchio the puppet, read it first to yourselves for the very fun of it. Then read it aloud to the young ones for their fun, their pleasure, and their educational introduction to a delight of which you were probably deprived.

J.T. Teahan

· ❖ ·

Foreword

*First, a word to English-speaking
boys and girls about this book.*

I know it may be hard for you to believe, but the real Pinocchio is more than a hundred years old! I say the real Pinocchio, because the one that you may already know is probably the imitation Pinocchio who appears in comic books and animated cartoons.

You may be surprised to learn that Pinocchio is an Italian. In fact, he was born a wooden puppet in 1881 in the northern region of Italy called Tuscany. Over the years since that time, Pinocchio's story has thrilled and delighted countless thousands of Italian boys and girls, and it is so well loved in Italy that children even study it in school!

When your grandparents were still little, the story of Pinocchio was put into English and the book became nearly as popular among the children of England and America as it was with Italian children. It became the practice of parents to read a chapter or two of the book at bedtime to little boys and girls who hadn't yet learned to read. Then, when at last they learned to read, those same children would read the book for themselves again and again, each time finding new pleasures and delights that they had missed before.

It's sad to think, though, that about forty years ago the *real* Pinocchio was lost to American children because he was put into an animated cartoon in which he appeared to be nothing more than a naughty but very cute little boy. In this way, then, your parents were cheated. They were robbed of the chance to relive the marvelous and exciting adventures of a disobedient wooden puppet who, because he really had a heart of gold, finally turned into a real boy. Those of you who have learned to read should read the footnotes carefully as you go along in order to understand fully Pinocchio's Italian background. Then, if you feel that you are really grown up—and you will know it when you are—you should read the notes for adults as well. Then you will know all about the life and times of one of childhood's greatest heroes—Pinocchio the puppet!

For the boy or girl who cannot read yet, I hope that some grownup will read this edition of *Pinocchio* to them and will pass on to them the important information I have provided in the footnotes for children and in the notes for adults.

❖

The Pinocchio
of C. Collodi

· ❖ ·

Chapter 1

How it happened that Mastro Cherry,[1]
the carpenter, found a piece of wood that
cried and laughed like a child.*

Once upon a time there was . . .

"A *king!*" my young readers will shout.

No, boys and girls—this time you're wrong. Once upon a time there was *a piece of wood!*

Now this wasn't a really fine piece of wood, you understand, but just an ordinary log from the woodpile.

I really don't know how it happened, but it seems that one fine day this piece of wood appeared in the workshop of an old carpenter whose name was *Mastr'* Antonio, although everyone called him *Mastro* Cherry because the end of his nose was always as red and shiny as a ripe cherry.

Well, when Mastro Cherry discovered this piece of wood, he rubbed his hands together and murmured to himself, "Ah now, this little piece of wood has come along at just the right time. I'll just use it to make a leg for that little table I've been working on."

With this, he took a sharp hatchet and got ready to take the bark off the little log. But just as he was about to make the first stroke with the hatchet, he stopped short with his arm up in the air because he thought he heard a soft little voice pleading, "Please don't hit me hard!"

*Mastro: This word is pronounced MAH-stroh and in Italian it means roughly the same as "master" in English. It is generally used, though, to refer to a master of a trade, as in the case of Mastro Cherry who is a carpenter.

3

Imagine how poor old Mastro Cherry felt at this! In fright he looked all around the room to see where this little voice could be coming from, but he couldn't see anybody. He looked under his workbench—nobody! He looked into his tool closet which he always kept shut up tight—nobody! He opened the door of his shop and looked up and down the street—still nobody! Where could that little voice be coming from?

"Ah! I think I know now," laughed Mastro Cherry as he scratched his wig, "I can see that that little voice was just my imagination. I think I'll just get back to work." Then he gave the piece of wood a hard whack with the hatchet.

"Ouch! That hurt!" the same soft little voice cried out.

This time Mastro Cherry was really shocked! His eyes bulged from his head with fright, and his mouth stood wide open, and his tongue hung out to his chin so his face looked just like the ugly face carved on the village fountain.*

Finally, after he managed to get his tongue back in his mouth,

*. . . the ugly face carved on the village fountain: Every village in Italy has a public water fountain in its *piazza* (pee-AH-tsa), or town square, where the villagers can draw water for use in their houses. The water is generally piped from a mountain spring and is allowed to pour freely from the tap of a stone fountain which is often carved in the form of a very ugly man's face with its tongue sticking far out. The water pours from the mouth with the long stone tongue serving as a spout. Most of the grotesque fountain faces date back to early Roman times when they were intended to represent the god which was supposed to frighten evil spirits away.

4

stammering and trembling, he said aloud, "But where the devil does that little voice come from? There certainly can't be anyone else in this place! Is it possible that this piece of wood has learned to whimper and cry like a baby? I just can't believe it! Here is this log—this chunk of firewood just like any other. You throw it on the fire and it'll make just enough heat to cook a pot of spaghetti. What could it be then? Could anybody be hiding inside it?[2] If there is, I'll take care of him right now!" and he seized that miserable piece of wood with both hands and began to beat it against the walls of the shop with all his might.

Then he stopped to see if he could still hear that little voice complaining. He waited two minutes and heard nothing. Five minutes—nothing. Ten minutes—still nothing!

"I see," he said to himself as he again ruffled his wig and forced himself to laugh. "I can see now that I only imagined that little voice that said 'Ouch!' All right, then, let's get back to work." But he was still very frightened, and he tried to keep his courage up by singing softly to himself.

Meanwhile, he set the hatchet aside and took up his carpenter's plane and began to plane and smooth off the piece of wood. This time, as he began to move the plane gently back and forth, he heard that same little voice saying with a giggle, "Oh-h, please stop! You're tickling me all over!"

This time poor old Mastro Cherry fell down as if he had been struck by lightning. When he finally opened his eyes, he found himself sitting on the floor. His face was completely changed, and even the tip of his nose, which was almost always bright red, had turned blue from fright.

· ❖ ·

Chapter 2

*Mastro Cherry presents the strange piece of wood
to his friend Mastro Geppetto¹ who wants to use it to
make a marvelous puppet that will be able to dance,
fence with a sword, and turn somersaults.*

Just then, someone knocked at the door.

"Come in," said Mastro Cherry who was still stretched out on
the floor.

The door opened and in walked a sprightly little old man
wearing a worn-out frock coat* and a bright yellow wig. This
old man was called Mastro Geppetto,† but all the boys in his
neighborhood, when they wanted to tease him, called him Mastro *Polendina*‡ because his wig looked so very much like a yellow
corn pudding. Mastro Geppetto was a very sensitive old man
and, when someone called him Polendina,² it made him very
angry. In an instant, he would turn into a ferocious animal that
nothing could hold back.

"Good morning, Mastr' Antonio," said Geppetto very sweetly. "Whatever are you doing lying there on the floor?"

"What does it look like? I'm teaching the alphabet to the ants!"

"*Bravo! bravissimo!*"** cried Geppetto, "Good for you!"

"Well, what brings you here at this time of day?" asked
Mastro Cherry.

*. . . *frock coat:* a dress coat with long, pointed skirts which was
worn by gentlemen in the 1800s.

†*Geppetto:* In the region of Tuscany, in northern Italy, where the
story of Pinocchio takes place, Geppetto (Jeh-PET-toh) is the nickname
for the name Giuseppe (Ju-SEP-peh) or Joseph. In English, then, Geppetto might be called "Little Joe," or even "Joey."

‡*Polendina:* This is the Tuscan word for the Italian *polenta*, which is
a delicious pudding made of yellow Indian corn meal and usually
served with tomato sauce and sometimes with grilled sausages on the
side. It is a favorite dish of the people of Tuscany, and if you'd like to
try it, I have given your mother the recipe for it in the notes.

***Bravo! bravissimo!:* Pronounce these words BRAH-voh! brah-
VEES-see-moh! When an Italian shouts *"Bravo!"* at a performer, for

"My own two legs! But, to tell you the truth, I have come to ask a favor of you."

"Well then, ask it! I'm ready to help you," said the old carpenter as he got to his knees.

---

example, a singer or an actor, he is letting him know that he has liked his performance. In English then, in this case, "Bravo!" means "Well done!" "Great job!" or, as Geppetto jokingly tells Mastro Cherry here, "Good for you!"

The -issimo ending on bravo gives the word a stronger meaning so that Bravissimo! might mean "Beautifully done!" or "Marvelous job!" What Geppetto says would simply be translated as "Good for you! *very* good for you!"

"This morning I had a wonderful idea," said Geppetto.

"Well, tell me all about it."

"I got to thinking," said Geppetto, "that I'd like to make myself a beautiful wooden puppet. Not just an ordinary puppet, you understand, but a marvelous one that could dance, fence with a little wooden sword, and turn somersaults in the air. Then, with this marvelous marionette, I could travel all over and make him perform for people.[3] This way I could earn enough money for my little bit of bread and my little glass of wine. What do you think about that?"

"*Eh, bravo* Polendina!" cried the same little voice that had been teasing Mastro Cherry.

Hearing himself called Polendina, Geppetto turned red as a chili pepper and, turning to the old carpenter, he said furiously, "Why do you insult me like that?"

"Who insulted you?"

"You did! You called me Polendina!"

"Not me!"

"I suppose, then, you'll say *I* said it! Well, I say *you* said it!"

"No, I didn't!"

"Yes, you did!"

"I didn't!"

"You did!"

"Didn't!"

"Did!"

Then, becoming angrier and angrier they went from words to blows and they fought, and they scratched, and they bit, and they mauled each other until, finally, when the fight ended, Mastro Cherry found old Geppetto's yellow wig clutched in his hands, and Geppetto found the carpenter's wig clenched firmly between his own teeth.

"All right," said Cherry, "give me back my wig."

"And you give me back mine and we can be friends again."

Then the two old men, after they exchanged wigs, shook hands and swore to remain good friends for the rest of their lives.

"Well now, old friend," said the carpenter, "what's the favor you want of me?"

"Well, I just need a piece of wood to make my puppet. Will you give it to me?"

When he heard this, Cherry had a wonderful thought! He went over to his workbench and picked up the piece of wood that had given him so much trouble. This would be his chance to get rid of it! But when he turned to give it to Geppetto, that wicked piece of wood, with a violent jerk, leaped out of the old carpenter's hands and banged with terrible force against poor Geppetto's dry old shins.

"Hey!" shouted the old man, "is this the way you make gifts? You've crippled me!"

"I swear I didn't do that!"

"I suppose then, you'll say *I* did it!"

"No, it was this piece of wood that did it. . . ."

"I *know* it was the piece of wood that hit me, but it was *you* who threw it at me!"

"You're a liar!"

"Geppetto! Don't insult me like that or I'll call you Polendina!"

"You donkey,* you!"

*. . . *donkey:* To call a person a "donkey" has always been an insult, it seems, in the language of every country that knows the tough little animal. The suggestion is that the person being so insulted is stupid or stubbornly dull-witted.

The fact is that the ass, or donkey, as we generally call him, while he is often stubborn, is anything but stupid and has been used for centuries as a work animal. It is believed that the domesticated donkey was known in Mesopotamia and Egypt as long ago as 4,000 years before Christ, and it is still used as a work animal in southern Europe, Africa, Asia, and in our own hemisphere in South and Central America, Mexico and even in the American Southwest.

The donkey is an incredibly sturdy and sure-footed little beast of burden. He has what most people consider a pretty face with large, beautiful brown eyes rimmed with black which give him a thoughtful, rather sad look. It may be the donkey's great long ears that make him look foolish to some, but he is quite intelligent, generally very patient, and when he is being stubborn, it is probably because he thinks what he is being asked to do by a human being is pretty dumb.

"Polendina!"

"Jackass!"

"Polendina!"

"Ugly baboon!"

"POLENDINA!"

When he heard himself called Polendina for the third time, Geppetto became blind with rage, and the two old men went at each other again, tooth and nail.

When this battle ended, Mastro Cherry found himself with two more scratches on his nose, and Mastro Geppetto with two fewer buttons on his frock coat. Then, the two shook hands again and swore to remain good friends for the rest of their lives. With this, Geppetto thanked Mastro Cherry and went limping off to his house carrying his fine new piece of wood under his arm.

Chapter 3

*Geppetto returns home and begins at once
to carve a puppet which he names Pinocchio.*
He also suffers the first pranks played by
the naughty puppet.*

Geppetto's home was actually just a little ground-floor room
which received its light only through a little window underneath
a staircase. His furniture could not have been simpler: There
was one broken chair, a miserable little bed, and a rickety old
table. At one end of the room there was a nice little fireplace
with a cheery fire blazing in it. But, if you looked real close, you
could see that the fireplace and the fire were really only painted
on the wall!† Over the painted fire there hung a painted pot that
seemed to be boiling merrily, sending up a cloud of steam that
really looked like steam.

As soon as he reached home, Geppetto took out his tools and
began to carve his puppet.

"Let's see, now—what name shall I give him?" he asked himself. "I know, I'll call him Pinocchio. That name should bring
him good luck—I once knew a whole family of that name. There
was Pinocchio the father, Pinocchia the mother, and Pinocchi‡

**Pinocchio:* This is what Italians call the seed of the pine tree.
Literally, it means "eye of the pine."

†*. . . the fireplace and the fire were really only painted on the wall:*
In northern Italy it used to be a common practice to paint on the walls
of a peasant cottage a picture of a blazing fireplace with a boiling pot
hanging over the painted fire. It was not unusual to see shuttered
windows and cupboards painted on walls simply as decorations.

‡*. . . Pinocchia . . . Pinocchi:* Actually there are no such words or
names in Italian. The "o" ending of an Italian noun usually means that
it is masculine gender; usually a noun ending with "a" means that it is
feminine gender. When a noun ends with "i," it usually means that it
is plural in number. Mister Collodi has jokingly changed the word
Pinocchio to *Pinocchia* to suggest the name of a woman, and to *Pinocchi* to suggest the plural, or several, children.

the children, and they all did very well indeed! And the richest one of them all was a beggar!"

After he decided to call his puppet Pinocchio, Geppetto began to work on him in earnest. He quickly fashioned his hair, his forehead, and then his eyes—his *eyes!* Imagine Geppetto's astonishment when he discovered that his puppet's eyes, which he had just finished carving, rolled around in his head wildly and then began to stare at him brazenly. When the old man found himself being stared at by those strange wooden eyes, he was offended, and he said in an angry voice, "You wicked eyes!*[1] Why do you stare at me like that?"

Of course, there was no answer.

Then, when he had finished the puppet's eyes, he made the nose. But that awful nose! No sooner had he fashioned it than it began to grow![†] It grew, and grew, and grew until, in a few minutes it had become such a huge nose that it never seemed to end! Poor Geppetto wore himself out trying to trim the nose to a proper size, but the more he carved, the longer it grew.

Finally, however, he was able to finish the nose and he began to work on the mouth. But even before he could finish the mouth, it began to laugh foolishly and to make fun of the old

*. . . *wicked eyes:* We know now that eyes are simply eyes and serve the purpose of letting our brains know what we see. For centuries, though, and perhaps since the beginning of time, people have believed that a person's real character could be read in his eyes. Thus we hear people say such things as "He has such shifty eyes, he must be a crook," or "She has such gentle eyes, she must be a very loving person," when what they are really seeing is only what they want to see in those eyes.

†. . . *that awful nose . . . began to grow:* Mister Collodi was really fascinated by the idea of growing noses. Here he has Pinocchio's nose growing long just to annoy poor *Mastro* Geppetto. In this same chapter, his long nose makes a fine handle for a policeman to seize, and in chapter 5 we find his nose growing longer because of hunger, while in chapter 17, because he is telling lies, his nose grows so big he can't get out of his bedroom.

man. "All right now, stop that laughing!" shouted Geppetto, but he might just as well have shouted at the wall.

"Stop that laughing!" he roared again in a threatening voice. At this, the mouth stopped laughing. Instead, it stuck out its tongue as far as it could go. This time, Geppetto wanted to get on with his work, so he pretended not to notice the tongue sticking out. He just went on working.

After he finished the puppet's mouth, he made the chin, then the neck, the shoulders, the belly, the arms, and the hands. When he finished the hands, Geppetto turned away for a moment only to feel his wig snatched from his bald head. When he turned back, what do you suppose he saw? He saw his yellow wig clutched in the puppet's new hands.

"Pinocchio! Give me back my wig this instant!"

But Pinocchio, instead of giving the wig back to Geppetto, mockingly put it on his own wooden head. It covered not only his head but his face as well so that he was nearly smothered by it. At this naughty behavior, Geppetto became terribly sad and downhearted and, turning to the puppet, he said, "You naughty boy! You're not even finished, and already you're showing disrespect for your old father! That's a very bad sign, my boy! Very bad, indeed!" And with this, he wiped away a tear.

Nevertheless, Geppetto went back to work to finish the legs and feet of the puppet. But, no sooner had he finished making the feet, than he received a hard kick right on the end of his nose.

"I really deserved that!" he said to himself. "I should have thought of it sooner, but now it's too late to do anything about it." Then, taking the puppet under its arms, he set it on the floor to teach it how to walk. As you can well imagine, Pinocchio's legs were quite stiff and he didn't know how to move them, but Geppetto took him by the hand and taught him how to place one foot before the other.

When his legs finally loosened up, Pinocchio began to walk by himself and began to run around the room. Then, making his way to the front door of the house, he leaped into the street and ran away. Poor old Geppetto ran after him as fast as he could but he couldn't catch him because that rascal Pinocchio leaped

ahead of him like a rabbit and the sound of his wooden feet on the pavement was like the sound of twenty pairs of wooden shoes clattering down the street.*

*. . . *wooden shoes clattering down the street:* When wooden shoes are mentioned, most young people think immediately of Holland and cute blond boys and girls dancing Dutch folk dances in their wooden shoes. You should know, though, that the wooden shoe was—and in some places, still is—worn by peasants all over Europe. You can imagine then what a loud noise twenty young Tuscans would make with their wooden shoes as they ran down a stone-paved village street.

"Stop him! Stop him!" cried Geppetto. But the people in the street, seeing a wooden puppet that ran like a racehorse, stopped dead in their tracks in astonishment, and laughed, and laughed, and laughed. At last, a big *carabiniere** appeared on the scene.[2] Thinking from the noise that a wild young colt had escaped from its owner, he planted himself bravely in the middle of the street with his legs spread wide apart to stop the runaway. Meanwhile, Pinocchio, still some distance away, saw the carabiniere blocking the street and tried to surprise him by running between his legs. But it was no use.

The carabiniere, without moving so much as an inch, seized the puppet neatly by the nose (it was that enormous nose of his, of course, which seemed to have been especially designed to be seized by policemen) and then he turned him over to Geppetto. To punish Pinocchio, the old man tried to pull his ears. But imagine how he felt when he couldn't find any because, in his hurry to finish the puppet, he completely forgot to make his ears![†]

Geppetto then seized him by the neck and began to lead him away, saying with a threatening shake of his head, "Let's go! I'll take care of you when we get home!" When Pinocchio heard this threat, he threw himself on the ground and wouldn't take another step. Meanwhile, a crowd of curious loafers began to gather in a circle around them. Some said one thing, others said another.

carabiniere (carah-bean-YAIR-eh): This is what a policeman is called in Italy. Originally, a carabiniere was a soldier on horseback who carried a short rifle called a *carabina* (in English, "carbine").

†*. . . forgot to make his ears:* This is not going to matter to you as much as it seems to matter to grownups, but when *Pinocchio* was first written, it was published as a serial in a weekly children's newspaper (*il Giornale dei bambini*) so that Mister Collodi seems to have written only one or two chapters each week and sometimes it looks as if he forgot little details such as Pinocchio's ears. In a later chapter we find a reference to his ears growing as long as a donkey's ears, and in the same chapter the author explains that puppets "from the time they are born, have tiny little ears—in fact, they are so tiny that you can't even see them." But what of it? It's a wonderful story that was written for you and not for picky grownups.

"Poor puppet!" said one of them, "He has good reason not to want to go home! Who knows how that mean old Geppetto may beat him!" To which some of the others added maliciously, "Sure! That Geppetto seems like a kind old man, but he's a regular tyrant with boys! If that poor puppet is left in his hands, he'll probably tear him to pieces!"

Finally, after hearing everything the crowd had to say, the big carabiniere set Pinocchio free and took poor old Geppetto off to prison.[3] The poor old man, who couldn't find words to defend himself, could only cry like a little calf, and as he was being locked in jail, he sobbed brokenly, "That miserable boy—! and to think that I worked so hard to make him a well-behaved puppet! But it serves me right—I should have thought of it before!"

What happened afterwards is a story that's very hard to believe, but I'll tell you all about it in the next chapter.[4]

· ❖ ·

Chapter 4

The story of Pinocchio and Talking Cricket[1]
from which we discover that naughty boys can't
stand to be corrected by those who know
more than they do.

Well then, boys and girls, I can tell you that while poor innocent Geppetto was being taken to prison, that rascal Pinocchio, finding himself free from the clutches of the policeman, took to his heels across the fields to return home as fast as he could run. And in his mad rush, he leaped over hillocks, over big bramble bushes, and across wide ditches full of water just as if he had been a rabbit or a wild goat chased by a hunter.

When he arrived at the house, he found the front door standing ajar. He pushed it open and went in. As soon as he bolted the door behind him, he threw himself on the floor where he sat sighing with contentment. But that feeling didn't last long, for soon he heard a little voice crying from somewhere in the room, "*crì-crì-crì!*"*[2]

"Who's that?" asked the frightened Pinocchio.

"It's me!"

Pinocchio turned around and saw a huge cricket crawling slowly up the wall. "Who are you?" he asked.

"My name is Talking Cricket, and I have lived in this room for more than a hundred years.

"Well, this room belongs to me now," said the puppet, "and if you'd like to do me a real favor, just go away and don't come back."

"I'm not going to leave here," replied Talking Cricket, "until I've told you a great truth."

"Well, tell me then—and be quick about it."

"There is only unhappiness in store for boys who turn against their parents and who run away from home. They will never come to any good in the world and, sooner or later, they will be bitterly sorry."

"Sing on as much as you like, Talking Cricket. I know that tomorrow morning at sunrise, I'll leave here, because if I stay I'll suffer the same fate as all other boys: I'll be sent to school and made to study whether I like it or not. As far as I'm concerned, I can tell you right now that I have no wish to learn anything. It's much more fun to chase butterflies and to climb trees and take little birds from their nests."[†]

"You poor little blockhead! Don't you know that if you lead a life like that you'll never be anything more than just a stupid donkey with everyone making fun of you?"

"Aw, keep still, you silly old cricket!"

---

crì-crì-crì: I really don't know how to write the sound that American or British crickets make. Anyway, this is the sound that Italian crickets make.

[†]*fun to . . . take little birds from their nests:* You will probably think this a cruel kind of fun because, since Pinocchio's time, we have been taught to respect nature and not to harm baby animals or birds or to steal eggs from birds' nests. However, country boys all over the world still do such things for sport.

But Talking Cricket, who by nature was very patient and understanding, instead of becoming angry at this sauciness, went on in the same even tone of voice ". . . and if you don't want to go to school, why don't you learn a trade? Then, at least, you'll be able to earn an honest living."

"Do you really want me to tell you why?" replied Pinocchio who was beginning to lose patience. "Of all the occupations of the world, there is only one that I care anything about."

"And what occupation might that be?"

"That of eating, drinking, sleeping, enjoying myself, and leading a lazy life from morning till night."

"As a rule," Talking Cricket went on in the same calm way, "whoever follows this kind of 'trade' ends up in a hospital or in jail."

"Be careful cricket! If I really get mad it'll be too bad for you!"

"Poor Pinocchio! I really feel sorry for you!"

"Why do you feel sorry for me?"

"Because you're only a puppet and, worse than that, because you have only a wooden head."

At these last words, Pinocchio jumped up in anger and, seizing a wooden mallet from the workbench, he threw it at Talking Cricket. Perhaps he didn't really mean to hit him but, unfortunately, the mallet struck him directly on the head and the poor cricket had hardly breath enough to say "crì-crì-crì!" After that, he remained dried up and flattened against the wall.*3

*. . . he remained dried up and flattened against the wall: Not to worry! Talking Cricket will be back, and in a way that will surprise you.

·❖·

Chapter 5

*Pinocchio is hungry and looks for an egg to
make an omelet. However, just at the most interesting
moment, the omelet flies out the window.*[1]*

Meanwhile, night was coming on, and Pinocchio, remembering
that he had eaten nothing, felt a rumbling in his stomach which
seemed very much like appetite. And the appetite of a boy grows
quickly. In fact, after a few minutes, his appetite became hunger,
and from raging hunger it became the hunger of a wolf, a
hunger that cut through him like a knife.

The poor puppet ran to the fireplace where he saw a pot
boiling. He was just going to take the lid off the pot to see what
was cooking in it when he discovered that the pot was only
painted on the wall. Imagine how he felt. His nose, which was
already a long one, became even longer by at least three inches.[2]

He raced about the room, rummaging in every possible hiding
place, looking for some little thing to eat, even if it was only a
bit of dry bread, a crust, an old bone left by a dog, a piece of
moldy corn pudding, a fishbone, a cherry stone—in fact, anything he could gnaw on. But he found nothing, . . . nothing,
. . . absolutely *nothing!*

Meanwhile, his hunger grew and grew, and poor Pinocchio
could only yawn for relief,[†] and his yawns became so big that
the corners of his mouth almost reached his ears. And after he
stopped yawning, he sputtered, and finally he felt as if his stomach had gone away and left him.

---

*. . . *the omelet flies out the window:* In the story, the "omelet"
that Mister Collodi refers to here is really a poached egg as you will
see. I mentioned this to the grownups in their notes and I was going to
let the matter rest, but then I figured that some smart aleck would
notice the mistake and make a big thing of it.

†. . . *could only yawn:* "To yawn from hunger" (*sbadigliare dal
fame*) is truly an Italian saying, and we don't seem to have anything
like it in English. It's a pretty good description of being hungry,
though. If you like it, use it on your parents.

At last, he began to weep, and in desperation he said to himself, "Talking Cricket was right! I was wrong to turn against my Daddy and run away from home! If my Daddy was only here, I wouldn't be dying of hunger! Oh, what a terrible disease hunger is!"

Suddenly, he thought he saw something in a pile of trash, something round and white that looked very much like an egg. The joy that he felt is really impossible to describe—it can only be imagined. Almost believing that it was a dream, he turned the egg over and over in his hands, petting it and kissing it and saying, "And now that I've found it, how shall I cook it? Shall I make an omelet out of it? No, it'd be better if I poached it. Or wouldn't it be even tastier if I fried it? Or instead, should I just drink it?* No, the best thing is to poach it—I'm in such a hurry to eat it!"

*Or, instead, should I just drink it: It is a common practice in Italy to eat hens' eggs raw by breaking a hole in both ends of the shell and sucking the egg out. An egg eaten like this is called *uovo da bere*, "an egg for drinking."

To poach the egg, he placed a small pan on a brazier* full of burning charcoal and, instead of using olive oil or butter, he poured a little water into the pan. Then, when the water began to boil—*crack!*—he broke the egg over the water. But neither the yolk nor the white of the egg appeared. Instead, a cheerful little yellow chick popped out of the shell and, making a polite bow, said to the puppet, "Thank you so much, Mastro Pinocchio, for saving me the trouble of breaking the shell open. Well, so long—take care of yourself and give my best regards to everyone at home." With this, the chick spread its little wings and, darting through the open window, flew off until it was completely out of sight.

The poor puppet stood there as if enchanted, his eyes staring, and his mouth wide open, and with the eggshell still clutched in his hand.

Finally, recovering from his first shock, he began to weep, then to howl, and then to stamp his feet in despair. Between sobs he said, "Talking Cricket was so right! If I hadn't run away from home, and if my Daddy was here, I wouldn't be dying of hunger now. Oh, what a terrible disease this hunger is!"

Then as his stomach went on rumbling worse than before, and not knowing how to keep it quiet, he decided to leave his house and to comb the neighborhood with the hope that some kind person would give him a crust of bread.

• ❖ •

Chapter 6

Pinocchio falls asleep with his feet
resting on the brazier and wakes up the next
morning with his feet burned off.

It was a stormy winter's night. With great claps of thunder, the lightning flashed as if the sky were on fire. A cold and biting

*a brazier: This is a metal pan on legs for holding burning charcoal. The brazier was used in Italian peasant cottages for cooking and for providing heat in the wintertime.

wind whistled fiercely, driving before it a great cloud of dust and making the trees creak and groan all over the countryside. Although Pinocchio was terribly afraid of thunder and lightning, his hunger was even stronger than his fear. Leaping out the door of the little house, he made a dash for the village which he reached in less than a hundred bounds, his tongue hanging out, and panting for breath like a dog after a rabbit. But he found everything dark and deserted. The shops were closed, the doors of the houses were locked, and in the street not so much as a stray dog appeared. It was like the land of the dead. Nevertheless, Pinocchio, mad with hunger, seized the bell-pull* of a

*Pinocchio . . . seized the bell-pull: Nowadays, to ring a doorbell, we push a little button which is really an electric switch. In old-fashioned houses, doorbells were not electric; instead, a "bell-pull" was fitted into the door frame. It looked much like a doorknob. This pull was attached to a chain which ran inside the house where it was con-

house and began to ring the bell with all his might, saying to himself, "That certainly ought to bring somebody."

As a matter of fact, it did bring somebody. A little old man with a nightcap on his head appeared at an upper window and shouted down angrily, "What do you want here at this time of the night?"

"Would you be so kind as to give me a little piece of bread?"

"Just wait there—I'll be right back," the old man replied, thinking that here was one of those young scamps who amuse themselves at night by ringing doorbells* to disturb respectable folk who are sleeping peacefully.

After a moment, the window opened again and the little old man called down to Pinocchio, "Stand under the window and hold out your cap."

Pinocchio, who still had no cap,[1] nevertheless stepped under the window as he was told, but, at that moment, the old man emptied a huge basin of water on him which drenched him from head to foot as if he had been a pot of withered geraniums. He

---

nected to a bell mounted on a big spring. When a person pulled this knob it would cause the bell to jangle loudly enough to awaken the whole house.

*. . . *young scamps. . . ringing doorbells:* Yes, they did it in those days, too—all over the world. When I was a kid, this was a silly trick we'd play on grownups on Hallowe'en. Nowadays, though, the custom seems to have died out and it's probably just as well.

24

went back home like a wet chicken, tired and weak from hunger. Because he was too weak to stand up, he sat on a chair and rested his wet, muddy feet on the edge of the brazier which was still full of hot burning coals. Then he fell asleep, but, as you might know, while he slept, his wooden feet caught fire. Then, little by little, they burned away until nothing was left of them but ashes. Even so, Pinocchio went on sleeping and snoring as if his feet really belonged to somebody else. At last, toward daybreak, he awoke because someone was knocking at the door. "Who's there?" he asked, yawning and rubbing his eyes.

"It's me," a voice answered.

And that voice was the voice of old Mastro Geppetto.

·❖·

Chapter 7

Mastro Geppetto returns home
and gives the puppet the breakfast
that he had bought for himself.

Poor Pinocchio, his eyes still half-closed with sleep, didn't even notice that his feet were burned off, but, hearing his father's voice, he slipped off the chair to run and open the door. However, after stumbling two or three times, he fell full length on the floor, and the noise he made falling sounded like a sackful of wooden spoons cascading from a fifth-story window.[1]

"Open the door!" Geppetto shouted from the street.

"But I can't," answered the puppet, weeping and rolling about on the floor.

"Why can't you?"

"Because my feet have been eaten up!"

"And who ate them?"

"The cat,"[2] said Pinocchio, seeing a cat amusing itself by making some wood-shavings dance about with its paws.

"Open up, I say!" called Geppetto. "If you don't, when I get into the house I'll give you the cat!"*

"Oh, please believe me . . . I can't stand up! Oh dear! I'll just have to walk on my knees for the rest of my life!"

Geppetto, thinking that all this weeping and wailing was just another one of the puppet's naughty tricks, decided once and for all to put an end to it. Climbing up the wall, he entered the house through the window. At first he was ready only to shout and scold, but when he saw Pinocchio stretched out on the floor with his feet burned off, he was moved to pity. He took him in his arms and began to kiss him and caress him, and then, with great tears running down his cheeks, he said sobbing, "My poor little Pinocchio! How ever did you burn your feet off?"

---

*. . . *the cat:* Mastro Geppetto is referring here to the "cat o' nine tails," a cruel whip made of nine braided strands of leather fastened to a short wooden handle and used to punish criminals and sometimes very naughty children.

"I don't know, Daddy, but believe me when I say that it has been an awful night that I'll remember as long as I live. It thundered and lightened, and I was terribly hungry, and then Talking Cricket said to me, 'It serves you right. You've been naughty, and you deserve it,' and then I said to him, 'Be careful, cricket!' and then he said to me, 'You're only a puppet with a wooden head,' and then I threw a mallet at him and he died, but it was his own fault because I didn't really mean to kill him, and the proof of it is that I put a pan on the charcoal in the brazier, but the little yellow chick flew out saying, 'So long—my best regards to everyone at home,' and then the hunger kept growing, and for that reason the little old man in the nightcap opened his window and said to me, 'Stand down there and hold out your cap,' and then he poured a basin of water on my head . . . to ask for a little bread isn't shameful, is it? . . . and then I came back home and then because I was still starved, I rested my feet on the brazier to dry them off, and then you came back, and then I saw they were burned off, and I'm not only still hungry, but I don't have any feet anymore, *Ih! Ih! Ih! Ih!*"* and poor Pinocchio began to sob and bellow so loudly that he could be heard five miles away.

Geppetto understood only one thing from this whole confusing story, and that was that the puppet felt that he was dying of hunger. He took three pears out of his pocket and gave them to the puppet saying, "I got these three pears for my own breakfast, but I'll gladly give them to you. Eat them, they'll do you good."

"If you expect me to eat them, you'll have to peel them for me."

"Peel them?" the astonished Geppetto replied. "I would never have believed, my boy, that you had such a delicate and refined appetite. That's too bad! In this world we should get used to eating everything because we never know what may become of us. There are so many dangers!"

"You're probably right," said Pinocchio, "but I will never eat fruit that hasn't been peeled. I can't bear to eat fruit rind." With

Ih! Ih! Ih! Ih!: For some reason that I can't explain, unhappy Italian children make this very sound when they are sobbing.

this, good old Geppetto took out a knife and patiently peeled the three pears and placed the rind on a corner of the table. After Pinocchio had eaten the first pear in two gulps, he was about to throw away the core, but Geppetto caught his arm and said to him, "Don't throw that away. Everything in this world can be of some use."

"But I'll never eat a core!" shouted the puppet, turning on him like a snake ready to strike.

"Who knows!" said Geppetto without losing his temper, "There are so many things that can happen!" Having said this, instead of throwing the three cores away, he placed them on the corner of the table together with the three rinds.

After having devoured the three pears, Pinocchio gave a great yawn* and said in a whining voice, "I'm still hungry!"

*Pinocchio gave a great yawn: Notice that Pinocchio is "yawning from hunger" (sbadigliando dal fame) here again just as he did in chapter 5.

"But, my dear boy, I have nothing more to give you."

"Really nothing? Nothing at all?"

"I have only the rind and the cores of the three pears."

"Well, all right," said Pinocchio, "if there's nothing else, I'll eat a rind."*

He began to chew. At first he made a wry face, but then, one after another, the rinds disappeared in a matter of moments. Then, after the rinds he also ate the cores, and when he had finished eating everything, he patted his stomach and said happily, "Now I feel better!"

"You see, then, don't you," Geppetto observed, "I was right when I told you that we mustn't get used to being too particular and too delicate in our tastes? Ah, my dear boy, one never knows what may happen in this world—there are so many dangers . . . !"

· ❖ ·

Chapter 8

Geppetto makes new feet
for Pinocchio, and sells his own coat
to buy him a schoolbook.

No sooner was the puppet's hunger relieved than he began to whine and grumble because he wanted a new pair of feet. But Geppetto, to punish him for his naughtiness, let him cry and whimper for half the day. Then he said to him, "Why should I make you new feet? Just so you can run away from home again?"

. . . I'll eat a rind: In America, it is not unusual for a person to eat an apple, a pear, a plum, or a peach, rind and all, although I don't think many would eat an orange or a grapefruit without first peeling it. Anyway, refined Italians and other European people like their fresh fruit peeled before they eat it and the rinds are just thrown away. Because Mastro Geppetto is a poor peasant, he doesn't want Pinocchio to put on airs and get into the habit of wasting food the way rich people do.

"Oh, I promise you," sobbed the puppet, "I'll be good from now on . . . !"

"All boys," replied Geppetto, "when they want something, say exactly the same thing."

"But I promise you that I'll go to school and study hard and make good grades . . . !"

"All boys, when they are determined to get something, tell the same old story."

"But I'm really not like other boys! I'm better than any of them, and I always tell the truth. I promise you, Daddy, I'll learn a trade[1] and then I'll be a comfort to you and support you in your old age."

Geppetto, who until now had kept a stern and angry look on his face, suddenly found his eyes full of tears and his heart aching with sadness to see his poor Pinocchio in such a state. Without saying another word, he took up his tools and two small pieces of seasoned wood, and began to work in great earnest.

In less than an hour's time, the feet were nicely finished—two slim but sturdy and nimble feet which might have been modeled by a great sculptor. Then Geppetto said to the puppet, "Now

close your eyes and go to sleep!" And Pinocchio shut his eyes and pretended to sleep. Then, with a little glue which he had melted* in a broken eggshell, Geppetto fastened the two feet in place, and he fastened them so well that you would never be able to see where they were glued.

When the puppet opened his eyes and looked down at his new feet, he jumped from the table he was lying on, and began to leap about, and he turned a thousand handsprings around the room as if he had gone crazy with joy. "To pay you back for everything you've done for me," said Pinocchio to his father, "I'll start school immediately."

"Good boy!"

*. . . a little glue which he had melted: A hundred years ago, "Elmer's Glue" hadn't been invented and carpenters and woodworkers used a glue made from animal hides which had to be melted over a fire before it could be used.

"But, if I go to school, I'll need some clothes."

Now, you must understand that old Geppetto was a very poor man. In fact, he didn't have so much as a penny in his pocket. Even so, he managed to make a little suit for Pinocchio out of a piece of wallpaper. Then, from the bark of a birch tree he made him a little pair of shoes. Finally, he took some bread crumbs, and from them he molded a nice little cap.

As soon as Pinocchio put on his new clothes he ran immediately to look at his reflection in a basin of clear water and he was so pleased with what he saw that he strutted about proudly saying, "Now I look like a real gentleman!"

"That's very true," replied Geppetto, "but, please bear in mind that it is not beautiful clothes that make a gentleman. Rather it is clean clothes."[2]

"By the way," said the puppet, "if I'm going to go to school, I'll need something else—the most important thing."

"What's that?"

"I'll need a reading book."[*3]

"Right! But how do we get one?"

"It's very easy—we simply go to a bookshop and buy one."

"And the money?"

"I don't have any money."

"Neither do I," replied the good old man very sadly.

Then Pinocchio, who up to now had been the happiest of boys, became sad too, because poverty, when it is real poverty, is understood by everyone, even by boys.

"Well, let's not worry about it!" cried Geppetto rising suddenly to his feet. Then, putting on his threadbare old coat, all patched and darned, he ran out of the house. In a little while he returned, and when he came back he had in his hand a reading book for Pinocchio. But he no longer had his old coat. The poor old man was now in his shirtsleeves, and outdoors it had begun to snow.

*I'll need a reading book: This was really a book of ABC's (called in Italian an *Abbecedario*) from which Pinocchio was to learn his letters and then how to read. In his time, schoolchildren had to provide their own schoolbooks, and this is why poor Geppetto had to sell his coat in order to pay for this book.

"But where's your coat, Daddy?" asked Pinocchio.

"I've sold it."

"But why did you sell it?"

"Because it made me too warm."

Immediately, Pinocchio understood what had happened and, his heart swelling with emotion, he leaped into old Geppetto's arms and smothered him with loving kisses.

· ❖ ·

Chapter 9

Pinocchio sells his reading book
to go to see a puppet show.

As soon as it stopped snowing, Pinocchio, with his fine new reading book under his arm, walked along the road that led to the school. And as he walked, he pictured a thousand things in his little wooden brain, and he built a thousand castles in the air, one more beautiful than another. Then, talking to himself, he said, "Today, at school, I'll learn to read. Tomorrow I'll learn to write, and the day after tomorrow, I'll learn arithmetic. Then, with my fine education, I'll make a lot of money and with the first money I have in my pocket I will immediately buy my Daddy a fine new cloth coat. But why do I say a *cloth* coat? I want it to be made out of silver and gold and with buttons made out of diamonds. And that poor man really deserves it too, because just to buy me books and to get me educated he has to go around in his shirtsleeves—in this cold! No other boy has a Daddy who will make such sacrifices!"

While he was saying all this with great feeling, it seemed to him that he could hear in the distance the high, piping music of fifes, and the bumbling sound of a brass drum: *pì-pì-pì! zum-zum-zum!** He stopped to listen. The music seemed to be

---

**pì-pì-pì! zum-zum-zum:* Italian boys and girls insist that this is the way fifes and bass drums sound, but, of course, we know that they really sound something like *toot-toot-toot! boom-boom-boom!* But then, you remember that Italian crickets don't sound the same as ours do.

coming from the end of a very long road which led to a little village near the seashore.

"What can that music be? It's a shame I have to go to school, otherwise . . ." and Pinocchio stood there wondering what he should do. In any case, however, he had to make up his mind. Should he go on to school, or should he follow that fascinating fife-and-drum music? It didn't take him long to decide.

"Today, I'll go listen to that wonderful music—there'll be time enough for school tomorrow!"

No sooner had he decided this than he turned down the long road and began to run swiftly. The farther he ran, the nearer sounded the fifes and the beat of that great drum: *pì-pì-pì! zum-zum-zum!*

At last he found himself in the middle of a village square filled with people who were crowded around the entrance of a building which was made of canvas and wood and painted in a thousand different bright colors.

"What's in that building?" Pinocchio asked a boy who lived in the village.

"It's all written there on that big sign. Just read it for yourself and then you'll know."

"I'd be happy to read it, but it so happens that, at the moment, I don't know how to read."

"You're a real dummy, aren't you? Well then, I'll read it for you. On that signboard up there it says in big red letters, *GRAN TEATRO dei BURRATINI*—GRAND PUPPET THEATER . . . !"*[1]

*. . . *GRAND PUPPET THEATER:* In Pinocchio's time, and long before that, puppet theaters were very common in Europe and even in America. Centuries ago, especially in Italy, puppets were used to dramatize the Christmas pageant of the Nativity. This apparently led to the use of puppets as characters in other religious dramas and later in simple plays which were usually comical. The puppet shows were presented at first on crude open-air stages by men who made their own puppets and controlled their antics from above and behind a curtain or sometimes from below the stage. Puppetmasters such as these traveled from village to village to present their puppet shows.

In the sixteenth century, almost 400 years before Pinocchio was "born," the big indoor puppet theater began to develop and more and

"Has the show started yet?"

"It's just beginning now."

"And how much does it cost to go in?"

"Four *soldi*."*

By this time, Pinocchio's curiosity was completely aroused and, with no feeling of shame at all, he said to the boy, "Would you lend me four soldi 'til tomorrow?"

"Look, I'd be glad to lend you four soldi," the boy replied in a mocking tone, "but just at the moment, all my money is tied up."

"Well, could I sell you my jacket for four soldi?"

"What would I ever do with a jacket made of wallpaper? If I ever got caught in the rain, I'd never be able to get it off my back."

"How'd you like to buy my shoes?"

"What? Shoes made of birch bark—? They'd only be good to light a fire with!"

"What'll you give me for my cap?"

"Now, that's a real bargain! A cap made of bread crumbs! Why, the mice would come and eat it off my head!"

---

more elaborate plays were presented. In these plays, certain characters appeared so regularly that audiences learned immediately to recognize them. Some of these regular puppet characters were the Harlequin (*Arlecchino*), the Punchinello (*Pulcinella*), and the *Signora* Rosaura, all of whom Pinocchio meets in chapter 10.

The Grand Puppet Theater here is a large tent in which you can assume will be presented its shows in that village for a week, two weeks, or perhaps a month, and then move on to another town, much as our circuses still do. However, in the cities there were regular puppet theaters like, for example, the wonderful Punch and Judy Theater in New York City which was set up like a regular theater with more than 300 seats and which presented puppet dramas until 1932. Such permanent puppet theaters sprang up all over Europe in the 1600s. In England, Punchinello became so popular that his name was shortened to "Punch" and he became the very symbol of English comedy and humor.

*. . . *four soldi:* In Pinocchio's time, the *soldo* (plural, soldi) was a copper coin which was one-twentieth of the Italian *lira* (LEE-rah) just as the American nickel is one-twentieth of a dollar.

Pinocchio was on pins and needles.[2] He wanted those four soldi desperately, but he felt guilty about offering for sale the only other thing he owned. Finally, and very hesitantly, he said to the boy, "Would you give me four soldi for this brand new reading book?"

"Now look," said the boy who had far more sense than the puppet, "I'm just a kid, and I don't go around buying things from other kids!"

"Hey! I'll take that schoolbook for four soldi!" called out a peddler of old clothes who had been listening to the conversation of the two boys. And the book was sold there and then. And to think that poor old Geppetto was at home shivering with cold in his shirtsleeves just so his silly son could have a reading book!

·❖·

Chapter 10

Harlequin¹ and Punchinello² recognize
their brother, Pinocchio, and hold a great celebration.
But suddenly the puppetmaster, Fire Eater, appears
and Pinocchio is in real danger.

When Pinocchio entered the puppet theater, something happened that almost caused a revolution. The curtain was already
up and the show had begun. Harlequin* and Punchinello† were
on the stage quarreling with each other as usual and, from one
moment to the next, threatening to beat each other with sticks.
The audience howled with laughter as they watched the antics of
these two puppet clowns as they insulted and threatened each
other like real human beings, like two real men of the world.
Then, suddenly, Harlequin stopped short and turned toward the
audience. He pointed toward the back and shouted, "Good heav-
ens! Am I dreaming? That looks like Pinocchio out there!"

"That's really Pinocchio!" exclaimed Punchinello.

"Yes! it's really Pinocchio!" shrieked the *signora*‡ Rosaura³ as
she peeked from behind the scenery.

Harlequin: In Italian, the name is *Arlecchino* (Arleck-KEE-noh). In
the early Italian theater, and in later puppet shows, Harlequin was the
foolish lover of the pretty Columbine. He appeared in a tight suit made
of many-colored cloth diamonds (lozenges) sewn together, and he wore
a small black mask that looked like the face of a cat.

†*Punchinello:* The Italian name is *Pulcinella* (Pull-chee-NELL-ah).
Like Harlequin, Punchinello also began as a character in the early
Italian theater, and later became a main figure in puppet shows. He
may still be seen as "Punch" in what came to be called in England the
"Punch and Judy Show." The original *Pulcinella* was a clown in a loose
white suit and cap. He wore a black mask with a huge hooked nose, and
was especially known for his terrible temper.

‡*. . . the signora Rosaura:* I guess I should explain *signora* and
signore at this point because you will find these common Italian words
used here and there in the story. Signora (seen-YOR-ah) means much
the same as the English word "Mistress" which, of course, we abbrevi-
ate to "Mrs." and pronounce "Missus." When you address an Italian

"Pinocchio! It's Pinocchio!" the puppets all shouted in a chorus, as they leaped from all sides on to the stage. "It's Pinocchio! It's our brother Pinocchio![4] Hooray for Pinocchio!"

"Pinocchio, come up here on the stage!" shouted Harlequin, "Come to the arms of your wooden brothers!"

Hearing this warm invitation, Pinocchio made a great leap

---

woman directly, you say simply, "*signora* Rosaura," but when you speak to someone else about her, you refer to her as "*la signora* Rosaura" (something like "the lady Rosaura") as Mister Collodi does here.

Signore (seen-YOR-eh) is about the same as our "Mister" (Mr.), although when you address an Italian man, you must drop the final -e (which makes it pronounced seen-YOR). Just as you do with *signora*, when you speak to a man, you call him "*signor* Collodi," but when you speak of him to another person, you say "*il signore* Collodi" ("the Mister Collodi," which doesn't make an awful lot of sense in English).

from the back of the audience into the reserved seats up front. Then, from the reserved seats, he leaped to the top of the orchestra leader's bald head, and from there he sprang on to the stage. It's really impossible to describe all the loving embraces, the hugging, the kissing, the handshaking, and all the affectionate little gestures of real brotherhood that Pinocchio received from this excited crowd of wooden actors and actresses.

It was a very moving spectacle indeed, but the audience didn't seem to like it at all. For them, the show had been spoiled and they began to shout impatiently, "On with the show! We want the regular show!" But they wasted their breath. The puppets, instead of going on with the show, doubled their noise and their shouting, and raising Pinocchio on their shoulders, they paraded him proudly before the footlights.

Just at that moment, out came the showman, the master of the puppets. He was a huge, ugly man who could strike fear into anyone's heart. He had a nasty black beard that was so long that it reached from his chin to the ground. In fact, he stepped on it when he walked. His mouth was as big as an oven, and his eyes looked like a pair of lighted red lanterns. With his right hand he snapped and cracked a huge whip which was made of foxes' tails and live snakes all braided together.

Everyone stopped talking when the puppetmaster appeared— no one dared even to breathe. It was so quiet you could have heard a fly walking on the wall, and the poor puppets trembled like so many leaves fluttering in the wind.

"Why are you disrupting my show?" the puppetmaster roared at Pinocchio in the harsh tones of an ogre with a very sore throat.

"Believe me, my dear *signore*, * it really wasn't my fault . . . !"

"That's enough out of you! We'll settle this matter later!"

As soon as the puppet show was over, the puppetmaster strode into his kitchen where, for his supper, he had been roasting a whole sheep which was turning slowly on a spit over a fire. He

*. . . *my dear signore:* In this case, signore means "sir." Pinocchio is addressing the puppetmaster as "my dear sir" which, of course, would have been considered very polite.

discovered that there wasn't enough firewood to finish roasting and browning the sheep, so he called out to Harlequin and Punchinello, "Bring that new puppet here to me! You'll find him hanging on a nail. He looks as if he's made of very dry wood. I'm sure if I throw him on the fire, he'll make a beautiful blaze to finish this roast mutton."

At first Harlequin and Punchinello hesitated, but they were so frightened by the look in the puppetmaster's eye that they obeyed him immediately. After a moment they came back to the kitchen carrying poor Pinocchio who squirmed and wriggled like an eel out of water. He screamed wildly, "Daddy! Daddy! Save me! I don't want to die! I don't want to die!"

·◆·

Chapter 11

*Fire Eater sneezes and pardons
Pinocchio, who then saves the life
of his friend Harlequin.*

The puppetmaster, Fire Eater—that was his name—was a frightful man, especially with that nasty black beard that covered his chest and his legs like a long apron. Deep down, however, he was not really a wicked man. As proof of this, when he saw poor Pinocchio carried before him struggling and screaming, "I don't want to die! I don't want to die!" he immediately began to feel sorry for him. He resisted it for a little while, but finally he couldn't stand it any longer and he let go a tremendous sneeze.

At the sound of the sneeze, Harlequin, who until that moment had been so frightened and upset that he was bent over like a weeping willow, suddenly became cheerful. He leaned toward Pinocchio and whispered softly, "Good news, brother! Fire Eater just sneezed, and that's a sign that he feels sorry for you, so you're saved!"

Now, there is something you should understand about this man Fire Eater. Most men, when they feel sorry for someone, shed tears, or at least they pretend to shed tears. But not Fire Eater. Whenever he was moved to pity, he *sneezed!* It was his way of showing just how soft his heart really was.

After he sneezed, the puppetmaster, still pretending to be mean, shouted at Pinocchio, "Stop that crying, boy! Your blubbering has given me a pain in my stomach. In fact, I feel a pain that almost . . . Ah-CHOO! Ah-CHOO!* and he sneezed twice more.

"Bless you!" said Pinocchio.

"Thank you. And your father and your mother, are they still alive?"

*Ah-CHOO! Ah-CHOO: This, of course, is the sound that a person makes when he sneezes in English. Actually, Fire Eater was sneezing in Italian and the sound he made was *Etci! Etci!* but I know you wouldn't believe it if it had been written like that here.

"My Daddy, yes, but I have never had a mother."

"Imagine how awful it would have been for your poor old father if I had really thrown you on that fire! Poor old man! I feel sorry for him . . . Ah-CHOO! Ah-CHOO! Ah-CHOO! and he sneezed three times more.

"Bless you!" said Pinocchio.

"Thank you! But just the same, I really should get some consideration, because as you can see, I have no more wood to finish roasting that sheep and to tell you the truth, in this case you would have made pretty good firewood. However, since I've already taken pity on you, I'll have to do something else. Instead of you I'll have to burn one of the puppets of my company." With this, he turned toward the door and shouted, "Hey there, police!"

At this command there immediately appeared two wooden policemen.[1] They were very tall and very skinny and on their heads they wore the cocked hats of the Italian *Carabinieri*, and in their hands they carried long wooden swords. Fire Eater said to them in his hoarse voice, "Seize that puppet, Harlequin, and tie him up tight, and then throw him on the fire! I want my sheep well roasted!"

Imagine poor Harlequin's fright! He was so scared that his

43

legs buckled under him and he fell to the floor on his face. Pinocchio, at this painful sight, threw himself at the puppetmaster's feet, and weeping bitterly, he soaked his great long beard with his tears, and in a pleading voice he said, "Oh, *signor* Fire Eater—! Please have pity on poor Harlequin!"

"Don't call me signore! I am not a signore!"* shouted the puppetmaster in his harsh voice.

"Have pity, then, *cavaliere* Fire Eater!"†

"Don't call me cavaliere! I am not a cavaliere!"

"Please, then, have pity *commendatore!*"‡

"And I'm no commendatore, either!"

"Ah, then, *eccellenza,***² please have pity on poor Harlequin!"

When he heard himself called "Your Excellency," the puppetmaster's manner became gentler, and he began to act a little more human. He then said to Pinocchio, "Well then, what do you want me to do?"

"Oh please, I beg you to let poor Harlequin go!"

"Ah, no! for him it can't be done! I have let you go, so he must be thrown on the fire in your place. I must have my mutton well done!"

"Well, if that's the case," cried Pinocchio proudly, rising from his knees and throwing off his cap of breadcrumbs, "I know what I have to do! Let's go, policemen! Tie me up and throw me into the flames! It's just not fair that poor Harlequin, my dear old friend, should have to die for my sake!" These brave words, which Pinocchio spoke in loud and heroic tones, made all the other puppets weep. Even the two policemen, although they were made of wood, cried like two babies.

---

*I am not a signore: The term *signore* suggests a "gentleman." In Pinocchio's time, because the puppetmaster was a man of the lower classes, he might have been addressed as *Mastro* Fire Eater just as Geppetto is sometimes called Mastro Geppetto. Pinocchio is trying to flatter Fire Eater by addressing him with high-sounding titles, as you will see.

†*. . . cavaliere Fire Eater:* Pinocchio continues his flattery by calling the puppetmaster "Sir Knight Fire Eater."

‡*. . . commendatore:* "Knight Commander."

***. . . eccellenza:* "Your Excellency."

Fire Eater at first remained as hard and cold as a block of ice. Then, little by little, he began to melt, and then he began to sneeze. After he sneezed four or five times, he spread his arms out affectionately and said to Pinocchio, "You're really a fine, brave boy! Come here and give me a big kiss."

Quickly, Pinocchio ran and climbed up the puppetmaster's beard like a squirrel and planted a smacking kiss on the end of his nose.

"Then I've been pardoned?" asked poor Harlequin in a faint little voice that could hardly be heard.

"You've been pardoned!" answered Fire Eater. Then, sighing and shaking his head, he added, "Well, what can I do? Tonight I'll just have to eat my mutton half raw, but the next time, look out!"

At the good news of Harlequin's pardon, the puppets ran joyfully out on the stage and, after lighting all the candles of the footlights and the chandeliers as if there were to be a regular performance, they began to leap and dance about with wild joy. When daylight came, they were still dancing.

· ❖ ·

Chapter 12

*Fire Eater gives Pinocchio a present
of five gold pieces to take to his father, but
Pinocchio lets himself be tricked by the Fox and the Cat
and foolishly goes off with them instead.*

The next day, Fire Eater called Pinocchio to him and asked him, "What is your father's name?"

"Geppetto," replied the puppet.

"And what does he do for a living?"

"Well, ah . . . he's a . . . well, I suppose you'd say he's a pauper."*[1]

. . . he's a pauper: The word "pauper" is not used much anymore. What Pinocchio means is that Geppetto is a very poor man. He is not a beggar, though, because later we find Pinocchio telling how his father had often told him that "it is shameful to beg for money."

45

"A pauper, eh? Does he earn much money?"

"Earn much? Why, he never has a penny in his pocket. Just think! In order to buy me a reading book, he had to sell the only coat he had—a coat so covered with patches and darns that it was a regular ruin."

"The poor old devil! I really feel sorry for him. Here's five gold pieces.[2] Go along home now and give them to your father with my best wishes." Then, as you can imagine, Pinocchio thanked the puppetmaster a thousand times. He hugged all the puppets of the company, one after another—even the wooden *carabinieri*—and then he started off for home with great joy in his heart.

He hadn't gone very far along the road home when he met two strange people walking toward him. One of these strangers was a shabby old Fox in ragged clothes and lame in one foot. The other was a seedy-looking old Cat[3] who wore dark glasses and had a sign hanging from his neck which read *CIECO—BLIND*. The Cat was pretending that he was blind in both eyes. The two of them were walking leisurely down the road, each helping the other along like two old cronies on a journey, the lame Fox leaning on the Cat, and the Cat allowing himself to be led along by the Fox.

"Good day, Pinocchio," said the Fox, greeting him politely.

"How do you happen to know my name?" asked the puppet.

"Oh, I know your father very well."

"Really? Where did you meet my father?"

"Why, I saw him only yesterday standing at the door of his house."

"And what was he doing?"

"He was standing there in his shirtsleeves and shivering with the cold."

"Poor Daddy! But if God is willing, from now on he won't shiver any more!"

"Why's that?"

"Because I have become a rich gentleman."

"A rich gentleman! You?" exclaimed the Fox with a rough, mocking laugh. The Cat began to laugh too, but to hide it, he pretended to be combing his whiskers with his paws.

"There's really nothing to laugh at," cried Pinocchio angrily.

46

"I really hate to make you envious, but these things, if you can recognize them, are five lovely gold pieces* I've got here in my hand!" And he showed them the money that Fire Eater had given him.

At the pleasant sound of the clinking gold pieces, the Fox, without realizing it, reached out with the paw that was supposed to be lame. Meanwhile, the Cat opened wide both his eyes like two big green lanterns, although he shut them again so quickly that Pinocchio saw nothing unusual.

"Well now," said the Fox, "what are you going to do with all that nice money?"

"First of all," he answered the puppet, "I want to buy my Daddy a beautiful new coat, all made out of gold and silver and with buttons made of diamonds. And then I want to buy a reading book for myself."

"For yourself?"

"Of course, that's because I want to go to school and study hard."

"You're making a big mistake there!" said the Fox. "Just because I wanted to go to school and study hard, I got a lame leg."

"And look at me!" said the Cat. "Just because I studied so hard, I ended up blind!"

At that moment, a white blackbird[4] perched in a bush beside the road and began his usual song, saying, "Pinocchio! Don't pay any attention to the advice of those two. If you do, you'll really be sorry for it!"

Poor blackbird! If only he had kept still! The Cat made one great leap and seized him without even giving him time to cry out, and then ate him up in one mouthful, feathers and all. After he ate him, he wiped his mouth and closed his eyes again and pretended to be blind as before.

"That poor little blackbird!" said Pinocchio to the Cat, "Why did you treat him so cruelly?"

"I did it to teach him a lesson. Next time he'll know better

*. . . *five lovely gold pieces:* I'm sure you know that today five gold pieces would be a real fortune. Well, in Pinocchio's time, as you can imagine, it would have been a huge amount of money, too!

than to interrupt the conversation of other people."

They had traveled some distance when the Fox stopped suddenly and said to the puppet, "Say, Pinocchio! How would you like to double the number of your gold pieces?"

"What do you mean?"

"How'd you like to make out of those miserable five gold pieces a hundred, . . ? a thousand, . . ? two thousand, . . ?"

"Would I! But how do I do that?"

"It's easy. Instead of going back home, you've got to come with us."

"And where do we have to go?"

"We have to go to Boobyland."[5]

Pinocchio thought this over for a moment, and then said very firmly, "No, I don't want to go. I'm nearly home now, and I want to get back to my Daddy who needs me. Who knows how the poor old man must have suffered when I didn't come back. I've really been a naughty boy and Talking Cricket was right when he said that disobedient boys never come to any good in this world, and I've proved this again and again because I've had all kinds of narrow escapes. Why, only yesterday, in Fire Eater's kitchen, I nearly . . . B-r-r-r! it makes me shiver just to think of it!"

"All right, then," said the Fox, "if you've really decided to go home it's just too bad for you!"

"Yes! Too bad for you!" repeated the Cat.

"Think it over real well, Pinocchio, because you're throwing away a fortune!"

"A fortune!" repeated the Cat.

"Between today and tomorrow, your five gold coins would become two thousand."

"Two thousand!" repeated the Cat.

"But how is that possible!" asked Pinocchio with his mouth wide open in wonder.

"I'll explain it to you," said the Fox. "You must understand that in Boobyland there is a marvelous field called the Field of Miracles. In this field all you have to do is dig a little hole and put in it, let's say, one gold piece. Then you cover it over with a little earth, and then you water it with two buckets of water from the spring, and then you sprinkle it with a little salt. Then, when night falls, you can go quietly to bed. Meanwhile, during the night, that gold piece will grow and blossom and then, the morning after, when you get up and go out to the field, what do you find? You find a beautiful tree loaded down with so many gold pieces that you couldn't carry them all home in a bushel basket in one trip."

"Well then, if that's the case," said Pinocchio, "if I planted all of my gold pieces in that field, how many gold pieces would I find the next morning?"

"That's easy," replied the Fox, "you can figure it out on your fingers. If every gold piece you plant turns into five hundred gold pieces, if you multiply five hundred by five, it means that the next morning you'll find yourself with two thousand, five hundred brand new, clinking gold pieces."

"Oh, beautiful!" cried Pinocchio as he danced with joy. "As soon as I've picked all these gold pieces off the tree, I'll take two thousand for myself, and I'll make a present of five hundred to you two."

"A present to us?" cried the Fox, "God forbid!"

"God forbid!" repeated the Cat.

"We don't work to make money," said the Fox, "we work only to make other people rich."

". . . to make other people rich!" repeated the Cat.

"What fine people these are!" Pinocchio thought to himself. And, in that very moment, forgetting his Daddy, the fine new coat, the new reading book, and all the fine promises he had made, he said to the Fox and the Cat, "All right, then, let's go! I'll go with you to Boobyland!"

Chapter 13

*An evening at the
Inn of The Red Lobster.*

They walked, and they walked, and they walked, until finally at evening, dead tired, they arrived at an inn called The Red Lobster.[1]

"Let's stop here a while," said the Fox, "just long enough to have a bite to eat and rest for a few hours. At midnight we can start again, and early tomorrow, we'll arrive at the Field of Miracles." So, they entered the inn, and all three sat down at the dining table, although none of them really had any appetite. The poor Cat, who had a bad stomachache, couldn't eat more than thirty-five baked red mullet with tomato sauce, and four portions of tripe in the Florentine style.[2] And then, because he found the tripe not properly seasoned, he had to call three times for more butter and grated cheese!

As far as the Fox was concerned, he would have been satisfied with just a light snack, but it seems his doctor had put him on a very strict diet. Because of this he was forced to be content with a simple meal of braised fat rabbit as it is prepared on the isle of Ischia[3] garnished with choice breasts of chicken *alla bolognese*.[4] When he finished this first course, he felt he should order a little something to settle his stomach. This special dish consisted only of some grilled partridge with young squirrel, frogs, lizards, and a few peacock eggs. After that, however, the Fox couldn't touch another thing—his appetite was so delicate, he said, that he really couldn't eat another mouthful. But Pinocchio was the one who ate the least. He had asked for a few walnuts* and a bit of

---

*. . . *a few walnuts:* The walnuts you probably know about are the dried ones you see around Thanksgiving and Christmas and which are sometimes eaten as a snack, used to decorate cakes, or chopped up for flavoring or for topping for desserts. The walnuts that Pinocchio has ordered for his meal are *fresh* walnuts. The green walnut, though, has a tough but moist shell and the walnut meat is covered by a thin moist skin which must be carefully removed because it is so terribly bitter.

bread, and then left everything on his plate. The poor boy, who thought about nothing but the Field of Miracles, had a terrible indigestion brought on by the thought of increasing his store of gold pieces.

After they finished eating, the Fox said to the innkeeper, "Give us two good rooms—one for *signor* Pinocchio* here, and one for me and my friend. Before we leave, we'd like to be waked up at midnight so we can go on our way."

"Certainly, gentlemen," replied the innkeeper, and he winked at the Fox and the Cat as if to say, "I know exactly what you're up to, and we understand each other perfectly well!"

As soon as Pinocchio got into bed he fell asleep and began to dream. He dreamt that he was in the middle of a field full of bushes covered with blossoms made of gold pieces which, as they swung in the wind, went *clink, clink, clink,* as if to say, "Whoever wants us can come and pick us." But just as Pinocchio was about to reach out to pick a few handfuls of those beautiful gold pieces and put them in his pocket, he was suddenly awakened by three loud knocks at his bedroom door. It was the innkeeper who had come to tell him that it was now midnight.

"And are my friends all ready?" the puppet asked.

"Ready? Why, they left two hours ago!"

"But, why were they in such a hurry?"

"Because the Cat received word that his eldest son was ill with blisters on his paws and was in danger of dying."

"And did they pay for the supper?"

"Why, how can you think such a thing? They're far too polite to insult a gentleman like you that way."

"Well, that's too bad! That's the kind of insult I wouldn't mind taking at all!" said Pinocchio as he scratched his head.

It's worth the trouble, though, because the meat has a most delicious walnut flavor that cannot be found in the dried nuts.

*. . . *signor* Pinocchio: Notice that the Fox is flattering Pinocchio here by referring to him as signore just as Pinocchio tried to flatter Fire Eater in chapter 11 by calling him signore. A signore (gentleman) in Italy at that time must have been born a gentleman. In other words, he would have to have been "of gentle birth."

Then he asked, "And where did my good friends say they'd meet me?'

"At the Field of Miracles, tomorrow morning at daybreak."

Pinocchio was forced to give the innkeeper one of his precious gold pieces[5] to pay for the huge meal his friends had eaten the evening before. Then, when he left the inn he found it so dark that he was only able to feel his way along the road. Not even a leaf stirred anywhere in the countryside. Only a few ugly night-birds flying across the road from one hedge to another brushed Pinocchio's nose with their wings. As he jumped back in fear, he shouted, "Who's that?" And the echo from the surrounding hills repeated in the distance, "Who's that? Who's that? Who's that?"

As he walked along, suddenly he discovered on the trunk of a tree a tiny figure that shone with a dull, pale light, like the little light of an old-fashioned porcelain night-lamp.

"Who are you?" asked Pinocchio.

"I am the ghost of Talking Cricket," replied the ghostly figure in a tiny voice so weak that it seemed to come from another world.

"What do you want?" asked the puppet.

"I want to give you some good advice. Turn back and take your four remaining gold pieces to your poor old Daddy who weeps in despair because you haven't gone back home to him."

"Well, I just want you to know that by tomorrow my Daddy will be a rich gentleman, because these four gold pieces are going to turn into two thousand!"

"My boy, never trust people who promise to make you rich overnight. Usually they are either lunatics or they are thieves! Take my advice and turn back."

"I'm sorry, but I want to go on."

"It's very late—!"

"I want to go on."

"It's very dark—!"

"I want to go on."

"The road is very dangerous—!"

"I still want to go on."

"Remember that foolish boys who insist on having their own way regret it sooner or later."

"The same old story! Good night, Cricket."

"Good night, Pinocchio, and may heaven protect you from the damp night air[6]—and from murderers!"

As soon as the ghost of Talking Cricket spoke these last words, he disappeared like a candle that has been blown out, and the road was darker than ever.

· ❖ ·

Chapter 14

Because he wouldn't listen to the advice of Talking Cricket, Pinocchio falls in with robbers.[1]

"Gee whiz," said the puppet to himself as he went on his way, "boys are really unlucky! Everybody scolds us, everybody gives us advice! If they had their way, they'd all become our lords and masters—all of them, even Talking Cricket. According to that boring old cricket, if I don't listen to him, I'll get into all kinds of trouble! According to him, I'll even meet up with robbers and murderers!* That's the least of my worries because I don't even believe in robbers and murderers, and I never did. As far as I'm concerned, they were invented on purpose to scare little boys who want to go out after dark. And even if I did meet robbers here on the road, they couldn't frighten me. I'd just meet 'em face to face and say, 'All right, you guys, what do you want of me? Just remember one thing—you can't fool around with me and get away with it! Now, get out of here and don't bother me!' After a speech like that, those robbers—I can just see 'em now—they'll run away like scared rabbits! On the other hand, if they didn't have sense enough to run away, I could always run away myself, and that'd be the end of that . . . !"

But Pinocchio didn't have time to finish this kind of thinking because he thought he heard a little rustling sound in the dry leaves behind him. He turned around to look, and in the shadows he could just make out two sinister black figures that were completely wrapped in charcoal sacks.† They were actually chasing after him on tiptoe like two black ghosts.

*. . . *robbers and murderers:* A hundred years ago, travel in Italy was very dangerous, especially travel on foot, because the countryside was infested with gangs of murderous thieves called *briganti* (in English, brigands). The government was quite unable to suppress these bandits for a very long time, and they may still be found in control of certain remote parts of the country.

†. . . *wrapped in charcoal sacks:* In those days, and in some places even now, cooking in Italian peasant kitchens was done over a charcoal fire. The charcoal they used was a lot different from what you have seen in the backyard cookout, though. There was a special class of peasants called *carbonai*—charcoal burners—who made a living by making charcoal by "baking" twigs and branches of hardwood trees at a very high temperature in crude ovens which they made by covering the piles of green wood with earth or clay. This carbonizing process simply burned out the sap and tarry substances leaving the twigs and branches just the way they were before, except that now they were very brittle, much, much lighter in weight, and jet black in color. They were then broken into small pieces and packed into cloth sacks which became very black themselves from the dust of the broken charcoal. You can see now why the figures chasing Pinocchio would look "like two black ghosts."

"Gee! They're really here!" he said to himself, and not having any other place to hide his gold pieces, he put them under his tongue and shut his mouth tightly. Then he tried to run away, but before he could take one step, he felt someone grab his arm and then he heard a horrible, hollow voice say, "Your money or your life!"[2]

Poor Pinocchio couldn't say a word because his mouth was full of gold pieces. In spite of all his brave ideas of the moment before, he could now only bow politely and pretend that he was only a poor puppet who didn't have so much as a penny in his pocket.

"Come on, now—never mind the nonsense! Out with the money!" shouted the two bandits.

When the puppet made signs with his hands as if to say, "I haven't any money," the taller of the two robbers said in a rough voice, "Just hand over your money or you're dead!"

". . . you're dead!" repeated the other robber.

"Then, after we kill you, we'll kill your father too."

"No! no! no! not my poor Daddy!" cried Pinocchio in a piteous voice but, as he shouted, the gold pieces clinked loudly in his mouth.

"Aha! You liar! So you've hidden your money under your tongue! All right, just spit it out!"

But Pinocchio stood his ground bravely.

"Oho! So you pretend you can't hear, eh? Well, we'll soon find a way to make you spit it out!"

With this, one of them seized the puppet by the end of his nose and the other took hold of his chin, and roughly they began to pull, one in one direction and the other in the opposite direction to try to make him open his mouth. However, it was of no use. The puppet's mouth was closed so tightly it seemed to be nailed shut. Then the smaller of the two bandits took out an ugly knife and tried to pry his mouth open by forcing it between his lips. But Pinocchio, quick as a flash, caught his hand between his teeth, and with one bite, bit it clean off and spat it out on the ground. Imagine his surprise when he discovered that instead of a hand he had spat out the paw of a cat!

After this victory, Pinocchio fought tooth and nail until, finally, he got out of the clutches of the two bandits. He made a

great leap over the hedge at the side of the road and raced like a madman across the fields. Of course, the robbers ran after him like two hounds chasing a rabbit, and the one that had lost the paw ran swiftly along on three legs, although nobody really knew how he did it.

After he had run about ten miles, Pinocchio found he could run no farther. Then, thinking his luck had completely run out, he climbed up the trunk of a very tall pine tree and perched on one of the topmost branches. The two robbers tried to climb up after him, but they were only able to get halfway up the tree when they slid down again, landing on the ground with their hands and feet badly skinned.

But they were not going to be stopped by a little thing like that. They gathered a big bundle of dry wood and piled it at the foot of the tree and then set fire to it. In no time at all, the tree began to burn and blaze like a huge bonfire. Pinocchio watched the flames climb higher and higher, but because he didn't want to end up like a roast pigeon, he made another great leap out of the treetop and began again to race across the fields and through the vineyards. And the bandits came close behind him without giving up for one moment.

When daylight finally came, they were still chasing him. Suddenly, Pinocchio came to a wide, deep ditch filled with nasty, muddy water. What in the world could he do now? Then, with a *one!* and a *two!* and a *THREE!* he made a big jump, but they didn't measure the distance very well and *Splash!*[3] they fell into the middle of the ditch. Pinocchio heard the terrible splash, and without stopping, he turned and shouted out with a laugh, "Have a nice bath, gentlemen!"

By this time, he was sure that the two bandits were drowned, but instead, when he turned to look, he discovered that they were still running after him, and still wrapped up in their black charcoal sacks, dripping water like two wet sponges.

Chapter 15

*The robbers chase Pinocchio,
and after they catch him, they hang him
from a branch of The Great Oak.*

When he discovered the robbers still chasing him, the puppet lost heart and was just about ready to throw himself on the ground and give up. But, as he looked wildly about him in every direction, at a distance he spied a snowy-white little house that stood out against the deep green of the old trees all around it.

"If only I had enough breath to get to that little house," he said to himself, "maybe I'd be saved."

Then, without wasting another moment, he began to run again through the woods as fast as he could with the bandits close behind him. At last, after running desperately for almost two hours, he arrived completely out of breath at the door of the little white house. He knocked on the door. No one answered. He knocked again—louder this time—for he could hear the awful sound of the running feet and the heavy breathing of his pursuers.

Still no answer.

When he saw that knocking was of no use, he began to kick the door and even to beat his wooden head against it. Suddenly, there appeared at a window a beautiful young girl with a face as white as the driven snow and hair the color of the blue sky.[1] Her

eyes were closed, and her arms were crossed on her breast. Without seeming to move her lips, she said in a voice that seemed to come from another world, "There is no one in this house. They are all dead."

"Then at least open the door for me yourself," cried Pinocchio as he wept and begged on his knees.

"I am dead, too."[2]

"Dead! Then how can you be standing at the window and talking to me?"

"I am waiting for the coffin to come to take me away."

"Oh, please, please, beautiful blue-haired girl!" cried poor Pinocchio, "Please, for heaven's sake, open the door! There are robbers after me who are going to kill . . ." But he couldn't finish his desperate plea, for at that very moment he was seized by the neck and he heard two voices growl, "We've got you! This time you won't get away from us again!"

The puppet, with death staring him in the face, began to tremble so violently that the joints of his legs creaked and the gold pieces which he had hidden under his tongue began to clink together loudly.

"Now then," demanded one of the two bandits, "are you going to open your mouth this time or not? Aha! So you won't talk! All right, then! this time we'll open it ourselves!" And the two whipped out long, ugly, razor-sharp knives and tried to stab Pinocchio in the back! Remember though, the puppet was made of very hard wood, and the two knives were simply shattered into a thousand pieces. The robbers just stood there looking foolishly at each other. "We've got to hang him! Let's go hang him right now!"

". . . right now!" repeated the other.

"Without wasting any more time, the pair of bandits tied poor Pinocchio's hands behind his back and put a rope around his neck and hanged him from the limb of a huge tree called The Great Oak. Then they sat down on the grass to wait until he made his last struggle, but after three hours of waiting, they found the puppet with his eyes still open and struggling harder than ever.

Finally, they grew bored with waiting and they turned to Pinocchio saying mockingly, "Well, so long, old boy! We'll

come back tomorrow morning. Maybe by that time you'll be kind enough to be good and dead with your mouth very conveniently hanging open."

With that, the two robbers left.

In the meantime, a wild north wind began to blow and rage angrily and the poor hanged puppet was swung back and forth like the clapper of a church bell ringing for a wedding. The swinging to and fro was very painful, and the rope around his neck choked him. Little by little his eyes grew dim, but even though he felt close to death, he hoped from one moment to the next that some kind soul would come to save him. But he waited, and waited, and waited, and yet no one came. Then he began to think of his poor old father, and when he was almost dead, Pinocchio stammered,

"Oh, Daddy! Daddy! if only you were here!"

After that he had no breath to say anything more. He shut his eyes, his mouth fell open, his legs stretched out, he gave a great shudder, and he hung there stiffly.

Chapter 16

The beautiful girl with the blue hair rescues
the puppet, puts him to bed, and calls in three doctors
to find out if he is alive or dead.

While poor Pinocchio hung more dead than alive from a limb of The Great Oak, the beautiful girl with the blue hair came again to the window of the little white house. When she saw the miserable puppet hanging by his neck and dancing up and down in the cold gusts of the north wind, she clapped her hands three times. At this signal, there was a great rushing sound of rapidly beating wings, and suddenly a huge Falcon alighted on the windowsill.

"What is it that you command, good Fairy?" asked the Falcon as he lowered his beak in a sign of deep respect. And now you should know that this young girl with the blue hair was really a beautiful Fairy who had lived in that little house for more than a thousand years.[1]

"Do you see that puppet hanging there from a limb of The Great Oak?" asked the Fairy.

"Yes, I see him."

"Well then, fly over there quickly, and with your strong beak untie the knot of the rope that has him hanging in the air, and then lay him gently on the grass at the foot of the tree."

The Falcon flew away and, within two minutes, he came back saying solemnly, "That which you have commanded has been done."

"And how was he? Alive or dead?"

"Well, to look at him, he seemed dead. But he can't really be dead because when I loosened the rope around his neck he heaved a great sigh and muttered, 'Ah! Now I feel better!' "

When she heard this, the Fairy clapped her hands twice and there appeared a magnificent Poodle that walked in on his hind legs just as if he were a man.

The Poodle was dressed in the full-dress livery* of a coach-

---

*. . . *full-dress livery:* In this instance, livery means the kind of

man, and on his head he wore a three-cornered hat decorated with gold lace over a white wig with curls that fell down to his shoulders. Also, he wore a chocolate-colored coat with diamond buttons and huge pockets in which he kept the bones his mistress, the Fairy, gave him at dinnertime. Besides this, he wore a pair of knee breeches of crimson velvet, silk stockings, and low-cut shoes, and behind him he wore a kind of umbrella case* made of blue satin in which he carried his tail when the weather was rainy.

The Fairy said to him, "Medoro,"—that was the Poodle's name—"I want you to take the finest carriage in my stable and go down the road to the woods. When you come to The Great Oak, you will find a poor puppet stretched out on the grass almost dead. Pick him up gently and lay him on the cushions of the carriage and bring him back here. Is that clear?"

The Poodle, to indicate that he understood perfectly, gave three or four shakes to the blue satin umbrella case that he wore behind, and then ran off like a racehorse. After a moment or two, a beautiful little carriage came out of the Fairy's carriage-house. It had soft cushions stuffed with canary feathers and its inside was lined with whipped cream, custard, and sweet lady-fingers. It was drawn by a hundred pairs of white mice, and the Poodle, seated on the coach-box, cracked his whip back and forth like a driver who is afraid he is going to be late.

Within a quarter of an hour, the little carriage returned. The Fairy, who was waiting at the door of the little house, immediately took poor Pinocchio in her arms and carried him to a little bedroom which was all decorated with mother-of-pearl. Then,

---

dress uniform worn by the coachmen and footmen, as well as by certain other servants, of a rich, aristocratic family.

*. . . *he wore a kind of umbrella case:* I'm not sure if umbrella cases are still used in America, although I know they are used in Europe. Anyway, this is a long, slender tube, closed at one end, and made of silk or similar material. When an umbrella is not being used, it is slipped into this case which keeps it tightly rolled up and protected from soil. In Pinocchio's time, umbrella cases were made of fine, brightly colored silk or satin and were often decorated with ruffles and ribbons.

she sent at once for the best physicians who could be found anywhere, and shortly afterwards three doctors arrived, one after another. One was a Cricket, the second was an Owl, and the third a Crow.[2]

"I would like to know from you gentlemen," said the Fairy to the three doctors who had gathered around Pinocchio's bed, "if this poor puppet is alive or dead."

At this, the Crow came forward and felt Pinocchio's pulse. Then he felt his nose, and then he felt his little toe. When he had felt everything very carefully, he very solemnly announced, "I am convinced that the puppet is quite dead. However, if by some misfortune he is not dead, it's a sure sign that he's still alive!"

"I'm very sorry," said the Owl,* "but I must disagree with my illustrious friend and colleague, the Crow. In my opinion, the puppet is still alive. However, if by some misfortune he is not alive, it's a sure sign that he's quite dead!"

"And you—have you nothing to say?" said the Fairy to the Cricket.

"I say that the careful physician, when he doesn't know what to say, should keep his mouth shut.[3] And besides," said the Cricket, "that puppet is no stranger to me. I have known him for some time, now!" Up to this moment, Pinocchio had been lying as still as any old piece of wood. Now he gave a kind of convulsive shudder that shook the whole bed.

Talking Cricket—this cricket doctor was the very same Talking Cricket, you will remember, whom Pinocchio killed with a mallet when he tried to give the puppet some very good advice—Talking Cricket went on to say, "That puppet is an absolute scoundrel!" Pinocchio opened his eyes at this and then quickly shut them again.

"He's a good-for-nothing, a loafer, a vagabond—!"

Pinocchio hid his head under the bedclothes.

*. . . the Owl: You must admit that what the Owl has to say about Pinocchio's condition is pretty dumb, but I explained earlier to the grownups that while Americans, for some reason, consider the owl to be a wise old bird, to most Europeans he represents stupidity.

"That puppet is a disobedient boy who will cause his poor Daddy to die of a broken heart!"

At this point, everyone in the room could hear the sound of weeping and sobbing. Imagine their surprise when they raised the bedclothes a little, and discovered that the weeping and sobbing came from Pinocchio.

"When a dead person weeps, it's a sure sign that he's on the road to recovery," was the solemn comment of the Crow.

"I hate to contradict my illustrious friend and colleague," said the Owl, "but as far as I'm concerned, when a dead man weeps it's a sure sign that he's sorry to die."

· ❖ ·

Chapter 17

*Pinocchio eats the sugar, but won't
take his medicine. However, when he sees the pallbearers
who have come to take him away, he finally takes it.
Then he tells a lie, and for punishment
his nose begins to grow.*

As soon as the three doctors had left the room, the Fairy went to Pinocchio and felt his forehead and discovered that he had a high fever. Quickly, she put some medicine in half a glass of water and offered it to the puppet, saying affectionately, "Here, drink this down, and soon you'll feel better."

Pinocchio looked at the glass, made a wry face, and then asked in a very unhappy voice, "Is it sweet or bitter?"

"It's bitter, but it'll help you."[1]

"If it's bitter, I won't drink it!"

"Now, see here—! Drink it!"

"I don't like bitter things!"

"Drink it down! Then after you've drunk it, I'll give you a lump of sugar to eat to take away the bitter taste."

"Where's the lump of sugar?"

"Right here," said the Fairy as she took a lump from a golden sugar bowl.

"First, give me the lump of sugar, and then I'll drink that glass of bitter medicine."

"Do you promise—?"

"Yes."

The Fairy gave him the lump of sugar and Pinocchio quickly crunched it between his teeth and swallowed it in an instant. Then, as he licked his lips, he said, "Wouldn't it be nice if sugar was medicine! I'd take it every day!"

"All right now, keep your promise and drink this little bit of medicine. It'll make you all better again."

Very unwillingly, Pinocchio took the glass of medicine in his hand. Then he put the tip of his nose to it and sniffed it. He brought the glass almost up to his lips, but then he stopped

68

again to sniff it. Finally, he said, "It's too bitter! too bitter! I can't drink it!"

"How can you say that when you haven't even tasted it?"*

"I can tell! I can tell from the smell of it! First give me another lump of sugar, and then I'll drink it!"

With all the patience of a little mother, the Fairy put another lump of sugar into Pinocchio's mouth. Then she gave him the glass of medicine again.

"I can't drink it like this!" cried the puppet as he made an awful face.

"Why not?"

"Well—because that pillow on my feet is uncomfortable."

The Fairy took the pillow away.

"It's no use! I still can't drink it."

"Now what's the matter?"

"That bedroom door bothers me. It's half open."

The Fairy went and closed the bedroom door.

"Even so," shouted Pinocchio as he burst into tears, "I won't take that bitter medicine—I won't! I won't! I won't!"

"Pinocchio, you'll be sorry if you don't take it."

"I don't care!"

"You're a very sick boy."

"I don't care!"

"In a very short while that fever is going to kill you."

"I don't care!"

"Aren't you afraid to die?"

"No, I'm not afraid! It'd be better to die than to drink that awful medicine!"

At this point, the door flew open and into the room marched four huge jet-black rabbits who carried a little coffin on their shoulders.²

"What do you want?" cried the terrified Pinocchio as he sat bolt upright in his bed.

*How can you say that when you haven't even tasted it: Are you surprised to learn that grownups were saying this to children a hundred years ago?

"We have come to take you away," replied the biggest of the black rabbits.

"Take me away—? But I'm not *dead* yet!"

"No, not yet. But you have only a few minutes left to live. You wouldn't take the medicine that would have cured your fever."

"Oh Fairy! dear Fairy!" the puppet screamed, "Give me that glass of medicine! Quick, for heaven's sake! I don't want to die—No! I don't want to die!" He then seized the glass in both hands and emptied it in a single gulp.

"Well, I guess we'll just have to wait," said the biggest of the black rabbits. "This time we came for nothing." Then, taking up the little coffin again, they put it on their shoulders and marched out of the room muttering and grumbling to themselves.

Hardly a moment later, Pinocchio leaped out of bed completely cured. As you probably know, wooden puppets don't often get sick, but when they do, they get well again very quickly.

The Fairy, seeing him running and romping about the room as frisky and happy as a young rooster, said to him, "Then my medicine was really good for you?"

"Good? More than good! It brought me back to life!"

"Then, why in the world did I have to beg you to take it?"

"Why? It's simply because boys are all alike! It's just because we're more afraid of the medicine than we are of the sickness."

"Shame on you! Boys should realize that good medicine taken in time can keep them from being very sick and perhaps even from dying. . . ."

"Ah yes, but the next time you won't have to beg me! I'll just remember those four black rabbits with the coffin on their shoulders—then I'll take up that glass of medicine and down it'll go!"

"All right, now suppose you tell me how you happened to fall into the hands of those murderous thieves."

"Well, it happens that the puppetmaster, Fire Eater, gave me some gold pieces and told me to take them to my Daddy. Instead, on the road I met a Fox and a Cat, two very honest and respectable people, who said, 'Would you like to see your money turn into a thousand—even two thousand—gold pieces? Come along with us and we'll take you to the Field of Miracles,' and then I said, 'Let's go!' and then they said, 'Let's stop for a while at the Inn of The Red Lobster, and after midnight we'll go on our way,' and then when I woke up, I discovered that they'd already left, and then I started out again and it was so dark you wouldn't believe it, and then, on the road I met two robbers wearing coal sacks who said, 'Give us your money!' and then I said, 'I haven't got any money,' 'cause I had hidden the four gold pieces in my mouth, and then one of the robbers tried to put his hand in my mouth, and then with one bite I bit off his hand and spat it out, but—and you know, it's a funny thing—it wasn't a hand at all, it was a cat's paw, and then the robbers chased me and I ran, till finally they caught me and hanged me by the neck from The Great Oak in the woods, and then they said, 'Tomorrow we'll come back and you'll be dead with your mouth hanging wide open and then it'll be easy to take out the money you hid under your tongue.' "

"And the gold pieces," asked the Fairy, "now where are they?"

"I lost them!" said Pinocchio with a perfectly straight face. But this was a lie, because he really had the money in his pocket. As soon as he told this lie, his nose—which, as you know, was already a pretty long nose—suddenly grew two inches longer.

"And where did you lose them?"

"In the woods."

With this second lie, Pinocchio's nose grew even longer.

"If you lost your gold pieces in the woods," said the Fairy, "we'll look for them there, and I know we'll find them, because anything that is lost there is always found."

"Ah! now I remember," the puppet stammered in confusion, "I didn't really lose the gold pieces. By accident I swallowed them while I was taking your medicine."

With this third lie, his nose grew so long that poor Pinocchio couldn't turn in any direction. If he turned this way, his nose would hit against the bed or the window panes. If he turned that way, it would bang against the walls or the bedroom door. If he even so much as raised his head, he ran the risk of sticking his nose into the Fairy's eye.

The Fairy just looked at him and laughed.

"What are you laughing at?" demanded the puppet who, by now, was completely confused and worried about his nose which had so quickly grown to such an enormous size.

"I'm laughing at the lie you told me."

"How could you ever know that I told a lie?"

"My dear boy," she replied, "it's so very easy to tell when someone is lying, because there are only two kinds of lie. There are lies that have short legs, and there are lies that have long noses.[3] It just so happens that your kind of lie is the kind with the long nose."

Pinocchio wanted to hide himself in shame, but when he tried to run out of the room, he couldn't do it because his nose had grown so long that he could no longer pass through the door.

· ❖ ·

Chapter 18

*Once again Pinocchio meets the Fox
and the Cat and goes with them to plant his
gold pieces in the Field of Miracles.*

For a good half-hour, the Fairy left the puppet by himself to weep and wail over the size of his nose which was so big he couldn't get it through the door of his bedroom. She left him alone like this, of course, to teach him a lesson, and to cure him of the nasty habit of telling lies—the worst habit a little boy can fall into. At last, however, she took pity on him. She clapped her hands and suddenly the bedroom window opened wide and through it flew at least a thousand red-headed woodpeckers. Immediately, those woodpeckers perched on Pinocchio's huge wooden nose and began to peck away at it fiercely, and in a very few minutes they had pecked the puppet's enormous and ridiculous nose down to its normal size.

"Dear Fairy, you're so good," said the puppet as he dried his eyes, "and I love you so much."

"I love you too," answered the Fairy, "and if you'd like to stay here with me, you can be my little brother and I'll be your loving sister."

"I would love to stay with you—but what about my poor Daddy?"

"I've thought of everything. I've already let your Daddy
know, and he'll be here before dark."

"Really?" shouted Pinocchio, jumping up and down. "Then,
little Fairy, if you'll let me, I'd like to go to meet him! I can
hardly wait to hug that poor old man who has suffered so much
for my sake!"

"All right, then—but be sure you don't get lost. Take the road
through the woods and I'm sure you'll meet him there."

Pinocchio immediately started out, and as soon as he reached
the woods he began to run like a deer. But when he came to one
certain spot, almost in front of The Great Oak, he stopped short
because it seemed to him that he heard something moving in the

bushes. Then, as a matter of fact, someone did come out of the bushes . . . can you guess who? It was his old friends, the Fox and the Cat with whom he had had supper at the Inn of The Red Lobster.

"Well, well, well," said the Fox as he gave the puppet a big hug, "if it isn't our dear old friend, Pinocchio. Well, Pinocchio, how do you happen to be here?"

"Yes, how do you happen to be here?" repeated the Cat.

"Ah well, it's a long story," said Pinocchio, "and I'll tell you about it when I have more time. But do you know that the other night, after you left me alone at the inn, I met robbers on the road—?"

"Robbers! Really? Oh, you poor boy! And what did they want from you?"

"They wanted to steal my gold pieces."

"Oh, those villains!"

"Those awful villains!" repeated the Cat.

"And then I tried to run away," continued the puppet, "but they chased me and finally they caught me and hanged me from the limb of that big tree . . ." and Pinocchio pointed to The Great Oak which was only a few steps away.

"Have you ever heard of anything so terrible?" cried the Fox. "Really, what an awful world this is we have to live in! Where can decent people like us find a safe place to live?"[1] Meanwhile, as the Fox was talking, Pinocchio noticed that the Cat was lame in his right foreleg—in fact, he had lost his whole paw with all its claws.

"Whatever happened to your paw?" he asked.

The Cat tried hard to say something sensible, but became confused. Seeing this, the Fox said very quickly, "My friend here is much too modest to answer your question, so I'll answer for him. Less than an hour ago we happened to meet an old wolf on the road who was starving to death and he begged us to give him something to eat. However, since we didn't have so much as a bare fishbone to offer him, what do you think my friend did? My friend here—who truly has a heart of gold—he actually cut off one of his own paws and threw it to that starving wolf so he could relieve his hunger—" and the Fox wiped away a tear.

When he heard this, Pinocchio was truly touched, and he went over to the Cat and softly whispered in his ear, "If all cats were like you, how lucky the mice would be!"

"Now then, what are you doing in this place?" the Fox asked the puppet.

"I'm waiting for my Daddy who should be coming along any time now."

"And what about your gold pieces?"

"Oh, I still have them in my pocket—that is, all but the one I had to spend at the Inn of The Red Lobster."

"Just think," said the Fox, "by tomorrow morning, those four gold pieces could become two *thousand* gold pieces! Why don't you take my advice? Why don't you just go and plant your gold pieces in the Field of Miracles right away?"

"Gee, I can't go today," said Pinocchio, "it'll have to be some other day."

"Well, that'll be too late," said the Fox.

"Why's that?"

"Because that field is going to be sold to a very rich *cavaliere*,* and after tomorrow nobody can plant money there anymore."

"How far is this Field of Miracles?"

"Why, about two miles from here. Why don't you come along with us? Within a half-hour you can be there. You can just plant your gold pieces and after a very little while you can collect two thousand. Then this evening you can go home with your pockets full. Well, do you want to come with us . . . ?"

Pinocchio hesitated a moment before answering as he thought about the good Fairy, about old Geppetto, and about the advice of Talking Cricket. But he ended up just the way all foolish and thoughtless boys do. He nodded his wooden head and said to the Fox and the Cat, "Let's go! I'm with you . . . !" and off they went together.

*. . . *a very rich cavaliere:* that is, "a very rich gentleman." However, *cavaliere* does not mean "gentleman" in the way we use the word. In Pinocchio's time, a cavaliere was a member of the lower nobility or, as we sometimes say, a person of "gentle birth." Remember in chapter 11 when Pinocchio tried to flatter the fierce puppet-master, Fire Eater, by addressing him as cavaliere Fire Eater, he was actually calling him something very like "Sir Knight."

After they had walked half the day, they came to a town called Fooltrap.[2] As soon as they entered the town, Pinocchio discovered that the streets were filled with mangy dogs who yawned with hunger, sheep shorn of their wool and shivering in the cold, roosters who had lost their beautiful combs and tail-feathers and who now begged for a little grain of corn, huge butterflies who could no longer fly because they had sold their lovely colored wings, peacocks who had sold their gorgeous tails and who were now ashamed to let themselves be seen, and pheasants who skulked about, mourning the loss of their brilliant gold and silver feathers which were gone forever. Through the midst of this crowd of miserable creatures there passed, from time to time, a fine carriage in which there rode a Fox, a thieving Magpie,[3] or some other ravenous bird or animal.

"This Field of Miracles—just exactly where is it?" asked Pinocchio.

"It's just a few steps from here."

After they passed through the town, they came to a lonely field which, when you looked at it carefully, seemed like any other field in Italy.

"Ah, here we are," said the Fox to the puppet. "Now, just dig a little hole in the ground with your hands and plant your gold pieces in it."

Pinocchio obeyed. He dug a little hole, put his last four gold pieces in it, and then covered them over with a little earth.

"Now then," said the Fox, "bring a pail of water from that spring over there, and water the soil where you planted your money."[4] Pinocchio went over to the spring, but because he had no pail, he took off his shoe and filled it with water. Then he asked, "What else do I have to do?"

"Nothing more," replied the Fox, "we can leave now, and in about half an hour you can come back and you'll find a bush pushing up through the ground with its branches loaded with gold pieces."

The poor foolish puppet was completely overjoyed. He thanked the Fox and the Cat a thousand times and promised to buy a beautiful gift for each of them.

"But we don't want any gifts," replied the two scoundrels. "It's quite enough for us that we've taught you how to grow rich without working hard. That's reward enough for us!" And with this, they said goodbye to Pinocchio, and wishing him a good harvest, they went about their business.

· ❖ ·

Chapter 19

*Pinocchio is robbed of his gold pieces
and he is punished for it by being put
in jail for four months.*

Pinocchio went back to Fooltrap and began to count the minutes one by one. Then, when he thought enough time had passed, he again took the road back to the Field of Miracles. As he hurried along, his heart beat hard: *tìc, tòc, tìc, tòc*—just like the sound of a big grandfather clock when it is well-oiled and running really well.

Meanwhile, he thought to himself, "Gee, maybe instead of two thousand gold pieces, I'll find three thousand on that bush! Suppose I find five thousand . . . or maybe even a hundred thousand . . . ! Boy, I'd really be rich then. I could have a thousand wooden ponies to ride, and I'd have a thousand stable boys just to take care of them. Then I'd have a wine cellar filled with barrels of *rosoli**[1] and *alchermes*!†[2] And then I'd have a big library, too, but there wouldn't be any books on the shelves, just sugar plums, *panettoni*,‡ pies and cakes, almond cakes, and cream puffs!"

He was still dreaming of these wonderful things when he

**rosoli:* the plural of *rosolio,* a cordial that Italians often make at home of alcohol, sugar, and raisins or other fruit.

†*alchermes:* This, too, was a strange kind of cordial which was beloved of Italians in Pinocchio's time. Later, it fell into disfavor because it was discovered that its principal ingredient was not really what people always thought it was.

‡*panettoni:* the plural of *panettone,* a rich, sweet, bread-like cake usually mixed with raisins and candied citron. Like bread, it contains yeast and rises to the shape of a beehive. It is delicious with hot tea, or cold milk.

came again to the Field of Miracles. When he arrived there, he looked all around for a bush loaded down with gold pieces, but he saw nothing. Then, he walked another hundred steps into the field—he still saw nothing. He walked directly to the spot where he had planted his four gold pieces—still nothing. He stood there puzzled, and as he scratched his head in confusion, he suddenly heard a loud burst of laughter. He looked up and saw a huge parrot perched on a branch above him. The parrot was preening the few feathers it had left.

"What are you laughing at?" asked Pinocchio angrily.

"I'm laughing," replied the parrot, "because when I was preening my feathers, I happened to tickle myself under my wing."

The puppet said nothing to this. Instead, he went back to the spring and again filled his shoe with water and once more he watered the ground where he had planted his gold pieces. At this, there was another loud burst of laughter—even louder than before—that broke the silence of that lonely field.

"Come on now, parrot—!" shouted Pinocchio in a rage, "What are you laughing at now?"

"I'm laughing at all those idiots[3] who believe every stupid thing they're told, and who let themselves be trapped and cheated by people who are sharper than they are."

"Do you . . . do you mean . . . are you talking about people like me?"

"I'm talking about *you*, poor little Pinocchio—about you who are silly enough to believe that money can be planted in the ground and raised like beans and corn. I believed in this nonsense once myself, and now I'm paying for it! And now, now when it's really too late, I've learned the hard way that to save a little money, you've got to earn it by hard work, or by the cleverness of your own brain."

"But, I don't understand," said the puppet who had begun to tremble with fear.

"Well, let's see if I can explain it better," replied the parrot. "As soon as you went back to Fooltrap, the Fox and the Cat came back here and dug up the gold pieces you planted and then they ran away like the wind. The one who can catch 'em now will have to be a pretty fast runner!"

Pinocchio just stood there with his mouth wide open. Then, because he didn't want simply to take the word of this shabby old bird, he got down on his knees and with his fingernails he began to dig up the ground he had so carefully watered. He dug, and he dug, and he dug until he had dug a hole deep enough to bury a haystack, but the money he had planted was no longer there.

Now, in wild desperation, he ran back to the town where he went directly to the courthouse to denounce the two thieves who had robbed him of his gold pieces. As it happened, the judge of the court turned out to be an ape of the gorilla family.[4] He was a very old ape and, because of his white hair and his long white beard, he looked very wise and respectable. But the thing that made him look especially dignified was the pair of gold-rimmed spectacles he wore—special spectacles without glasses in them which he was forced to wear because of some eye trouble he had suffered for several years.

Pinocchio stood before the judge and told the whole story of how the two thieves had robbed him of his gold pieces. He gave a complete description of the Fox and the Cat and all the details he could think of that would prove his case and help bring the robbers to justice. When he had finished his story, the judge said sympathetically, "Ah, now I understand everything." And with this, he reached out his hand and rang a little bell.

At the sound of the bell, two huge, ugly dogs appeared dressed

in the uniform of the *Carabinieri*.[5] Then the judge, pointing to Pinocchio, said to them, "All right, officers, I want you to know that this poor little devil has been robbed of his four gold pieces. Take him away and throw him in jail immediately!"[6]

Pinocchio was flabbergasted when he heard this. He tried to protest, but the carabinieri didn't want to waste time, so they stopped up his mouth with their paws and hustled him off to the lockup. And there he stayed for four months—four whole months! And he might still be there if it hadn't been for a stroke of luck. It seems that the young prince who ruled over the town of Fooltrap had won a great victory over his enemies, and had ordered a big celebration with bright colored lights, fireworks, horse races, and bicycle races. Furthermore, he commanded that all the jails and the prisons be opened and all criminals be released.

"Look," said Pinocchio to his jailer, "if you let the others go, I want to go too!"

"Ah no!" answered the jailer, "I'm afraid you've got to be a *real* criminal for me to let you go, y'see."

"Now just a minute!" shouted Pinocchio, "Don't you realize I *am* a real criminal?"

"Well then, that's different," said the jailer, "if you're a real criminal, I've got to let you go—that's the law!"[7]

Chapter 20

When Pinocchio gets out of jail,
he sets out for the house of the Fairy.
On the way he meets a horrible snake, and
afterwards he is caught in a trap.

Just imagine Pinocchio's joy when he found himself free again! Without wasting a moment, he hurried out of the town of Fooltrap and took the road that led to the Fairy's little house. It had been raining very hard for a long time, the road had become a regular swamp, and he sank into mud up to his knees. But the puppet would not give up. He was so eager to see his father again, and his little sister with the blue hair, that he ran and leaped like a greyhound, and as he splashed through the mud puddles he became covered with mud from head to foot.

While he was running, he kept saying to himself, "My goodness! So many terrible things have happened to me! And I deserved every one of them, too, because I'm just a stubborn, hard-headed, whining puppet! I've always had to have my own way about everything, and I've never listened to the people who love me and who have a thousand times more common sense than I have! But from now on, I'm going to change my ways and be a really good, obedient boy. After all this time, I've finally learned that disobedient boys always lose out in the end and never amount to anything. And will my poor old Daddy be waiting for me? I wonder if I'll find him at the Fairy's house. Poor man! It's so long since I last saw him that I can hardly wait to hug him and kiss him a thousand times. And will the Fairy forgive me for all the naughty things I've done? To think of all the kindness and the loving care she gave me! And then to think that if I'm alive today, it's just because of her! There couldn't possibly be a more ungrateful or stupid boy than I am!" He had hardly finished saying all this to himself when he stopped suddenly and took four steps backward in fright!

What did he see—?

He saw a huge snake stretched across the road. Its skin was green, its eyes glowed like fire, and its long tail was smoking like a chimney. You can't really imagine how frightened Pinocchio was! He turned and ran back to a safe distance, and then he sat down on a little pile of stones to wait for the big snake to go about its business and leave the road clear for him to go by.

He waited an hour, two hours, three hours, but the snake was still there, and even from where he was sitting, he could see the red glow of its fiery eyes and the column of smoke rising from its tail. Finally, Pinocchio took courage, and walking up to within a few steps of the snake he said in a soft, sweet little voice, "Excuse me, *signor* Snake,* but would you be so kind as

*signor *Snake:* Here's that word *signor* again. As you can well understand, Pinocchio is being very cautious with this great snake and addresses him respectfully as "Sir Snake."

to move over a little to one side of the road, just enough to let me go by?"

He might as well have been talking to a wall, for there was no answer.

He tried again in that same silly little voice, "You must understand, signor Snake, that I am on my way home where my father is waiting for me and it's been such a long time since I last saw him! Please then, will you kindly step aside and let me go on my way?" He waited for some little sign in answer to his polite request, but nothing happened. Instead, the snake, which up until now seemed so full of life, became completely still and almost stiff. Its eyes were closed* and its tail had stopped smoking.

*Its eyes were closed: Mister Collodi was pulling our legs when he said that this snake's tail smoked "like a chimney," and he is doing it again here. As you probably know, snakes, like fish, have no eyelids so this monster could not possibly have closed its eyes!

"Could it be dead?" wondered Pinocchio as he rubbed his hands together. Then, without stopping to think, he made a leap over the snake, but as he did, the snake coiled itself up like a steel spring and tripped the puppet and made him fall head first into the mud. There he was, standing on his head, stuck fast in the mud with his legs wiggling foolishly in the air.

At the sight of the puppet with his head stuck in the mud and kicking with all his might, the snake burst out laughing, and it laughed, and laughed, and laughed until finally it suffered a heart attack and died. And this time it was really dead.

Now Pinocchio began to run again as fast as he could so that he might reach the Fairy's house before dark. As he ran along, however, he began to get terribly hungry. He got hungrier and hungrier until finally he decided to leave the road to pick a few bunches of grapes he saw on a grapevine in a field. He was sorry he ever thought of it!

He had hardly reached the grapevine when . . . *Crack!* his legs were caught fast between two sharp irons,[1] and the pain was so terrible that he saw every star in the sky! The poor puppet had been caught in an iron trap which had been set to catch some big polecats*[2] that had been killing chickens all over the neighborhood.

· ❖ ·

Chapter 21

*Pinocchio is captured by a farmer
who makes him work as a watchdog.*

Pinocchio, as you can well imagine, began to cry and scream, but all his tears were wasted for there wasn't a house anywhere in sight, and not a living soul could be seen on the road.

*. . . *big polecats:* Collodi is referring to the European polecat (in Italian, *faina*) which is related to the weasel. It can reach a length of 30 inches measured from the tip of its pointed nose to the end of its bushy tail. It is brown and black with yellowish patches on its face. It hunts small animals for food, and has a special appetite for poultry, as we shall see later. It also has a bad smell, which is probably why the American skunk is often called a polecat.

At last darkness fell.

Partly because of the pain caused by the trap which cut into his shins, and partly because he was afraid of being left alone in the dark in that field, Pinocchio was ready to faint, when suddenly he saw a little firefly*[1] fluttering above his head. Calling out to it, he said, "Please, little firefly, won't you take pity on me and set me free from this awful trap?"

"Poor little boy!" answered the firefly, "How did you ever get caught in a thing like that?"

"Well, I came into this field to pick a few bunches of grapes, and . . . ."

"But, do these grapes belong to you?"

"Well—no."

"Then who told you that you could take things that don't belong to you?"

"But I was hungry."

"My dear boy, just because you're hungry isn't a good reason for taking something that doesn't belong to you."

"I know, I know—that's true!" said Pinocchio as he burst into tears, "I'll never, ever do it again!"

At this point, the conversation was interrupted by the sound of soft footsteps which came closer and closer. They were the footsteps of the farmer who owned the field who was coming on tiptoe to see if he had caught one of the polecats that were killing his chickens every night. When he raised his lantern over his head and looked closely, he was astonished to discover that, instead of a polecat, he had caught—a boy!

---

*. . . *little firefly:* Surely, every boy and girl has seen fireflies flickering in the dark shadow of a hedge in the dusk of a summer's evening. Some have even captured these gentle little creatures and watched them flash their little lights in a handkerchief or in a glass jar. Sometimes they are known as "lightning bugs," and when I was a little boy, I was told that the Indians call them *wa-wa-ta-see.* I believed this then, but when I grew up, I forgot to ask an Indian if he really called them that. Anyway, in Italian, the firefly is called *lucciola* (lou-chee-OH-lah) "little light," and they are as fascinating to Italian children as to any other children in the world.

"Aha, you little thief!" said the angry farmer, "So you're the one who's been stealing my chickens!"

"No! no!" cried Pinocchio, sobbing, "I only came into your field to pick a couple of bunches of grapes!"

"Well, anybody who'd steal grapes'd steal chickens, too. Just you wait! I'll teach you a lesson you'll remember for a while!" Then the farmer opened the trap, seized the puppet around his neck, and carried him off to his farmhouse as if he were carrying a newborn lamb.

When he reached the barnyard, the farmer threw Pinocchio on the ground and, putting his heavy foot on his neck, he said, "Well, it's getting late, and I want to go to bed. I'll settle with you first thing tomorrow. Meanwhile, my old watchdog died today, so you can just take his place. You can be my new watchdog." With this, he put a huge collar all covered with sharp

brass studs around poor Pinocchio's neck and pulled it up so
tightly that he could not slip his head through it. Attached to
this terrible collar was a long iron chain that was fastened firmly
to the wall.

"If it rains tonight," said the farmer, "you can lie down in
that kennel over there. For a bed you can use the straw that my
poor old dog used for four years. Remember, keep your ears
pricked, and if chicken thieves come around, don't forget to
bark." With these final instructions, the farmer went into the
house and locked the door tightly, leaving poor Pinocchio lying
in the yard nearly dead from cold, hunger, and fright.

From time to time, the puppet desperately seized the collar
that choked him, crying, "It serves me right! It really serves me
right! I wanted to be a good-for-nothing, a vagabond! I was only
too ready to listen to evil companions and because of that I've
always had bad luck. If I'd only been a good boy like all the
others—if I'd only stayed at home with my poor Daddy, I
wouldn't be here now in this barnyard working as a watchdog
for a farmer! Oh, if only I could be born again! But, now it's too
late and here I am . . . !" And with this outburst which came
from the bottom of his heart, he crawled into the kennel and fell
fast asleep.

Chapter 22

*Pinocchio discovers the
chicken thieves and as a reward for
his loyalty he is set free.*

He had been sleeping soundly for more than two hours when,
about midnight, Pinocchio was awakened by the whispering of
strange voices that seemed to come from the barnyard. He stuck
the tip of his nose out the door of his kennel and saw four
dark-colored animals that looked a little like big cats who seemed
to be holding a kind of council-meeting. But they were not
really cats at all, they were polecats, wild, meat-eating animals
that are especially greedy for eggs and young chickens. One of

these polecats went over to the door of the kennel and said in a soft voice, "Good evening, Melampo."[1]

"My name isn't Melampo," answered the puppet.

"Oh, who are you then?"

"I'm Pinocchio."

"And what're you doing here?"

"I'm acting as watchdog."

"But where's Melampo? Where's the old dog that lives in this kennel?"

"He died this morning."

"Died? Oh, the poor old boy! He was such a kind old dog! But, then, judging by your face, you seem to be a pretty good dog, too."

"I beg your pardon, but I'm *not* a dog!"

"Oh? What are you then?"

"I'm a puppet."

"And you're acting as watchdog?"

"I'm afraid so! I have to do it as punishment."

"Well then, I suppose we can make the same arrangement with you that we had with old Melampo. I'm sure you'll be happy with it."

"And what kind of an arrangement is that?"

"One night a week we'll come to this chicken coop as we always have done in the past, and we'll carry off eight chickens. We'll eat seven of those chickens and we'll give one to you. You've got to understand, though, that you must never bark and wake up the farmer."

"Is this the same agreement you had with Melampo?" asked Pinocchio.

"Exactly, and we always got along very well together. You just sleep peacefully, and you can be sure that before we go, we'll leave you a fine fat chicken, all plucked and ready for your breakfast next morning. Now, do we understand each other quite well?"

"Oh yes, very well!" answered Pinocchio, who at the same time shook his head and thought to himself, "We'll soon see about that!"

The four polecats, thinking they were perfectly safe, went immediately into the chicken coop which was close by the kennel. With their teeth and claws, they quickly opened the wooden gate and slipped inside, one after the other. But they were hardly inside the chicken coop when they heard the gate slam shut behind them. It was Pinocchio who had closed the gate and, to keep it shut tight, he rolled a huge stone against it. Then he began to bark just like a watchdog, "*Bù-bù-bù!*"*

When the farmer heard the barking, he jumped out of bed. Taking his gun, he went to the window and shouted, "What's going on out there?"

"Thieves!" cried Pinocchio.

"Where?"

"In the chicken coop!"

"I'll be right down!"

And quicker than you can say "Polecat!" the farmer was in the barnyard. He went straightway to the chicken coop, caught the polecats, and after putting them into a sack, he spoke to them with great satisfaction: "Well, I've finally caught you! I could very well punish you myself, but I'm not a cruel man. Instead, I'll just take you tomorrow to the innkeeper in the village who can cook you in a nice sweet-and-sour sauce and serve you up for stewed rabbit.² It's an honor you don't really deserve, but generous people like me aren't fussy about such little matters."

Then, turning to Pinocchio, the farmer patted him on the head and, among other things, he asked him, "How did you ever discover these wicked little thieves? Melampo, my faithful old Melampo, could never discover anything!" At this point, the puppet could very easily have told the farmer about the shameful agreement that his dog had made with the thieving polecats. But he suddenly remembered that the old dog was dead now, and he thought to himself, "What's the use of denouncing the dead? The dead are dead, and it's just as well to leave them in peace!"

*. . . *Bù-bù-bù:* We know, of course, that this should be *Bow-wow-wow* but it seems that Italian animals simply will not talk right— even when they are being imitated by a puppet. I have been told, though, that Tuscan dogs really bark like this.

"When those thieves came into the barnyard, were you awake or asleep?" asked the farmer.

"I was asleep," answered Pinocchio, "but they woke me up with their loud talk. Then finally, one of them came over to me and said, "If you promise not to bark and wake up the farmer, we'll make you a present of a nicely plucked young chicken.[3] How about that—? The nerve of that polecat making a proposition like that! I may be only a wooden puppet with every fault in the world, but I would never make a deal with thieves or share anything they stole from others!"

"Good boy!" said the farmer, patting him on the back. "That's a fine attitude—and just to show you how grateful I am, I'm going to set you free right now so you can go home."

And with this, he took the heavy collar off the puppet's neck.

· ❖ ·

Chapter 23

Pinocchio mourns the death of the beautiful girl with the blue hair. Then he meets a Pigeon who carries him to the seashore where he dives into the water to try to save his father.

When Pinocchio no longer felt the heavy weight of that awful dog collar around his neck, he started out across the fields without stopping for a single moment until he reached the main road that led to the Fairy's little house.

Once he reached the road, he turned to look down over the countryside. With his naked eye he could clearly see the woods where he had met those two robbers, the Fox and the Cat. Above all the other trees, he could clearly see the top of The Great Oak on which the robbers had hanged him. But, although he looked around in every direction, he could not see the little house of the beautiful girl with the blue hair.

Then a strange, sad feeling came over him, and he began to run with all his might, and in a few minutes he reached the field where the little white house had stood. But the little white house was no longer there. Instead, in its place, he found a little

marble tablet, and carved into the cold stone were these sad words:

HERE LIES

THE GIRL WITH THE BLUE HAIR

WHO DIED OF SORROW

BECAUSE SHE WAS ABANDONED BY HER

LITTLE BROTHER,

PINOCCHIO[1]

You can imagine how the poor puppet must have felt after he had slowly spelled out those terrible words.[*2] He threw himself on the ground, and covering the little marble gravestone with a thousand kisses, he burst into a great flood of tears. He cried all night, and the next morning and well into the day he went on crying although he had no tears left. His cries and his wails were

*. . . *he had slowly spelled out those terrible words:* Here we find Pinocchio reading the words on the little gravestone even though we know he can't read because he has never gone to school. You probably noticed this just the way I did when I was a boy, but I'm sure it doesn't bother you any more than it did me. It's just that some wise guy is going to make a fuss about it when it doesn't really matter.

so heartbreaking and so loud that all the hills around him echoed their sound.

As he wept he said, "Oh, dear little Fairy, why did you die? Why didn't I die instead of you? I'm such a wicked boy, and you were so good. And my Daddy—where is he? Oh, dear little Fairy, tell me where I can find him, for I want to stay with him forever and never leave him again—never! Oh, dear Fairy, tell me it's not true that you're dead! If you love me—if you really love your little brother, come back to life again—come back as you were before! Doesn't it make you unhappy to see me alone and abandoned by everyone? If those robbers come back, they'll hang me again from The Great Oak, and then I'll be dead forever. What can I do now, all alone in the world? Now that I've lost you and my Daddy, who will feed me? Where will I sleep at night? Who'll make me a new jacket when I need one? Oh! it would be better—a hundred, hundred times better—if I died instead of you! Oh, yes! I want to die too! *Ih! Ih! Ih . . . !*" and in his misery he tried to tear his hair, but because his hair was really only made of wood, he couldn't even stick his fingers into it.

Just then a big Pigeon flew overhead and, soaring on out-spread wings, it called down to the puppet from a great height, "Tell me, little boy, what are you doing down there?"

"Can't you see what I'm doing? I'm crying!" said Pinocchio, looking up at the sky and wiping his eyes with the sleeve of his jacket.

"Tell me," the Pigeon went on, "do you happen to know a puppet called Pinocchio?"

"Pinocchio! Did I hear you say Pinocchio?" shouted the puppet, jumping quickly to his feet. "I'm Pinocchio!"

At this, the pigeon flew quickly down to the ground. It was a huge bird—larger, even, than a turkey. "Do you know Mastro Geppetto, too?" it asked.

"Do I *know* him? He's my poor old Daddy! Has he spoken to you about me? Will you show me where he is? Is he still alive? Tell me quickly, for heaven's sake—! is he still alive?"

"Well, he was still alive when I left him three days ago on the seashore. He was building a little boat to cross the ocean in. For more than four months, that poor old man has wandered all over the land looking for you. Since he couldn't find you, he decided that he'd have to search for you in faraway countries in the New World."

"How far is it to the seashore?" Pinocchio asked anxiously.

"More than six hundred miles."[3]

"Six hundred miles! Oh, dear Pigeon, how wonderful it would be to have wings like yours!"

"If you really want to go, I'll carry you there."

"How?"

"Why, on my back just as if you were riding a horse. Are you heavy or light?"

"Heavy? No, not at all! I'm as light as a stick of wood."

Without saying another word, Pinocchio jumped on the Pigeon's back with a leg on each side like a horseman and he shouted happily, "Gallop! Gallop away little horse—I must get there quickly!"

The Pigeon flew up into the air with the puppet on his back, and in a few minutes they were up so high that they almost touched the clouds. When he found himself so high in the air, Pinocchio became curious and looked down at the ground, but the sight made him so frightened and dizzy that he put his arms tightly around the neck of his feathered horse and hung on for dear life.

They flew all day long. Toward evening, the Pigeon suddenly said, "I'm thirsty!"

"And I'm so hungry!" added Pinocchio.

"I'll tell you what," said the Pigeon, "let's stop at that pigeon house down there for a few minutes. Then we can go on our way and be at the seashore by early tomorrow morning." However, when they landed at the old pigeon house, it was empty and they could find nothing but a basin of water and a basket of fava beans.*[4]

---

*. . . *fava beans:* Italians love these huge beans which are among the earliest spring vegetables in Italy. The bean is encased in a thick, leathery skin that becomes quite loose and easy to strip off when it is boiled or steamed. When the skins are taken off before serving, fava beans look a little like huge lima beans. In England and America, favas are sometimes called "broad beans" or "horse beans."

Now, the puppet had never in his life been able to stand fava beans because, to hear him tell it, they upset his stomach and made him very sick. But that evening he ate beans until he was full, and when the basket was almost empty, he turned to the Pigeon and said, "Gee, I never would have believed that fava beans could taste so good!"

"Well, you'll just have to learn, my dear boy," replied the Pigeon, "that when you're really hungry, and there's nothing else to eat, even beans can be delicious. In fact, there is even a very old saying, 'Hunger makes hard beans sweet'."[5]

After they finished their little lunch of beans and water, they began their journey again, and away they flew. Early the next morning they arrived at the seashore. The Pigeon set Pinocchio gently on the ground, and because it didn't really want to be thanked for its kind deed, it quickly flew away and disappeared in the clouds.

The beach was crowded with people who were waving their arms and shouting as they looked out to sea. Pinocchio went up to an old woman and asked, "What's going on here?"

"Well," said the woman, "it seems that some poor old man has lost his son and he's gone off in a little boat to look for him across the sea. But the sea is so rough and stormy, I'm afraid his little boat'll sink."

"Where is the boat?" asked Pinocchio anxiously.

"It's right out there where I'm pointing," said the old woman as she pointed her finger out to sea at a little boat that, at such a great distance, looked like a nutshell with a tiny man in it. Pinocchio strained his eyes out to sea and, after peering hard for a long time, he gave a shout, "Hey—! that's my Daddy out there! That's my poor old Daddy!"

Meanwhile, the little boat, tossed about by the wild sea, once disappeared completely, but in the next moment it appeared again riding high on the crest of a huge wave. Pinocchio stood on top of a high rock and called again and again to his father, signaling to him desperately with his hands, with his handkerchief, and with his cap. And it seemed as though old Geppetto had recognized his son even though he was so far from shore, for he too waved his cap, and by making wild gestures, he indicated that he would like to go back to shore, but he couldn't because the sea was so rough he couldn't use his oars. Suddenly there came a tremendous wave and the little boat disappeared again. Everyone waited for it to come to the surface again, but it was no more to be seen.

"Oh, the poor old man!" cried the fishermen who stood in a little group on the shore, and after murmuring a prayer for poor Geppetto, they turned away to go back to their cottages. Just then they heard a wild cry, and when they looked back, they saw a little boy leap from a rock into the sea shouting wildly, "I'll save my Daddy—! I'll save him!"

Now you remember, of course, that Pinocchio was made entirely of wood, and because of this he floated lightly on top of the water and, besides, he could swim like a fish. In one moment the people on the beach saw him disappear under the water,

96

carried down by the force of the waves. In the next moment, far, far from shore, they could see now a leg, and now an arm, appear above the surface, but at last they lost sight of him altogether, and he was seen no more.

"Oh, the poor little boy," muttered the fishermen on the beach and, after murmuring a prayer for the poor puppet, they turned away again to go back to their cottages.

· ❖ ·

Chapter 24

Pinocchio lands on Busy Bee Island
and finds the Fairy again.

Hoping to be in time to save his poor father, Pinocchio swam all night long, and what a terrible night it was! The rain came down in a flood with hailstones and loud claps of thunder, while flashes of lightning made the whole world as bright as day. Toward morning, he saw a long strip of land a short distance away from him. It was an island in the middle of the sea.

He tried vainly to reach the shore of the island, but the waves tossed him about as if he had been just any old stick of wood. At last, luckily for him, there came a huge wave with such force that it lifted him up high and threw him violently on the beach. He came down so hard that when he struck the ground all his ribs and joints rattled and cracked. But he comforted himself by saying, "Well, that's another lucky escape I've had!"

Then, little by little, the sky cleared, the sun came out in all its brilliance, and the sea became as calm and smooth as a huge pool of oil. The puppet spread his clothes out to dry in the sun, and began to look in every direction to see if he could discover on that vast ocean a little boat with a man in it. But, although he strained his eyes with looking, he saw nothing before him but the sky, the great wide sea, and the sail of a ship that was so far, far away that it looked no bigger than a little white moth.

"I wonder what this island is called," he said to himself. "I wonder if the people who live here are at least civilized, that is, people who don't have the nasty habit of hanging boys on oak

trees! But who can I ask? What if there's nobody here at all?"

The thought of being alone, alone, all alone in this land where nobody lived made him so unhappy that he was almost ready to cry when, all of a sudden, he saw a big fish swimming near the shore. It was quietly going about its own business with its head raised out of the water. Not knowing how to call the fish by name, the puppet shouted loudly to make himself heard, "Hey there, signor Fish! May I have a word with you?"

"You may even have two words, if you like," answered the big fish who happened to be a Dolphin,[1] but so very polite that there are few other fish like him in any sea in the world.*

"Would you be so kind, then, as to tell me if there is a place on this island where I can get something to eat without being eaten up myself?"

*. . . a Dolphin . . . so polite that there are few other fish like him . . . in the world: The dolphin, sometimes mistakenly called "porpoise" in the United States, besides being very polite, is also a very intelligent sea creature which, as you probably already know, is not a fish at all, but a mammal like the whale, the seal, and the sea otter. The dolphin has always been considered friendly and helpful to mankind, and many stories have been told about how these wonderful sea animals have pushed drowning sailors to safety ashore.

"There certainly is," replied the Dolphin. "In fact, there's a place not far from here."

"And what road should I take to get there?"

"Take that path on your left, and just follow your nose. You can't miss it."

"Tell me something else . . . you swim about the sea all day and all night. By any chance, have you ever seen a little boat with my Daddy in it?"

"And who is your Daddy?" asked the Dolphin.

"He's the best Daddy in the whole world," said Pinocchio, "and I'm probably the worst son in the whole world."

"With that terrible storm we had last night," said the Dolphin, "that little boat probably sank right to the bottom."

"And my Daddy—?"

"By this time, he certainly must have been swallowed up, boat and all, by that huge Shark* that's been spreading death and destruction in these waters for a long time now."

"And is he very big, this Shark?" asked Pinocchio who had begun to shake with fear.

"Is he big? Just to give you an idea, I only need to say that he's as big as a five-story building, and he has a mouth so wide and deep that it could easily swallow a freight train, locomotive and all!"

"*Mamma mia*—!" exclaimed the terrified puppet. Then, quickly putting his clothes on, he turned again to the Dolphin and said, "Good bye, signor Fish, please excuse the trouble I've caused you, and many thanks for your kindness."

He turned then and hurried down the path, walking so fast that he was almost running. And at every little noise he heard, he turned to look behind him, afraid that he might see following him that terrible Shark as big as a five-story building with a freight train in its mouth. After he had walked for a good half-hour, he came at last to a village which was called Busy Bee. The streets of the village were swarming with people who hurried here and there on business—everyone had something to do, and

---

*. . . *that huge Shark:* In Italian, the shark is called *pesce-cane* (pesh-eh-CA-neh) which means "dog-fish."

everyone was busy. You couldn't have found an idler or a loafer if you had looked for one with a bright lantern!

"I can see right now," said the lazy Pinocchio to himself, "this is no place for me! I was never born to work!"

Meanwhile, he had become terribly hungry for he had had nothing to eat for more than twenty-four hours, not even a dish of fava beans. What could he do? There were only two ways for him to get some food: he could look for work, or he could beg for a little money to buy some bread. But it is shameful to beg for money. His father had often preached to him that no one has the right to beg but old people and cripples. The really poor people in this world, the ones who truly deserve pity and charity, are those who are so old and sick that they can't earn a living with their own hands. It is the duty of everyone to work, and if they won't work, it's too bad for them if they go hungry![2]

At that moment, a man passed by, tired and breathing heavily. He was pulling two heavy carts full of charcoal. Pinocchio could tell by his face that he was a kind man, so he approached him and, lowering his eyes in shame, he said to him softly, "Please, signore, will you give me a *soldo**—I'm dying of hunger."

"Not one soldo," answered the man, "but I'll give you four *soldi* if you'll help me pull these loads of charcoal home."

"Really signore! I'm surprised at you!" cried the puppet as if he had been insulted. "For your information, I'm not a donkey—! I have never hauled a cart in my life!"

"Well, good for you!" said the man, "if you're really dying of hunger, you can just eat a couple of slices of your own pride! But be careful it doesn't upset your stomach."

A few minutes later, a mason walked down the street, carrying a load of mortar on his shoulder. "Please, signore," said the

*. . . *a* soldo: Once before I explained soldo, but that was way back in chapter 9. Just in case you don't remember, I will repeat the explanation here:

"In Pinocchio's time, the soldo (plural, *soldi*) was a copper coin which was one-twentieth of the Italian *lira,* just as the American nickel is one-twentieth of a dollar."

puppet to the mason, "would you be so kind as to give a soldo to a poor boy who is yawning with hunger?"

"I'd be glad to," answered the mason, "and, instead of just one soldo, I'll give you *five* if you'll come and carry mortar for me."

"But mortar is so heavy," replied Pinocchio, "and I don't want to tire myself out."

"Well then, if you don't want to tire yourself out, my boy, you can just amuse yourself by yawning, for all the good it may do you!"

In less than half an hour, twenty people passed by, and Pinocchio tried to beg money of all of them, but they all said the same thing: "Aren't you ashamed of yourself? Instead of loafing about the streets, go and look for work and learn to earn your own living!"

Finally, there passed by a pretty young lady, carrying two big jars of water.* "Would you mind, *signorina*, if I took a sip of water from one of your jars?" asked Pinocchio who was burning with thirst.

"Of course not—drink, you poor boy!" said the young lady as she put her jars on the ground.

When Pinocchio had finished soaking up water like a sponge, he wiped his mouth and mumbled, "I'm not thirsty anymore. Now if only I wasn't hungry anymore!"

When she heard this, the pretty lady said, "If you'll carry one of these jars of water to my house, I'll give you a big piece of bread."

Pinocchio took another look at the jar, but he didn't say yes and he didn't say no.

". . . and besides the bread I'll give you a lovely big plate of spaghetti with tomato sauce and grated cheese."[3]

*. . . *carrying two big jars of water:* The pretty young lady had drawn the jars of water from the village fountain. This was the custom in Italian villages a hundred years ago—and still is the custom in many small country towns—because there was no running water in the houses. The fountain very probably had an ugly man's face carved on it that looked like the one mentioned in chapter 1.

Pinocchio took another look at the jar, but still he didn't say yes or no.

". . . and after you finish the spaghetti, I'll give you some ice cream."

This last temptation was just too much for Pinocchio, and he said with great determination, "All right, then, I'll carry the jar all the way to your house!" The water jar was very heavy, and the puppet, not being strong enough to carry it by hand, had to carry it on his head instead.

When they arrived at the house, the lady seated Pinocchio at a little table and placed before him everything she had promised him. The hungry puppet didn't simply eat, he gobbled everything down. His stomach was like a vacant house that hadn't been lived in for five months. Little by little his hunger was satisfied, and he raised his head to thank the kind lady. But when he looked at her he suddenly uttered a long "O-o-o-oh!" of astonishment, and he sat there enchanted, his eyes staring, his fork in the air, and his mouth full of spaghetti.

"Well, what's all this surprise about?" she asked, laughing.

"It's . . . it's . . . ," stammered Pinocchio, "it's . . . you look like . . . you remind me of . . . yes! yes! yes! the same voice the same eyes—the hair—yes! yes! yes! you even have blue hair, just like hers! Oh, dear Fairy, little Fairy, tell me, is it you? Is it really you? Don't make me cry anymore! If you only knew! I have cried so much! I have suffered so much!" And as he said this, Pinocchio burst into tears and, falling to his knees, he put his arms lovingly about that mysterious lady.

. ❖ .

Chapter 25

Pinocchio promises the Fairy that
he will be good and that he will study hard
because he is tired of being a puppet and
would like to become a real boy.

At first, the nice little lady would not admit that she was the little Fairy with the blue hair, but when she saw that she had finally been found out, she said, "You little rascal! How did you ever discover who I was?"

"It was my great love for you that told me."[1]

"Did you really remember? When you left me, I was only a girl, and now you find me a woman—a woman old enough to be your mother."

"I like that very much, because now instead of calling you 'little sister,' I can call you 'mother.' I've always wanted to have a mother like all the other boys. But tell me, how did you manage to grow up so fast?"

"That's a secret!"

"Then teach it to me—I'd like to grow up a little, too. I've never been bigger than a penny's worth of cheese."

"But you can't grow up," replied the Fairy.

"Why not?"

"Because puppets never grow up. They are born puppets, they live puppets, and they die puppets."

"Oh gee! I'm fed up with always being a puppet!" cried Pinocchio, and he rapped his wooden head with his wooden knuckles. "It's about time I became a real man, the way others do."

"You could become a man, too, if you really deserved it."

"I could? And what can I do to deserve it?"

"That's easy, you begin by being a good boy."

"And you think I'm not a good boy?"

"Now see here! You're anything but a good boy! Good boys are obedient, and you . . ."

"I'm never obedient."

"Good boys like to work and study hard, and you . . ."

"And I'm a lazy loafer all year round."

"Good boys always tell the truth, and you . . ."

"And I always tell lies."

"Good boys like to go to school, and you . . ."

"And school gives me a real pain. But, I promise you that from today on I'll change my ways."

"Is that a real promise?"

"Yes, it is—I'll become a good boy and be a comfort to my Daddy, but where can my poor Daddy be?"

"I don't know."

"Will I ever be lucky enough to see him again?"

"I think so—yes, I'm quite sure of it."

At this, Pinocchio became so mad with joy that he seized the Fairy's hands and smothered them with kisses. Then, raising his face, he looked at her lovingly and said, "Tell me, dear little mother, you weren't really dead, were you?"

"It doesn't seem so, does it?" answered the Fairy with a little smile.

"If you only knew how sad and heartbroken I was when I read 'Here lies . . .'!"

"But I *do* know, and that's why I have forgiven you. Because you were truly heartbroken, I was sure you had a good heart. If a boy has a good heart—even if he's naughty and full of bad habits—there's always hope for him. That is, there's always hope that he'll be back on the right path. That's why I came here to look for you. I'll be a little mother to you."

"Oh, how wonderful!" shouted Pinocchio as he jumped for joy.

"However, you must obey me and do everything I tell you to do."

"Oh, I will! I will!"

"Tomorrow, then," the Fairy went on, "you will start school."

Immediately Pinocchio became a little less joyful.

"Then you will have to choose some profession or some trade."

Pinocchio made a sour face and then lowered his head.

"What are you muttering between your teeth?" the Fairy asked in an angry tone.

"I was only saying," answered the puppet in a whining voice, "that it seems to be a little late for me to be going to school now."

"No sir—! Just get it through your head right now that it's never too late to learn and to get an education."

"But I don't want to enter a profession or follow a trade."

"Why not?"

"Because working makes me tired!"

"My dear boy," said the Fairy, "people who talk that way almost always end up in jail or in the hospital. Just remember that every man in this world, rich or poor, must work at something. Heaven help the lazy man! Laziness is a terrible disease which must be cured in childhood, and if it's not cured then, it can never be cured after you grow up."

Pinocchio was deeply moved by these wise words, and raising his head again, he said to the Fairy, "I'll study! I'll work! I'll do anything you tell me to do because I'm really sick of being a puppet. I want to become a real boy no matter what it takes to be one! You promised that I could, didn't you?"

"That's right, I did promise—and now, the rest depends on you."

· ❖ ·

Chapter 26

*Pinocchio and his schoolmates go
to the seashore to see the terrible shark.*

The very next day, Pinocchio went to school. Imagine what those mischievous children did when they saw a puppet come to their school! It seemed as if they would never stop laughing. One of them pulled at his jacket from behind; another snatched off his cap and ran off with it. One tried to draw a mustache under his nose, and one even tried to tie strings to his hands and feet to make him dance!

For a little while, Pinocchio pretended not to notice them, but at last he lost all patience and, turning on the ones who were teasing him the most, he said in an angry voice, "Watch out, now! I didn't come here to be a clown for you! I respect other people, and I want to be respected myself!"

"*Bravo*, puppet! You sound just like a book!" shouted the rascally schoolboys as they shouted with laughter. Then one of them who was meaner than the others, reached out his hand and seized the puppet by his long nose. But he wasn't quick enough, for Pinocchio quickly stuck his foot out from under his desk and kicked him in the shins.

"Wow! what hard feet!" cried the boy as he rubbed the bruises on his shins.

"Hey! what hard elbows he's got! They're even harder than his feet!" cried another who had been hit in the stomach.

The fact is, that after a few kicks of his hard feet, and a few blows of his sharp elbows, Pinocchio quickly earned the respect of all the boys in the school, and they all finally made friends with him. And even the old schoolmaster praised him because he was intelligent, because he paid attention in class, and because he studied hard. Besides, he was the first one to arrive at school in the morning, and the last one to leave when school was let out.

Pinocchio's only fault was that he made too many friends, and among these were several good-for-nothing boys who loved mischief and hated school. The schoolmaster warned him about these friends every day, and even the good Fairy told him again and again, "Be careful, Pinocchio! Those naughty friends of yours will end up by making you lose interest in your books, and may even lead you into some big trouble."

"Oh, there's no danger of that," answered the puppet as he

touched his forehead with his finger as if to say, "There's really too much sense up here for that!"

Now it happened one fine day, as he was walking to school,[1] he met some of his friends who asked him excitedly, "Have you heard the big news?"

'No," replied Pinocchio.

"Well, they say there's a shark in the sea near here, and it's as big as a mountain."

"Really—? I wonder if it could be the same shark[2] that was there when my poor Daddy was lost."

"We're all going down to the beach to see it. Do you want to come too?"

"Oh, no, I couldn't. I have to go to school."

"Aw, why go to school? You can always go to school tomorrow. With one lesson more or less, we'll still be the same jackasses we are now!"

"And the schoolmaster—? What'll he say?"

"Oh, let him say what he likes. He's paid to grumble and complain all day long."

"And my mother?"

"Oh, mothers never know anything that happens!"

"I know what I'll do," said Pinocchio, "I have a very good reason to see that shark—but I'll have to go to see it after school."

"Don't be silly! Do you really think a huge shark like that is going to wait around until you're ready to look at him? As soon as he gets tired of being in one place, he'll just go off to another place, and that'll be the end of that."

"How long does it take to go from here to the beach?" asked the puppet.

"We can be there and back in an hour."

"Well, let's go, then!" Pinocchio shouted, "and the one who runs the fastest is the best man!"

With this, the gang of boys, with their books and their notebooks under their arms, dashed across the fields, and Pinocchio ran ahead of them all, for he seemed to have wings on his feet. Now and then, he turned to make fun of his friends who were a long way behind, and when he saw them all covered with dust and panting with their tongues hanging out, he laughed and laughed. Poor puppet! How could he know at that moment just what horrible disasters he was going to meet with?

❖

Chapter 27

A great fight between Pinocchio
and his friends in which one of them is hurt,
and Pinocchio is arrested.

As soon as he arrived at the seashore, Pinocchio took a long look at the sea, but he couldn't see the shark anywhere. The sea was as smooth as a huge mirror.

"Well, where's the shark?" he asked, turning to his friends.

"He must be out to lunch," said one of them, laughing.

"Or maybe he went to bed to take a little nap," said another, laughing even harder.

From their silly answers and their stupid laughter, Pinocchio could see that his friends were making fun of him by trying to make him believe something that was not true. He took the joke very badly and he asked angrily, "All right, now! What's the idea of telling me that crazy story about the shark?"

"Oh, it was a good joke!" they all answered in a chorus.

"Well, what was it all about?"

"Just to make you miss school and come with us. Aren't you ashamed to be so careful and fussy about your schoolwork? Aren't you ashamed to be studying so hard all the time?"

"And what do you care how hard I study?"

"Just because it makes the rest of us look bad to the school-master."

"Why's that?"

"Because boys who study hard make the ones who don't like to study look bad, and we don't like that. We have our pride too, you know."

"Then what can I do to make up for it?"

"Be just like us! We hate school, we hate books, and we hate the schoolmaster—our three worst enemies!"

"And what if I want to keep on studying?"

"Then we won't have anything more to do with you, and the first chance we get, we'll get even with you!"

"Really, don't make me laugh," said the puppet with a toss of his head.

"Now look, Pinocchio—!" said the biggest one of the boys, "don't think you can bluff us! Don't think you can push us around! If you're not afraid of us, then we're not afraid of you! Remember, you're all alone, and there's seven of us!"

"Yeah, seven, like the Seven Deadly Sins,"[1] said Pinocchio with a laugh.

"Did you hear that? He's insulting us! He called us the Seven Deadly Sins!"*

"Pinocchio, you'd better say you're sorry for that, or it'll be too bad for you!"

"Cuckoo!" called the puppet as he thumbed his nose at them.

"Pinocchio, you'll be sorry!"

"Cuckoo!"

"We'll beat you like a donkey!"

"Cuckoo!"

"You'll go home with a broken nose!"

"Cuckoo!"

"I'll give you 'Cuckoo!' " shouted the toughest one of the boys. "Take that and have it for your supper!" and with that, he punched the puppet in the head with his fist.

But this wasn't the end of it because Pinocchio immediately punched the boy back, and in a moment, all the boys joined in a furious free-for-all. Pinocchio was all alone, but he fought like a regular hero. With those hard wooden feet of his, he was able to keep his enemy at a respectful distance. Wherever those feet struck, they left a black-and-blue mark that wasn't easy to ignore.

Then the boys, angry because they couldn't get close enough to the puppet to hit him with their fists, decided to use other

---

*He called us the Seven Deadly Sins: In the teachings of the Roman Catholic Church, these are also called the *capital* sins and are supposed to be the source of all the other sins of mankind. You can understand, then, why Pinocchio's Italian Catholic schoolmates would be insulted by being called "the Seven Deadly Sins."

weapons. Opening up their schoolbags, they took out their schoolbooks—grammars, geographies, arithmetics, and readers—and began to throw them at Pinocchio. But the puppet had very sharp eyes, and he could duck so quickly that the books just passed over his head and fell into the sea. But just imagine the surprise of the fish! Thinking that the schoolbooks were something good to eat, they rushed to the surface in schools, but after they had tasted a few pages, they spat them out making sour faces as much as to say, "This is food—? We're certainly used to eating better things than this!"

Meanwhile, the fight became even more furious, and a huge old crab came out of the water and climbed slowly on to the beach and called out in a loud voice that sounded like a trombone with a bad cold, "Stop it, you young good-for-nothings! These schoolboy fistfights always end up badly! Something terrible will surely come of it!"

Poor old crab! He might just as well have talked to the wind. Pinocchio, who was as bad as the rest of them, turned to him and said rudely, "Aw shut up, you silly old crab! Why don't

you go home and take some cough syrup for that sore throat of yours? Just go to bed and take some medicine!"

Just then, the boys, who had thrown away all their own books, spied the puppet's schoolbag lying on the ground and, quicker than you can tell about it, they seized it. Among the books in the bag was a big one bound in heavy cardboard with a leather back and leather corners. It was called *A Treatise on Mathematics*, and you can just imagine how big and heavy that must have been!

One of the boys picked up the heavy book, and aiming it at Pinocchio's head, he threw it with all his strength. But instead of hitting the puppet, it struck one of his own friends in the head. The poor boy turned white as a sheet and cried out, "O, *mamma mia*! Help me! I'm dying—!" And he fell his full length on the sand. Thinking he was dead, the frightened boys ran off as fast as their legs could carry them, and in a moment they were nowhere to be seen.

But Pinocchio stayed there, although he was so frightened he was really more dead than alive. Nevertheless, he dipped his handkerchief in sea water and bathed the poor boy's forehead to try to bring him back to life. Weeping bitterly, he called to him saying, "Eugenio! Hey, Eugenio—! Open your eyes and look at me! Why don't you answer me? I wasn't the one who did it! Believe me, I didn't do it! Open your eyes, Eugenio! If you keep them closed like that, I'm going to die too! Oh dear, what can I do? How can I ever have the nerve to face my little mother? Where can I run and hide? Oh, how much better—a thousand times better—it would have been if I had only gone to school! Why did I listen to those boys who've done nothing but get me into this terrible trouble? And the schoolmaster warned me, and my dear little mother repeated the warning, 'Beware of evil companions!' but I've always been a hard-headed fool! I let them talk and then I do whatever I please. Then, afterwards, I have to suffer for it, and that's the way it's been ever since I came into this world, I've never had a happy half-hour in my whole life! Whatever will become of me? What will *become* of me? What *will* become of me?"

Pinocchio went on crying and sobbing and beating his head with his fists as he called out poor Eugenio's name. Suddenly he heard the sound of footsteps. He turned around and saw two carabinieri coming toward him.[2]

"What're you doing there stretched out on the ground?" asked one of the carabinieri.

"I'm trying to help my schoolmate."

"Why, has he been hurt?"

"Oh, yes . . . !"

"Yes, he certainly has been hurt!" said one of the policemen as he bent over Eugenio and looked at him closely. "This boy has a bad wound on his head. Who did it?"

"Not m-m-me," said Pinocchio nervously.

"Well then, what was he wounded with?"

"With this big b-b-book," and the puppet picked up the heavy *Treatise on Mathematics*, all bound in cardboard and leather, and showed it to the policemen.

"And whose book is this?"

"It's m-m-mine . . . ."

"Well, that's all we need to know. Get up out of there and come along with us."

"But I . . ."

"Come along, now!"

"But I haven't done anything wrong!"

"Come along!"

Before leaving, one of the policemen called to some fishermen whose boat was just passing close to the beach, "This boy has been badly hurt. Take him home with you and look after him. We'll come back to see him tomorrow." Then, turning to Pinocchio and placing him between the two of them, one of the policemen commanded, "Forward, march! and step lively, or it will really go hard with you!"

Without waiting to hear it a second time, Pinocchio began to walk with them along the path that led to the village, but the poor little devil hardly knew what he was doing. He seemed to be dreaming—and what a horrible dream! He seemed to be out of his mind—his eyes were crossed, his legs shook, and his tongue stuck to the roof of his mouth so he couldn't utter a single word. Yet, frightened and dazed as he was, one thought pierced his heart like a thorn—he would have to pass beneath the window of the good Fairy as he marched along between the two carabinieri. He would rather have died than have her see him like this!

Just as they were about to enter the village, a sudden gust of wind blew Pinocchio's cap off his head and carried it a good ten yards away.

"Is it all right," he asked, "if I go and get my cap?"

"All right, go, but be quick about it!"

Pinocchio went, but when he picked up his cap, instead of putting it on his head, he took it between his teeth and began to run like a rabbit back toward the beach. The carabinieri, realizing that they couldn't possibly catch him, sent a huge police dog to chase him. This was a dog that had taken first prize in all the local dog races and, while Pinocchio ran fast, the dog ran even faster. The villagers all came to their windows or crowded into the street to see the end of that wild race, but they couldn't see it, for Pinocchio and the dog raised so much dust that in a few moments they couldn't see anything at all.

·❖·

Chapter 28

*Pinocchio is in danger of being
fried like a fish and eaten.*

There were moments during that awful race when Pinocchio was sure he was going to lose, because Alidoro[1]—this was the police

dog's name—ran so furiously that several times he almost caught him. He could hear the fierce animal panting only inches behind him, and he could even feel its hot breath on the back of his neck. Lucky for him that he was close to the beach and the water was only a few steps away.

As soon as he reached the beach, the puppet made a great leap like a bullfrog and landed far out in the water. Alidoro tried to stop, but he was running so fast that he too was carried out into the sea. Unfortunately, the huge dog had never learned to swim, and he thrashed about wildly with his paws to keep his head above the water. But the more he struggled, the deeper he sank! When he came to the surface, the poor dog's eyes were rolling with fear, and he barked out, "I'm drowning! I'm drowning!"

"Go ahead and drown!" called Pinocchio, who was now a safe distance away.

"Help me, Pinocchio . . . ! Don't let me drown!"

When he heard that desperate cry, the puppet, who really had a heart of gold, took pity on the poor dog and turning to him he said, "If I help you, will you promise not to chase me anymore?"

"I promise! Oh yes, I promise! But please hurry! If you wait another minute I'll drown!"

Pinocchio hesitated for a moment, but then, remembering that his Daddy had always told him that one never loses out by doing a good deed, he swam toward Alidoro. He took the drowning dog by the tail with both hands and dragged him safe and sound up on the dry sand of the beach. The poor dog could hardly

stand on his feet, and he had swallowed so much salt water that he was blown up like a balloon. However, Pinocchio didn't dare trust him too much, and with another bullfrog leap, he threw himself back into the water and began to swim away. When he was some distance away from the shore, he turned and called back, "Goodbye, Alidoro, take care of yourself, and give my best to everybody at home!"

"Goodbye, Pinocchio," answered the dog, "a thousand thanks for saving my life. You've been kind to me, and in this world, one good deed deserves another. If you ever need me, remember, I'll pay you back."

Pinocchio went on swimming, all the while keeping close to the rocky shore. At last he came to a place that looked safe, and looking up and down the beach, he finally spied in the rocks the opening of a cave from which great billows of smoke were pouring. "There must be a fire in that cave," he said to himself. "That's great! I'll just go in there and dry myself off and get warm by the fire, and then we'll see what's what!"

With that, the puppet began to swim directly toward the cave. He had not quite reached the shore when suddenly he felt something rise up under him. This strange thing, whatever it was, was lifting him up . . . up . . . up . . . until he found himself lifted completely out of the water and dropped on the ground. He tried hard to escape but, to his astonishment, he found himself trapped in a big fishnet together with a huge mess of fish of all shapes and sizes that were flipping and flopping about like mad.

Pinocchio looked wildly around him and suddenly saw someone coming out of the cave. It was a fisherman*—but *what* a fisherman! He was so ugly—so horribly ugly—that he looked more like a sea monster than a human being. His skin was bright green, his eyes were green and, instead of hair, there grew on his head a clump of wet, green seaweed. His beard, which was really a tangle of green seagrass, was so long that it touched the ground. He looked more like some great green lizard walking on two feet!

The Green Fisherman[2] looked happily at all the fish he had caught in his net and shouted, "Hey! This is wonderful! What a seafood dinner I'm going to have today!"

When he heard this, Pinocchio gathered a little courage and said to himself, "Boy, am I ever lucky I'm not a fish!"

The Green Fisherman then dragged the net full of fish into his cave, a dark, smoky place in the middle of which was a huge frying pan full of steaming hot oil which gave off a smell of garlic that would take your breath away! "Now, let's see what kind of fish we have here!" he cried. Then, reaching into the net with a hand as big as a shovel, he pulled out a great fistful of mullet.

"Ah! these are good mullet!" he said as he looked them over, and after sniffing each one carefully, he threw them all into a big wooden tub. He repeated this operation again and again, and as he pulled each kind of fish out of the net, his mouth watered and he chortled to himself,

It was a fisherman: This is not the kind of fisherman that you probably know about. In Pinocchio's time—and to this day in some wild coastal areas of Italy—a peasant class of fishermen called *pescatori* (pes-ca-TOW-ree) actually lived in caves, or right on the beaches in rude huts which were often made from the overturned wrecks of fishing boats. These rough people lived almost entirely upon the fish they caught in the sea and what they didn't eat themselves was taken to the inland villages and sold there in the street markets.

"Ah, what fine mackerel!"

"Hm-m-m, such lovely sardines!"

"Oh, what beautiful sole!"

"Ah, these herring will really be delicious!"

"Oh, and this haddock will be excellent!" And each batch of fish—the mackerel, the sardines, the sole, the herring, and the haddock—went into the big tub to keep company with the mullet.

The last thing left in the net was poor Pinocchio.

When the Green Fisherman finally pulled him out, his horrible green eyes opened wide with astonishment and he cried out almost in fright, "What in the world kind of fish is this? I don't think I have ever in my whole life eaten a fish like this one!"

He turned the puppet over and over in his huge hands, examining him closely from every angle. Finally he said, "Now I know—it must be some new kind of crab!"

Now Pinocchio, very upset at being mistaken for a crab, said to the Green Fisherman in an angry voice, "Just what do you mean, *crab?* Be careful what you call me! I'll have you know I'm *not* a crab, I'm a puppet!"

"A puppet, eh? Well, to tell you the truth, a puppet fish is a new one on me. Even so, I'll be very happy to eat you!"

"Eat me! But can't you get it through your head that I'm really not a fish? Can't you see that I can talk and think just the way you do?"

"I see," said the Green Fisherman as he scratched the clump of seaweed on his head. "Well then, since you're a fish that talks and thinks like me, I'm going to give you special treatment."

"And what kind of treatment will that be?"

"Because I like you and want to be your friend, I'm going to let you choose the way you want to be cooked. You have a choice of being fried in oil, or stewed in tomato sauce with garlic."

"To tell you the truth," replied Pinocchio, "As long as I have a choice, I choose to be set free and sent home."

"You must be joking! Do you think for one minute that I'd miss this chance to taste a rare fish like you? It isn't every day I catch a puppet fish in these waters. Well, leave it to me then, I'll

just fry you in oil with all the other fish. You'll be happier that way—it's always a comfort to get fried with friends."[3]

At this, the unhappy puppet began to cry and scream and beg for mercy. Then, over and over, he repeated the same refrain as he always did when he found himself in trouble: "Oh, why didn't I go to school the way I should have? Why did I ever listen to those awful boys—? And now I'm going to pay for it!" and all the while he wriggled and twisted like a slippery eel as he tried to escape from the huge green hands that held him tightly.

The Green Fisherman, growing tired of the puppet's struggles, took a long piece of string and tied him up like a salami.* Then he simply threw him into the tub with the mullet, the mackerel, and all the other fish. Now, taking out a big wooden bowl of flour, he began to roll the fish in it, and as soon as each fish was nicely floured, he tossed it into the frying pan to cook for his supper.

The first to dance in the hot boiling oil were the poor mullet; then came the mackerel, then the sardines, then the sole, the herring, and the haddock. And then, at last, it was Pinocchio's turn, and the poor puppet, seeing himself so close to death (and what a terrible death it would be!) shook so hard and was so frightened that he could no longer find the breath to beg for mercy; all he could do was to beg with his eyes.

But the Green Fisherman, paying not the slightest attention to him, plunged poor Pinocchio into the wooden bowl and rolled him in the flour five or six times until he was so covered with white that he looked like a puppet made of plaster.

Then, he picked him up by the head and. . . .

*. . . *tied him up like a salami:* In Italy you can find many, many different kinds of salami. (It might interest you to know that in Italian the name of that wonderful sausage is *salame* which is pronounced sa-LAH-meh.) Among the different kinds are the dried and the smoked salami which are tied up in a net of linen string with a loop at one end to allow it to be hung from a hook or a nail while it is being dried or smoked.

· ❖ ·

Chapter 29

Pinocchio goes back to the house of
the Fairy who promises him that the next day
he will no longer be a puppet but a real boy.
There is to be a grand breakfast of hot chocolate
and whipped cream, and rolls buttered on both
sides to celebrate the happy event.

Just as the Green Fisherman was about to throw poor Pinocchio
into the frying pan, a big dog, attracted by the delicious smell of
fried fish, entered the cave.

"Get out of here!" shouted the Fisherman at the dog, still
clutching the floury puppet in his big fist.

But the poor dog who was starving, simply whined and
wagged his tail as if to say, "Please, just give me one little
mouthful of fried fish, and I'll leave you alone."

"Get out of here, I said!" repeated the Green Fisherman as he
raised his foot to give the dog a kick. But the dog, who was
much too hungry to worry about a little kick, turned on the
fisherman, snarling and showing his long, sharp teeth. At that
moment, the big dog heard a weak little voice cry out, "Save me,
Alidoro—oh, save me! If you don't save me, I'll be fried like a
fish!"

The dog immediately recognized Pinocchio's voice, but he was
amazed to hear that little voice coming from the floury bundle
the fisherman held in his hand. But what do you suppose he
did? He made one great leap and seized that floury bundle in his
mouth, and holding it gently between his teeth, he tore out of
the cave and vanished like a flash of lightning!

The Green Fisherman, furious at having snatched from his
hands the one fish that he had wanted so much to taste, dropped
everything and ran as fast as he could after the big dog. But he
was able to run only a little distance when he began to cough,
and the cough became so violent that he had to give up the chase
and go back to his cave to sulk. As soon as Alidoro reached the
path that led to the village, he stopped and gently put his friend,
Pinocchio, on the ground.

"How can I ever thank you enough?" said the puppet to the big dog.

"You don't have to thank me at all," said Alidoro. "You saved my life, and as I told you at the time, in this world one good turn deserves another."

"But how did you ever happen to come to that awful cave?"

"It's simple—I was lying on the beach more dead than alive after you pulled me out of the water. Then the wind brought the lovely smell of frying fish toward me—and, you know, there's nothing in this whole world that I love more than fried fish! Well, that delicious smell gave me an appetite, so I just followed my nose to the cave. If I had arrived just one minute later . . . !"

"Please, just don't talk about it!" groaned Pinocchio who was trembling at the thought of the terrible experience, "Don't talk about it! If you had arrived a minute later, right now I'd be nicely fried, eaten, and digested. B-r-r-r! I shiver to think about it!"

At this, Alidoro laughed and put out his right paw to the puppet who shook it firmly as a sign of friendship. Then they parted company. The big dog took the road home, but Pinocchio, left to himself, walked toward a little cottage near by where a little old man sat sunning himself in the dooryard.

"Tell me, *signore*," the puppet asked him, "do you know anything about a poor boy named Eugenio who was wounded in the head?"

"Sure," said the old man, "that boy was brought here to this cottage by some fishermen, but now . . ."

"But now he's dead!" interrupted Pinocchio with a sob.

"No, now he's alive and he's already gone home."

"Really? Really?" cried the puppet, jumping for joy. "Then his wound wasn't very serious after all?"

"It could have been very serious, it could even have killed him," answered the old man. "They threw a very heavy book at his head, y'know."

"Who threw it at him?"

"Well, it was one of his schoolmates—some boy called Pinocchio."

"And just who is this Pinocchio?" asked the puppet, pretend-ing not to know.

"They say he's a real bad boy—a regular good-for-nothing."

"That's a big lie!"

"Why do you say that? Do you know this Pinocchio?"

"Well yes, I know him by sight," replied the puppet.

"And just what do you think of him?" asked the old man.

"He seems to me to be a pretty good boy—he likes to study, he's very obedient, and he's very, very fond of his Daddy and the rest of his family."

While the puppet was telling these barefaced lies, he happened to touch his nose and discovered that it had grown several inches longer. This frightened him so much that he cried out, "Please, signore, don't believe a word I said! I know this Pinocchio very well and I can tell you right now that he's really a bad boy—a very bad boy, disobedient and lazy, and when he is supposed to be in school, he goes off instead with evil companions!"

As soon as he had spoken these words, he felt his nose becoming shorter until, finally, it was back to its regular size.

"Why are you all white like that?" the old man asked suddenly.

"Well, I'll tell you—I accidentally brushed against a wall that had just been freshly whitewashed," answered the puppet who was really too ashamed to admit that he had been rolled in flour like a fish ready to be fried.

"But what happened to your clothes?"

"Well, it's like this—I met some thieves and they not only took all my money, but they took all my clothes, too.[1] But, tell me, signore, could you give me some old clothes to go home in?"

"My dear boy, I have nothing but an old burlap bag that I keep beans in, but if you want that, you can have it."

Pinocchio didn't have to be asked twice. He took the empty bean bag and with a pair of scissors he cut a hole in the bottom of it for his head to go through, and a hole on each side for his arms, and he put it on like a shirt. Dressed like this, he started off toward the village.

As he walked along, however, the puppet began to feel disturbed. In fact, he felt so disturbed that he finally stopped walking and began to pace up and down, saying to himself, "How can I ever face my good Fairy again? What'll she say when she sees me? Will she forgive this second naughty thing that I've done? I bet she won't—oh, I'm sure she won't forgive me this time! And it serves me right, too, because I'm nothing but a good-for-nothing. I keep promising to do the right things and then I always break my promises."

Pinocchio didn't reach the village until long after dark. It was a stormy night, and the rain came down in buckets, but he went straightway to the house of the good Fairy, determined to knock at the door until somebody opened it. But, when he reached the door, he lost courage and instead of knocking, he backed off about twenty steps. He went back a second time, but he still couldn't make up his mind . . . a third time, still the same. The fourth time he went up to the door, took the big iron knocker in his hand and, trembling, he gave it a little tap.

Then he waited, and waited, and waited, and finally, after half an hour, a window was thrown open on the top floor—the Fairy's house had four floors, you understand—and a Snail carrying a lighted candle on her head looked out and called down, "Who's that pounding on the door at this hour of the night?"

"Is the Fairy home?" asked the puppet.

"The Fairy's sleeping and she doesn't want to be disturbed! But who are you?"

"It's me!"

"Me who?"

"Me. Pinocchio!"

"Pinocchio who?"

"Pinocchio, the puppet—the one who lives here with the Fairy."

"Ah, yes, I see!" said the Snail. "Just wait right there and I'll come right down and let you in."

"Well, for goodness sake, please hurry! I'm freezing to death!"

"My dear boy, you must realize that I'm just a snail, and we snails are never in a hurry."

One whole hour passed, then two hours, and still the door didn't open. Pinocchio, who was soaked to the skin and shivering from the cold, gathered his courage and knocked at the door a second time—this time much harder. At this second knock, a window on the third floor was thrown open and the Snail looked out again.

"Please, dear little Snail," pleaded Pinocchio, "I've been waiting here for two hours! And two hours in this kind of weather is like two years. Please hurry, for heaven's sake!"

"My boy," replied the Snail in a soft, weary voice, "my dear boy, I'm just a snail, and as you know, snails never, ever hurry!" and the window was slammed shut.

A little later, the big clock in the village square struck midnight, then one o'clock, two o'clock, and still the door was closed. By this time, Pinocchio had lost all patience. In a rage, he seized the doorknocker to give a knock at the door that would echo through the whole house. But the iron knocker suddenly turned into a live, slippery eel² that wriggled out of his hand and slipped into the stream of rainwater rushing down the gutter, and disappeared down the street.

"Oh, so that's how it's going to be!" cried Pinocchio, blind with rage. "Well, if the doorknocker can swim down the street, I can still bang on the door with my foot!" and with this, he backed off and aimed a tremendous kick at the door. But he kicked so hard that his foot went all the way through the wooden panel. When he tried to pull it out, he found that he couldn't because it was stuck in the wood as hard as a nail that had been hammered in by a carpenter. Just think of it! Poor Pinocchio had to spend the rest of the night with one foot on the ground and the other stuck in the door.

At last, at dawn the next morning, the door opened. That clever little snail had taken only nine hours to come down from the fourth floor to the front door. But then, of course, she had really hurried. She took one look at the puppet and laughed, "What in the world are you doing with your foot stuck through our front door?"

"It was just an accident," Pinocchio explained. "But, please, little Snail, see if you can get me out of this terrible jam I'm in."

"My dear young man," said the Snail very severely, "that's a job for a carpenter, and I have never been a carpenter in my whole life!"

"Then, will you ask the Fairy to help me?"

"I told you, the Fairy's sleeping and she can't be disturbed."

"But what do you expect me to do all day long with my foot stuck in the door like this?"

"Well, for one thing, you could amuse yourself by counting the ants as they pass by."

"Then could you at least bring me something to eat? I'm really starved."

"Yes sir, right away!" said the Snail as she hurried off into the house.

Then, sure enough, three and a half hours later, Pinocchio saw her coming back balancing a silver tray on the tips of her horns. On the tray there was a whole roast chicken, some bread, and four beautiful ripe plums.

"Here's the breakfast the Fairy has sent you," said the Snail as she set down the tray.

The food seemed like a gift from heaven to the overjoyed puppet. But, when he tried to eat it, his joy turned to bitter disappointment, for he discovered that the bread was really only made of cardboard, the chicken was made of plaster, and the four lovely plums were made of colored marble. He felt like crying, and in his despair, he tried to throw away the tray and everything that was on it. Instead, because he was weak from pain and hunger, all he could do was to faint dead away.

When he came to, he found himself lying on a couch with the Fairy seated next to him. "You've been punished enough for your naughtiness," she said, "and I'll forgive you just once more. But I warn you, you'll be sorry if you're ever naughty again. I won't forgive you a third time."

When he heard this, Pinocchio gave his word of honor that he would go back to school and study hard. And, as a matter of fact, he did keep his word, because for all the rest of the year he did study hard and got higher grades than anyone else in the school, and, after final examinations, he even made the honor roll. He had behaved himself so well, and he had done so well at school that the good Fairy was delighted and proud. Finally, one day she said to him, "At last, tomorrow, your biggest wish will come true!"

"You mean . . . ? do you really mean it?" shouted the beaming Pinocchio.

"Yes, I really mean it. By this time tomorrow you will no longer be a puppet, and you will turn into a real boy."

You can't possibly imagine Pinocchio's wild joy when he heard this news, the news he had waited so long to hear. All his friends from school, then, were invited to the Fairy's house the next morning for a grand breakfast party to celebrate the big event. And for this breakfast, the Fairy set about preparing two hundred cups of hot chocolate with whipped cream,[3] and four hundred hot, buttered sweet rolls—and they were even to be buttered on both sides! It looked as if it would be a lovely, happy day for everyone, but. . . .

Unfortunately, there is always a *but* in the life of a puppet, and that *but* spoils everything!

· ❖ ·

Chapter 30

Pinocchio, instead of becoming a boy, sneaks off to Toyland[1] with his friend Lampwick.

While preparations were being made for the breakfast-party, Pinocchio asked the Fairy if he could go through the village and invite all his friends for the next morning. The Fairy agreed that it would be a good idea, but before he left the house, she said very plainly, "Remember, though, I want you to come back home before dark. Do you understand that?"

"Oh, yes!" replied the puppet, "I won't be gone more than an hour."

"Be careful with your promises, now! Boys are always quick to make promises, but most of the time, they are quick to forget them, too."

"But, really—I'm not like the others! When I say I'll do a thing, I do it."

"Well, we'll see about that. But remember, if you disobey me this time, it will really go bad with you!"

"Why?"

"Why? I'll tell you why—because boys who don't listen to those who know better than they do always end up in trouble."

"Well . . . yes . . . I guess I've proved that all right!" said Pinocchio, "But I won't make that mistake again, I promise you!"

"Well, we'll see. . . ."

Without saying another word, the puppet skipped out of the house singing at the top of his voice. Within an hour's time, he had gone through the village, inviting all his friends to the party. Some of them eagerly agreed to come; others had to be talked into it, but when they heard about the sweet rolls that would be buttered on both sides, they soon agreed to come too.

Now, it so happens that Pinocchio had a friend whom he liked more than any of the other boys at school. This boy's real name was Romeo, but because he was so thin and tall, everyone called him Lampwick.* It also happens that this boy Lampwick was the laziest and naughtiest boy in the whole school, and this, of course, is why Pinocchio admired him. In fact, the first one he went to look for was Lampwick, but he wasn't at home. He went back to his house a second time, and still he didn't find him. A third time, and still no Lampwick. But where else could he look for him? He looked in one place after another until, finally, he discovered him hiding under the porch of a villager's house.

"What in the world are you doing under here?" asked Pinocchio as he too crawled under the porch.

"I'm waiting for midnight to come so I can leave."

"Leave? But where are you going?"

"Far, far away!"

"But I've gone to look for you at your house three times!"

"What were you looking for me for?"

---

*. . . *everyone called him Lampwick:* Just as we call a tall, thin boy "Skinny," or "Stringy," or "Slim," Italians call him *Lucignolo* (lou-CHEEN-yo-loh) which means "Lampwick," because as you probably know, the wick of an old-fashioned oil lamp is very long and thin.

"You mean you haven't heard the big news? You haven't heard what's going to happen to me tomorrow?"

"What's that?"

"Tomorrow I stop being a wooden puppet and I turn into a real boy just like you and all the others."

"Well, good for you!"

"So, tomorrow morning I'd like you to come to my house for a big breakfast-party."

"But I already told you I'm going away tonight."

"At what time?"

"At midnight."

"And where are you going?"

"I'm going off to live in another country—the most wonderful country in the world—a regular land of dreams."

"Really? and what's it called?"

"It's called Toyland . . . But, why don't you come too?"

"Who, me? Oh no, I could never do that!"

"You're making a big mistake, Pinocchio! Believe me, if you don't come, you'll really be sorry. Where could you ever find a better place for kids like us? There are no schools, there are no schoolmasters, and there are no schoolbooks! In Toyland nobody ever studies. They don't have school on Thursday, and the nice thing about that is that there are six Thursdays in every week, and one Sunday.* And just think—vacation starts the first day of January and ends on the last day of December! Now that's the kind of place for me! That's the way they should run every country!"

"Gee! But how do they spend their time in Toyland?"

"How? Why, they play and have fun from morning till night. At night they go to bed, and the next morning when they get up, they start having fun all over again."

"H-m-m-m," muttered Pinocchio, and he wagged his head as if to say, "Now that's the kind of life I wouldn't mind having at all!"

*. . . six Thursdays in every week and one Sunday: You may notice that nothing is said here about Saturdays. Italian boys and girls have to go to school on Saturday (ugh!), so the six Thursday holidays in Toyland also eliminate Saturday school.

"Well," said Lampwick, "do you want to go or not? Is it yes or no? Make up your mind."

"Oh, no! No, I couldn't do it. I just promised my good Fairy I'd behave myself, and I want to keep that promise. It's beginning to get dark, too, and I've got to go home right away. Goodbye, Lampwick. Have a good trip."

"Where are you rushing off to in such a big hurry?"

"Home—the Fairy told me to be sure to get home before dark."

"Aw, just wait a couple minutes more."

"I can't, I'll be late!"

"Just two minutes more."

"But the Fairy will scold me!"

"Aw, let her scold. When she gets tired of scolding, she'll stop," said Lampwick.

"But how are you going?" asked the puppet. "Are you going alone, or is someone else going with you?"

"Alone? Why there'll be more than a hundred other boys going too."

"Are you going to walk all the way?"

"Oh no, at midnight there'll be a big coach coming by here to pick us up and take us away to that wonderful country."

"Gee, I'd give a lot to see that coach come along right now," said Pinocchio with a sigh.

"What for?"

"Because I'd love to see you all going off together."

"Well, just stay a little while longer and you can," said Lampwick.

"No, no, I've got to go home now."

"Just wait a little while longer."

"Really, I can't, I've waited too long already, the Fairy will be worried about me."

"Aw, the poor Fairy—! Is she afraid the bats will eat you up?"

"No, not really, but tell me," Pinocchio went on, "are you really and truly sure there are no schools in that country?"

"Not a one!"

"And no schoolmasters?"

"Nope, not a single one!"

"And you never have to study?"

"Never ever!"

"Boy, what a great country!" sighed Pinocchio, and as he thought about it, he actually felt his mouth watering. "What a wonderful country! Of course I've never seen it, but I can just imagine how it must be."

"Look, why don't you come along with us?" Lampwick insisted.

"No, it's no use trying to tempt me. I've promised my good Fairy I'd be a good boy, and I don't want to break my word."

"Well, goodbye then, and give my regards to all the kids at school when you see them."

"Goodbye, Lampwick. Have a good trip. Have fun, and think about your friends once in a while." As he said this, the puppet took a couple of steps as if to leave, but then he stopped, and turning to his friend, he asked, "Are you absolutely sure that in Toyland there are really six Thursdays and one Sunday in every week?"

"Absolutely!"

"And are you positively sure that vacation starts the first day of January, and ends on the last day of December?"

"Positively!"

"What a great country!" said Pinocchio again, bubbling with enthusiasm. But then, becoming very serious, he added, "Well, Lampwick, this time it's really goodbye. Have a good time."

"Goodbye."

The puppet hesitated a moment and then asked, "How long will it be before you leave?"

"Oh, not long," answered Lampwick, "maybe another couple of hours."

"That's too bad. If it was only about an hour, I might have waited to see you off."

"And what about the Fairy?"

"Well, it's been dark a long time already. One hour more wouldn't make much difference."

"Poor little Pinocchio!" said Lampwick with a wicked laugh, "What if the Fairy scolds you?"

"Aw, let her scold. When she gets tired of scolding, she'll stop."

Meanwhile, the night had become darker and darker. Suddenly, after what seemed only a few minutes, they saw a tiny light in the distance. Now they began to hear the faint jingling of little bells. Now the sound of a coach horn so soft that it sounded more like the hum of a mosquito.

"Here it comes!" shouted Lampwick as he jumped to his feet.

"What's coming?" asked Pinocchio in a whisper.

"The coach that's going to take me to Toyland. Well, are you going to come or not?"

"But, is it really, really true," asked the puppet, "that you never have to study in that country?"

"I *told* you—never, never, never!"

"What a great country—what a *great* country—what a great *country!*"

· ❖ ·

Chapter 31

After spending five happy months in Toyland, Pinocchio wakes up one morning to a nasty surprise.

At last the coach arrived, and it came without making the least bit of noise because its wheels had been carefully wrapped and padded with rags.* Pulling the coach were twelve pairs of donkeys,† all exactly the same size, but each one a different color. Some were gray, some were white, some were spotted like salt and pepper, while others had big stripes of red and blue. But

---

*. . . *its wheels . . . wrapped and padded with rags:* This, of course, was so the parents of the runaway boys wouldn't be able to hear them sneaking off to Toyland.

†. . . *twelve pairs of donkeys:* If Pinocchio had not had a wooden head he might have seen something fishy about a team of donkeys pulling a coach (and there was actually something really fishy about it as we find out a little later). Teams of horses or mules were used to pull wagons or coaches, not because the intelligent little donkey is not strong enough, but because he is too independent to work in harness with other donkeys. It is still not unusual, however, to see a donkey teamed with a horse or a mule to draw a wagon or to pull a plow.

the strangest thing about these donkeys was that they were not shod with iron shoes like regular donkeys. Instead, they were all wearing the kind of leather shoes that schoolboys wear.

And what about the coachman?

Imagine to yourselves a little man who is wider than he is tall; soft and oily as a lump of butter, with a little face that looks like a ripe, red apple; a tiny, laughing mouth, and the soft, sweet voice of a pussycat begging her mistress for a bowl of cream. The boys all loved this jolly little coachman[1] as soon as they saw him, and they pushed and shoved each other to get the best seats on his coach which was to take them all to the wonderful country called Toyland.

In fact, by the time the coach arrived at the village, it was already full of boys from eight to twelve years old, jammed in like so many salted anchovies.* They were so uncomfortable and crowded that they could hardly breathe, but nobody said a word, nobody complained, because they all knew that in just a few hours they would be in a happy land where there were no schools, no schoolbooks, and no schoolmasters. They were so contented that they felt no discomfort, no weariness, no hunger, and no thirst.

As soon as the coach stopped, the little coachman looked down at Lampwick and said, "Well, my boy, would you like to come with us to that wonderful country?"

"Would I? of course I would!"

"Well, there's only one difficulty. There's really no room left in the coach. As you can see, all the seats are full."

*. . . jammed in like so many salted anchovies: We would probably describe these boys as being "jammed in like *sardines* in a can," or, in Britain, "in a tin." However, anchovies seem to be more popular in Italy, especially in the south. The anchovy, like the sardine, is a small silvery fish that belongs to the herring family. While sardines are packed whole, except for their heads, in oil or salt water, anchovies not only lose their heads and tails, but they are sliced into two strips (fillets) and packed either in coarse salt or in olive oil. Because anchovies are generally smaller than sardines, and because they lose so much more of themselves, you can pack many more of them in the same space.

"Oh, that's all right," replied Lampwick, "if there's no place for me inside, I'll just ride on the tongue between the donkeys." And with this, he jumped up and seated himself astride the harness pole of the coach.

'And what about you, my boy?" the little coachman asked Pinocchio with a broad grin, "What are you going to do? Are you coming with us or not?"

"No, I'm staying here," said Pinocchio, "I have to go home and study, because I want to get good grades in school the way a good boy should."

"Well then, lots of luck to you!"

"Hey, Pinocchio!" called Lampwick, "Listen, come along with us, we'll really have a great time!"

"No . . . no . . . no. . . !"

"Aw, come on! Come with us, we'll have lots of fun where we're going!" shouted a hundred boys' voices from inside the coach.

"But if I go with you, what will my good Fairy say?" asked Pinocchio, although you could easily see that he was beginning to weaken.

"Aw, don't bother yourself with that kind of nonsense! Just remember that we're going to a country where we can raise the devil from morning to night!"

To this, Pinocchio made no answer, but he sighed, then he sighed again, and after he had sighed a third time, he said, "Oh, all right. Make room for me, I'm coming too!"

"Well," said the little coachman, "all the seats in the coach are taken, but I'll tell you what—if you really want to come, you can take my seat on the driver's box!"

"But you, what'll you do?"

"Oh, that's all right, I can walk."

"No sir!" cried Pinocchio, "I couldn't let you do that! I'd rather ride one of these donkeys than let you walk all the way to Toyland."

No sooner had he said this than he went up to the right-hand donkey of the very first pair in the team and tried to climb on his back, but the little animal suddenly gave the puppet a hard kick in the stomach and sent him flying with his legs in the air. How the other boys laughed at this sight! But the little coachman didn't laugh. Instead, he walked up to the rebellious little donkey and, pretending to give him an affectionate kiss, he bit off half of his right ear!

In the meantime, Pinocchio had got up off the ground and, still angry, he again leaped on the donkey's back. It was such a beautiful leap that all the boys in the coach burst into laughter and shouted, "*Bravo! bravissimo*, Pinocchio!" and they all clapped their hands in wild applause.

Suddenly, however, the little donkey reared up and kicked so hard with his hind legs that the puppet was thrown off on top of a pile of stones beside the road. Again, all the boys roared with laughter, but the little coachman didn't laugh. Once again he went lovingly up to the naughty little donkey and gave him another kiss which, this time, took off half of his left ear. Then he turned to the puppet and said, "It's all right now, you can get on his back without being afraid. That donkey had some funny notion in his head, but I just whispered a few words in his ear that have made him calm and reasonable."

Pinocchio mounted the donkey once more and immediately the coach began to move. But, while the donkeys galloped along, and the coach rumbled over the paving stones, he thought he heard a little voice saying softly, "You fool, you poor little fool! You just had to do things your own way, but you're going to be sorry for it!"

Pinocchio was frightened, and he looked all about him to see if he could discover where this voice came from, but he could discover nothing. The donkeys galloped, the coach rumbled on, the boys inside the coach all slept soundly, Lampwick snored like a dormouse,[2] and all the while the little coachman sat up on the box singing softly between his teeth,

> *They sleep and they sleep*
> *The whole night through,*
> *But me, I never sleep at all . . .*

When they had gone another mile or two, Pinocchio once again heard the little voice say, "Remember, you poor little simpleton, boys who won't study, who skip school, and who turn their backs on books and on schoolmasters just to spend their time having fun always wind up in bad trouble! I know, I tried it, and I know what I'm talking about! The time will come when you'll be weeping just the way I'm weeping now, but then it'll be too late, too late!"

When he heard these words, the puppet was more frightened than ever. He quickly jumped off his donkey's back, and seizing him by the nose, he was surprised to see that the poor little animal was crying[3] like a little boy!

"Hey, signor Coachman!" shouted Pinocchio to the driver of the coach, "You know what? This poor little donkey's crying."

"That's all right, let him cry. He'll laugh on his wedding night!"[4]

"But, did you teach him to talk, too?"

"Ah, no, but he spent three years in a show with some trained dogs, and he learned to speak a few words from them."

"Poor little animal—!"

"Come on! come on!" cried the little coachman, "Don't waste time watching a donkey cry. Get up on his back again and let's go! It's a cold night and there's still a long way to go!"

Pinocchio obeyed without saying another word. The coach rumbled on again and, just about daybreak, they all arrived safely in Toyland. As it turned out, Toyland was like no other country in the whole world. Its entire population consisted of boys, and the oldest boys were no more than fourteen, while the youngest were scarcely eight years old. As you can well imagine, the excitement, the shouting, and the racket in the streets were loud enough to drive a grownup crazy.

There were crowds and crowds of boys everywhere! Some were playing marbles,[5] some were playing ball, and some were playing ducks and drakes[6] with flat stones in the village fountain. Others were riding on tricycles and bicycles;[7] still others were riding wooden hobbyhorses. They played hide-and-seek, they played tag, they rolled hoops, they ran foot races and they turned cartwheels, stood on their heads, and walked on their hands with their feet in the air. Some older boys dressed up like clowns and pretended to be magicians and fire-eaters, while others dressed up like army officers with helmets made of folded newspaper, and marched up and down with squads of cardboard soldiers.[8] They laughed, they shouted, they hooted, they whistled, they cackled like hens, they crowed like roosters—in fact, there was such an infernal racket, such a furious uproar, that you would have had to stuff your ears with cotton to keep from becoming deaf! There were big circus tents everywhere, and they were crowded with boys from morning till night. All over the walls of every building there were misspelled inscriptions:

We luv fun!
Down wit skool & skoolmasters too!
No more ritmetick an stuf like that!

As soon as they set foot in this capital city of Toyland, Pinocchio, Lampwick, and all the other boys who had made the long journey with the little coachman, hurried to join the other boys in the wild confusion in the streets. Immediately, they made friends with everybody, and who could have been happier, who could have been more contented than they were to live in a land like that?

Then, after that, the hours, the days, the weeks passed like lightning. Every time Pinocchio saw Lampwick on the street, he shouted out, "Hey, Lampwick, this is the life!" And each time, Lampwick would answer, "Well, I told you, didn't I, and you were the one who didn't want to come! You were the one who wanted to go back to your old Fairy. You were the one who wanted to waste your time studying! Well, if you don't have to worry about school and schoolbooks anymore, it's all because of me! I was the one who gave you the good advice to come to Toyland. Just don't forget, only a real friend will do you a favor like that!"

"Yeah, you're right, Lampwick! If I'm living a happy life now, it's all because of you. But, do you know what the schoolmaster used to tell me about you? He used to say, 'Pinocchio, you musn't have anything to do with that good-for-nothing, Lampwick—he's a bad boy, and he'll only get you into trouble!'"

"That poor old fool!" replied Lampwick as he shook his head, "I know he didn't like me, and I know he used to tell all kinds of lies about me, but even so, I'm good-hearted, and I forgive him."

"Golly, Lampwick, you're really a great guy!" said Pinocchio

as he put his arms around his friend and gave him an affectionate hug.

The happy life in Toyland went on and on for five long, happy
months. Pinocchio spent all his days having a good time without
having to look at a book, or a school, or a schoolmaster.

Then, one morning, he woke up and had a nasty surprise that
put him in a very bad mood!

· ❖ ·

Chapter 32

*Pinocchio discovers he has
sprouted a beautiful pair of donkey's ears.
Then he turns into a real donkey
with a tail and everything.*

And what, exactly, was that nasty surprise?

Well, I'll tell you, dear boys and girls, the surprise was that
when Pinocchio woke up, he naturally reached up and scratched
his head, and while he was scratching he discovered . . . would
you believe what he discovered. . . ? He discovered that overnight his ears had grown[1] at least five inches longer!

Now, you must realize that puppets, from the time they are
born, have tiny little ears—in fact, they are so tiny that you
can't even see them. Imagine then how shocked Pinocchio was to
find that his ears had grown so long during the night that they
stuck out of his head like two brooms!

Immediately he went to look for a mirror so he could look at
himself closely. But he couldn't find a regular mirror, so he
filled his washbasin with water and looked at his reflection in it.
Then he saw what he really never wanted to see. He saw his
head decorated with the most beautiful pair of donkey's ears!

Just think of the horror, the shame, and the sorrow that poor
Pinocchio must have felt when he saw this! First he cried, and
then he screamed, and then he beat his head against the wall,
but the more he cried, the longer those ears grew. They grew,
and they grew, and finally they became hairy at the very tips
exactly like a donkey's hairy ears.

Hearing his loud screaming and crying, a pretty little Marmot*
who lived on the floor above came into his room. When she found
the puppet in such a terrible state, she asked politely, "Why,
whatever has happened to you, my dear young neighbor?"

"I'm sick, little Marmot—I'm very sick! I seem to have some
terrible disease. Could you tell if I have a fever?"

"Yes, I think so."

"Well will you please see if I have one?"

The little Marmot reached out and touched Pinocchio's forehead with her paw, and then she said with a sigh, "Ah, my dear
boy, I'm afraid I have very bad news for you."

"What's that?"

"You have a very bad fever."

"What kind of fever is it?"

"It's donkey fever!"

"Why, I never heard of donkey fever!" cried the puppet,
although he knew perfectly well what she meant.

"Well then, I'll explain it to you," answered the little Mar-

*. . . *a pretty little Marmot:* The marmot is a burrowing animal
which is closely related to the ground squirrel. He has a stocky body,
powerful digging claws, and a coat of thick, coarse, brown fur. The
best-known marmot in America is the common woodchuck, or
groundhog.

mot. "You may as well know that in two or three hours you'll no longer be a puppet."

"But, what *will* I be?"

"In just a few hours, you'll turn into a real donkey just like the ones that draw carts and haul lettuce and cabbage to the market."

"Oh! Oh! Poor me!" cried Pinocchio, and he seized his huge ears and pulled and jerked them furiously as if they belonged to somebody else.

"You poor dear," said the little Marmot sympathetically, "there's nothing you can do about it, it's simply your destiny. Ancient books of wisdom tell us that lazy boys who hate books, and who hate school and schoolmasters, and who spend all their time playing and having fun, must end up, sooner or later, by turning into little donkeys."

"But, is that really true?" sobbed the puppet.

"Yes, unfortunately, it's really true! But it's too late to cry now, you should have thought of that before it was too late."

"But it wasn't my fault! Believe me, little Marmot, it was all Lampwick's fault!"

"And just who is this Lampwick?"

"He's my friend from school. I was the one who wanted to go home. I was the one who wanted to be good. I was the one who wanted to study hard and make the honor roll. But Lampwick was the one who said, 'What do you care about studying hard? What do you want to go to school for? Why don't you come with me to Toyland? You won't have to study anymore, and you can do nothing but have fun every day from morning till night!'"

"And why did you take the advice of that naughty boy?"

"Why? Because, dear little Marmot, I'm only a thoughtless puppet with no common sense at all! Oh, if I only had just a little consideration for others, I never would have gone away and left that good Fairy who was like a mother to me, and who did so much for me! By this time I wouldn't be a puppet anymore, I'd be a real boy like all the others! Boy! When I see that Lampwick again, he'll be sorry! I'm really going to let him have it!"

With that, Pinocchio started to leave the house, but when he reached the door, he happened to remember his long donkey ears. He was too ashamed to let people see them, but then, what could he do? He got a big cotton cap and pulled it down over his ears and his head and right down to the top of his nose. Then he went out to look for Lampwick. He looked for him in the streets, in the playground, in the circus tents. He looked for him everywhere, but he couldn't find him. He asked everybody he met, but nobody had seen him. Finally, he went to Lampwick's house and knocked at the door.

"Who is it?" shouted Lampwick from inside.

"It's me, Pinocchio!" answered the puppet.

"Wait just a minute and I'll let you in."

After a good half hour, the door finally opened. Imagine Pinocchio's surprise when he went in and found his friend wearing a huge cotton cap that came down to the top of *his* nose. At the sight of that cap, the puppet felt a little better, and he thought to himself, "Could it be that Lampwick has the same sickness I have? Do you suppose he's got donkey fever, too?"

Then he pretended that he hadn't really noticed anything, and with a broad smile he said, "Well, Lampwick, how are you feeling today?"

"Hey, Pinocchio, I feel just fine! I'm as happy as a mouse in a piece of Parmesan cheese!"

"Do you really mean that?"

"Would I lie to you?"

"Well then, why are you wearing that silly cotton cap pulled down over your ears?"

"Uh—well, you see, my doctor told me to wear it because the other day I skinned my knee. But, how about you? Why're you wearing that silly cotton cap that comes down over your nose?"

"Well, uh—my doctor prescribed it because I stubbed my toe."

"Aw, poor Pinocchio!"

"Aw, poor Lampwick!"

After this, the two kept very still for a very long time, although they looked at each other suspiciously. Finally, the puppet said softly, "Tell me, Lampwick, have you ever had any trouble with your ears?"

"No—never. How about you?"

"Me neither, except, this morning, I had an awful earache."

"Yeah, I did too!"

"Really? But which one?"

"Well, it was both of 'em. How about you?"

"Both of 'em. Do you think maybe we have the same disease?"

"Yeah, I'm afraid so."

"Hey, Lampwick, do me a favor, will you?"

"What kind of a favor?"

"Just let me look at your ears!"

"Well—why not? But first I want to look at your ears."

"Aw, no, you've got to be first."

"No, first you, then me."

"Well then," said the puppet at last, "let's compromise."

"How?"

"Let's both take these caps off at the same time. All right with you?"

"All right!"

"All right, then," said Pinocchio, and he began to count in a loud voice, "One—! Two—! THREE!"

At the count of three, the two boys took off their caps and threw them up in the air.

What happened then was ridiculous. When Pinocchio and Lampwick saw that they both had grown long donkey ears, instead of being ashamed and embarrassed, they began to waggle them at each other as they pranced about the room roaring with laughter. They laughed, and they laughed, and they laughed until it hurt so much they had to hold their sides.

Then, all of a sudden, Lampwick began to stagger and grow very pale as he called to his friend, "Help me, Pinocchio—help me!"

"What's the matter?"

"I . . . I can't . . . I just can't stand up straight anymore!"

"Gee, neither can I!" cried Pinocchio as he, too, began to weep and stumble about.

Then, even while they were talking, they doubled over and began to run around the room on all fours. As they ran about like this, their hands and feet gradually turned into hoofs, their faces got longer and longer till they turned into donkey's muzzles, and their backs finally became covered over with a coat of light gray hair sprinkled with black.

But that wasn't the worst of all! The most horrible thing that happened to those miserable boys was that they began to grow tails. They became so upset and ashamed that they began to cry loudly at the thought of it.

Ah, but they should have kept quiet! Instead of making the sounds of weeping and wailing, they brayed! Together, they brayed loud and long like a pair of donkeys, "Hee-haw! hee-haw! hee-haw!"*

Meanwhile, as they trotted around the room braying at the top of their lungs, there came a knock at the door, and a voice shouted, "Hey, in there! Open the door! I'm the coachman who brought you to Toyland! Now, open up, or you'll be sorry!"

*. . . hee-haw: In English, donkeys seem to make this sound, but if you listen to Italian donkeys closely, they don't sound like this at all. According to Mister Collodi, Pinocchio and Lampwick made braying sounds that he wrote like this: *ih-à, ih-à!* However, I know that when you try to say it, this doesn't sound right, so I'll explain it this way: there was a pretty little donkey in a pasture near our house in Piedmont who, when he was happy or unhappy, would utter a series of noises that sounded like a Cub Scout learning to play the bugle.

· ❖ ·

Chapter 33

*Pinocchio is now a real little donkey
and he is sold to the ringmaster of a circus.
His new master teaches him how to dance and jump
through a hoop, but he falls and becomes
lame and is sold to a man who wants to
use his skin to make a drumhead.*

When he saw that nobody was going to open the door, the little coachman broke it down with a violent kick. As he entered the room, he said to Pinocchio and Lampwick with his usual jolly laugh, "*Bravo! bravissimo!* You two boys really bray very well! I recognized your voices right away, and now I've come for you!"

At these words the two little donkeys hung their heads, and with their ears lowered, and their tails between their legs, they stood silently. At first, the little man treated them kindly, stroking and patting them gently. Then, he took out a currycomb* and combed them until their coats were so shiny he could see his face in them. When he had finished currying them, he put halters on them and led them off to the market place where he expected to sell them for a lot of money.

As a matter of fact, there were plenty of buyers. Lampwick was sold immediately to a farmer whose old donkey had died just the day before. Then Pinocchio was sold to the ringmaster of a circus who planned to teach him to leap and dance like his other animals.

Now, it's easy to see, boys and girls, what a fine business that little coachman was in. This wicked little monster with the sweet, lovable face went all over the world picking up lazy boys who hated school and schoolbooks. As soon as his coach was full,

*. . . *he took out a currycomb:* A currycomb is an oblong instrument that looks a little like a man's hairbrush, but instead of bristles, it is fitted with rows of sharp metal teeth. It is used for the rough grooming of the coats of donkeys, horses, and mules, after which a finer, stiff-bristle brush is used to give the coats a glossy look.

he would carry them off to Toyland where they would spend all their time playing, making noise, and having fun. Then, after a long time of endless play and no study, these poor silly boys would turn into so many little donkeys, and the coachman would simply take them off to market and sell them. In this way he became a millionaire in just a few years.

Whatever happened to poor Lampwick, I can't say,[1] but I do know that, from the very first day, Pinocchio led a hard, rough life. As soon as he was put into his stall in the circus stable, the ringmaster threw some straw into his manger. No sooner did Pinocchio taste the straw than he spat it out. Then the ringmaster, grumbling at him, put some hay in the manger, but Pinocchio didn't like that either. "Oho! so you don't even like hay!" shouted the ringmaster angrily. "Well then, if you're going to be so fussy, I can fix that!" and he began to beat the poor little donkey's legs with his whip.

This hurt Pinocchio terribly and he began to cry and bray, "Hee-haw! I can't eat straw!"

"All right, then," said the ringmaster, who understood donkey language perfectly, "you can eat hay instead!"

"Hee-haw! Hay gives me a bellyache!"

"Do you mean to tell me that I have to feed a donkey like you on veal cutlets and pork sausage?" said the angry ringmaster as he whipped him again.

After the second whipping, poor Pinocchio decided that it would be much wiser to hold his tongue, and he said nothing more. Then the ringmaster went out and closed the door of the stall behind him, and Pinocchio was left all alone. It had been a long time since he had eaten anything and he was so hungry that he began to yawn, and when he yawned, he opened his mouth as wide as an oven. But there was nothing to eat in the manger but hay, so he decided to eat that. He took a mouthful of it and chewed and chewed for a long time. Then he shut his eyes and swallowed it.

"Well, this hay's not so bad, after all," he said to himself, "but how much better off I'd be now if only I had kept up my schoolwork! Instead of this dry old hay, I could be eating a lovely salami sandwich! But—there's nothing I can do about that now."

147

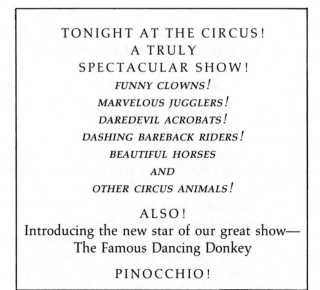

TONIGHT AT THE CIRCUS!
A TRULY
SPECTACULAR SHOW!
FUNNY CLOWNS!
MARVELOUS JUGGLERS!
DAREDEVIL ACROBATS!
DASHING BAREBACK RIDERS!
BEAUTIFUL HORSES
AND
OTHER CIRCUS ANIMALS!

ALSO!
Introducing the new star of our great show—
The Famous Dancing Donkey

PINOCCHIO!

Next morning when he woke up, he looked for another bit of hay in the manger, but there wasn't any left because he had eaten it all up during the night. Then he tried a mouthful of chopped straw, but as he chewed it, he had to admit to himself that chopped straw didn't taste nearly as good as a nice plate of rice *alla milanese* or a dish of macaroni *alla napoletana*. "Well, no matter—" he said, and he went on chewing the straw. "I just hope my misfortune will be a good lesson to other naughty boys who don't want to study hard—" and he went on grumbling, "No matter, no matter."

"What do you mean, 'No matter'?" shouted the ringmaster who had come into the stable just at that moment. "You little jackass, do you think I bought you just for the fun of feeding you? Well, you're wrong! I bought you so you can work hard for me so I can make a lot of money! So, get up out of there and let's go into the circus ring. I'm going to teach you to jump through a paper-covered hoop, breaking the paper with your head. I'm going to teach you to stand on your hind legs, and then I'm going to teach you to dance the waltz and the polka." So, poor Pinocchio, whether he liked it or not, had to learn to do all these cute things. But it took him more than three months to learn, and all during that time the ringmaster whipped him so hard he thought surely he'd lose his skin.

Then, at last the day came when the ringmaster decided that the little donkey could put on a really great performance. He had a thousand beautiful posters printed in brilliant colors, and then had them put up on every street corner and on every post and wall in the town.

That night, then, as you can well imagine, the circus was jammed with people an hour before the show started. Not another single person could buy a seat even if he paid his own weight in gold! All the seats around the ring were packed with boys and girls of all ages who were eager to see the wonderful new star, the famous dancing donkey called Pinocchio.

As soon as the regular performance was finished, the ringmaster went to the center of the ring. He was carrying his long whip, and he was wearing a handsome black cutaway coat, tight white breeches, and great, shiny leather boots that came way up above his knees. He then bowed low to the audience and with a perfectly straight face, he delivered this pompous speech:

"Most respectable and honorable *signore e signori**. . . !

"This most unworthy person, who is but a mere temporary resident of this, your fair city, wishes to take unto himself the glorious honor—indeed, the prodigious pleasure—of presenting to this profoundly intelligent and eminently illustrious audience, a famous little dancing donkey who has the most enviable distinction of having performed in the magnificent presence of His Most Gorgeous Majesty, the Emperor of all Europe. . . !

"And now. . . ! with the deepest and most profound pleasure and gratitude, I humbly beg your kindest indulgence in allowing me to present the new scintillating star of our great circus— PINOCCHIO!"

When the ringmaster finished this ridiculous speech, the audience broke into loud laughter and applause, and then, when the star of the show, Pinocchio, appeared in the ring, the applause became as loud as a thunderstorm. He was brilliantly decked out for the occasion[2] with a brand new shiny patent leather bridle with polished brass buckles and studs, and a beautiful white ca-

---

*. . . *signore e signori:* By now, you know enough Italian to know that this means "ladies and gentlemen."

mellia behind each ear. His mane was parted into curly locks, and each lock was tied with a red silk bow. He wore around his middle a broad girth of gold and silver, and his tail was decorated with pretty blue and scarlet ribbons. He was truly an adorable donkey!

Now the ringmaster, as he presented Pinocchio to the audience, had this to say:

"Most illustrious signore and signori! I do not propose to lie to you about the tremendous difficulties I had to overcome in capturing and taming this wild beast* as he roamed from mountaintop to mountaintop in the deserts of the torrid zone! I would like you to observe, if you will, the savage gleam in his eye! I tried every way I could think of to tame him like other gentle domestic animals, but finally I was forced to use the whip on him. Yet, even with all the kindness I showed him—which really should have made him very affectionate toward me—he became more and more savage every day. However, by following the scientific method of ancient Gaul, I discovered a little bump on his skull which, according to the Royal French Institute of Medical Science at Paris, is the bump that makes new hair grow on bald heads, and makes people dance. Therefore, I have taught this little donkey not only to dance beautifully, but also to leap through paper-covered hoops. Watch him, then, and judge for yourselves! But. . . ! before I leave you, I would like to take this opportunity to invite you to come to our show tomorrow night, and if the weather is bad, then our evening show will be given at eleven o'clock in the morning."

Once again the ringmaster bowed low and, turning to Pinocchio, he cracked his whip and said, "All right—! Look alive! Now, before you begin, I want you to make a nice bow to this lovely audience of ladies and gentlemen and children!"

At this command, Pinocchio went down on his knees and stayed there until the ringmaster cracked his whip and shouted, "All right, now—*walk!*" and the little donkey obediently walked slowly around the ring.

*. . . *this wild beast:* This is pure nonsense, and just circus talk. The pretty, gentle, intelligent, and marvelously strong—and sometimes very stubborn—little donkey is anything *but* the savage animal that this pompous ringmaster describes.

After a little of this, the ringmaster cracked his whip again and shouted, "Now, *trot!*" Once again Pinocchio obeyed and he began to trot around the ring.

"Now, *at a canter!*" and Pinocchio immediately broke into a gentle canter.

"Now then—*at a fast gallop!*" and Pinocchio galloped around the ring as fast as he could go. Then, suddenly, the ringmaster raised his arm and fired a pistol, and the little donkey, pretending he had been shot, fell down as if he were dead.

Then, as the audience applauded and cheered, he got up off the ground and, as he did so, he naturally raised his head and looked around him. And as he looked, he saw in the crowd a beautiful lady who was wearing a gold chain about her neck, and from that gold chain there hung a medallion,* and painted on that medallion was the portrait of a puppet.

*. . . *a medallion:* A medallion is a kind of large medal on which is sometimes painted a "miniature," a small portrait of a loved one, which is worn like a locket about the neck on a slender chain. Here we find the Fairy wearing such a medallion which bears the miniature of her beloved Pinocchio.

"That's my picture! That lady is my good Fairy!" said Pinocchio to himself as he recognized her immediately. Then, in his excitement, he tried to cry out, "Oh, dear Fairy! My dear, dear, good Fairy!" But instead of these words, there came from his mouth a donkey's bray so loud and long that the whole audience—especially the children—laughed and laughed.

At this, the ringmaster became very angry, and to teach Pinocchio that it was bad manners to bray at the audience, he gave him a cruel rap on the muzzle* with the butt of his whip. Of course this hurt terribly, and the poor little donkey stuck out his tongue a good four inches and licked his sore nose for several minutes.

But then, when Pinocchio had recovered enough to look again for the Fairy, to his terrible disappointment, he found the seat empty. His good Fairy had disappeared! He felt like dying! His big, soft eyes filled with tears and he began to weep sadly although nobody even noticed it, least of all the ringmaster who cracked his whip and shouted, "Now then, Pinocchio—! Let's show these lovely people how gracefully you can jump through the hoop!"

Pinocchio tried this two or three times, but every time he came up to the hoop, he found it much easier to duck under it than to jump through it. On the last try, he leaped directly through it, but as he did so, his hind legs caught in the hoop and he fell in a heap on the ground. As he struggled to get up, he found that he was quite lame, and it was all he could do to limp painfully back to his stall in the stable.

"We want Pinocchio! We want the little donkey! Bring back the little donkey!" shouted all the children in the audience who were upset and sad about the accident. But the poor little donkey did not appear again that evening.

The very next morning, the veterinarian—that is, the doctor who takes care of animals—examined Pinocchio. When he fin-

*. . . a cruel rap on the muzzle: The "muzzle" of a donkey—just as it is of the horse, the mule, the cow, etc.—is the soft end of his nose which is not covered with hair. A donkey's muzzle, then, is so tender and sensitive that you can easily imagine how it must hurt him to be struck there with the hard handle of a whip.

ished his examination he sadly announced that the little donkey would be lame the rest of his life.

When he heard this, the ringmaster said, "What am I supposed to do with a lame donkey? He can't work, and he'd only eat me out of house and home!" and with this, he turned to a stable boy and said, "Here, you! take this worthless donkey to the market place and sell him for what you can get for him!"

No sooner had the stable boy arrived in the market place with Pinocchio when a shrewd donkey trader appeared. Gruffly he asked, "Well boy, how much do you want for that lame donkey?"

"Twenty *lire*—"

"Twenty *lire!* you can't be serious! I'll give you twenty *soldi**

Twenty lire . . . twenty soldi: Remember way back in chapter 9 I explained the *soldo* as a small-value copper coin something like the

for him.[3] Remember, I'm not buying him so he can work for me—I only want him for his skin.[4] I can see he has a very tough hide and I want to use it to make a bass drum for the town band."

Just imagine, boys and girls, how poor Pinocchio must have felt when he heard that his skin was going to be used for a drumhead!

As soon as the donkey trader had paid the twenty *soldi*, he led the little donkey to a rock high above the seashore. He then tied a heavy stone to his neck, and fastened the end of a long rope to one of his hind legs. Then he gave him a quick push, and poor Pinocchio fell into the water. With that heavy stone tied to his neck, he went straight to the bottom of the sea. Meanwhile, the donkey trader held the long rope tight and sat down on the rock to wait until he was sure the little donkey was quite drowned so he could skin him.

Chapter 34

*Pinocchio, having been thrown into
the sea, is eaten by the fishes and becomes a
puppet again. While he is swimming to save his own
life, he is swallowed up by a terrible Shark.*[1]

When the poor little donkey had been under water for almost an hour, the donkey trader thought to himself, "Well, by this time that lame donkey must be dead. I'll just pull him back up. That skin of his is going to make a beautiful drumhead." Then he began to haul in the rope he had tied to the donkey's hind leg.

American five-cent piece (the nickel) and the *lira* as something like the American dollar? Well, now we find Pinocchio as a lame donkey offered for sale for an "asking price" of twenty lire which would have been a ridiculously high price to ask even for a horse in sound condition. The donkey trader is no fool, though, and he buys Pinocchio for only twenty soldi: one-tenth of what the stable boy asks for him.

He hauled, and hauled, and hauled, until suddenly there appeared on the surface of the water—what do you suppose? Instead of a dead donkey, there was a live wooden puppet wriggling like a slippery eel!

The man took one look at this puppet he had hauled in and thought he was dreaming. He couldn't utter a word, but just stood there with his mouth open and his eyes popping out of his head. When he finally recovered a little, he stammered, "B-b-but . . . where's the d-donkey I threw in the sea?"

To this the puppet answered with a laugh, "Well, I'm sorry, but I happen to be that little donkey!"

"You?"

"Yes, me!"

"Now look, you little thief! Don't you get funny with me!"

"Who, me? I'm not trying to be funny, I'm serious!"

"But . . . but, only an hour ago you were a donkey I tried to drown in the sea! How can you be a wooden puppet now?"

"I guess it must be the effect of the seawater. It makes things change, you know."

"Now, just a minute, puppet, don't you try to fool me! Don't make me mad, or you'll be sorry for it!"

"Well, *signor* donkey trader, do you want to hear the real story? Just take this rope off my leg, and I'll tell you all about it."

The donkey trader, who was really curious to hear the real story, quickly untied the rope and took it off the puppet's leg. When Pinocchio found himself free as a bird once more, he began to tell his story:

"The truth of the matter is, I was once a wooden puppet, just as I am now. I had just reached the point where I was going to be turned into a real boy like all the others in the world. But, because I didn't like school and because I took the advice of other naughty boys, I ran away from home. Then one day I woke up and found myself changed into a donkey with long ears, and a long tail, and everything! I was so terribly ashamed. Oh, I only hope, dear *signore*, that the good Saint Anthony[2] never puts such a shameful punishment on you. And then I was taken off to the donkey market and sold to the ringmaster of a circus who taught me to dance and jump through a hoop—and then one night during a performance, I had a bad fall and lamed my legs—and then, when the ringmaster didn't know what he could do with a lame donkey, he sent me back to the market, and there you bought me!"

"I sure did! I paid twenty *soldi* for you. So, now how am I going to get my money back?"

"But why did you buy me in the first place? I'll tell you why. You just wanted me to make a drumhead out of my skin! Imagine, a drumhead!"

"Yes, that's right! And now where do I find another donkey skin?"

"Aw, don't feel bad, good signor donkey trader. There are so many other little donkeys in the world!"

"Well then, you little brat, is that the end of your story?"

"No," answered the puppet, "I have a few more words to say before I'm finished. After you so kindly bought me, you brought me here to kill me for my skin. And then, because you're such a soft-hearted man, you decided to tie a stone round my neck and just throw me into the sea. I want you to know that this kind-hearted deed does you great credit, and I will always be grateful to you for it! On the other hand, dear donkey trader, when you tried to drown me, you didn't count on the good Fairy."

"The good Fairy? Who's she?"

"She's my mother, and she's just like all good mothers who love their children and never let them out of their sight, and who always help them when they get into trouble, even if they're naughty and do foolish things and don't really deserve to be helped. Anyway, I started to say that as soon as the good Fairy saw that I was in danger of drowning, immediately she sent a huge school of fish who thought I was just a dead donkey, and they began to eat me.[3] And what big bites they took out of me! I would never have thought that little fish could be greedier than little boys!

"Some ate my long ears, some ate my muzzle, my neck, and my mane. Others chewed away at my hoofs and the skin of my legs and my back, while one of them very kindly chewed off my tail."

"Well, I just want to say this," said the horrified donkey trader, "I'll never eat fish again! Imagine opening up a grilled mackerel or a fried mullet and finding a donkey's tail inside!"

"I see what you mean," replied Pinocchio, laughing, "but, I should tell you that when those fish finished chewing off that donkey hide that covered me from head to foot, they naturally came to the bone—or, I should say, they naturally came to the wood, because, as you can see, I'm made out of very hard wood. But after they tried one bite, those greedy fish discovered that they really didn't like the taste of wood after all, and they were so disgusted that they swam off in all directions without even saying 'Thank you.' And now you know why, when you hauled in your rope, you found a live puppet instead of a drowned donkey."

"All right!" shouted the donkey trader in a rage, "I've heard just about enough of this nonsense! All I know is I paid twenty soldi for you, and I want my money back! Well, I know what I can do. I can just take you back to the market and sell you as a bundle of kindling wood."

"Oh, that's all right," said Pinocchio, "I don't mind at all," but as he said it, he made a beautiful leap and plunged into the sea, and, as he swam gaily away, he shouted back to the man, "*Ciào*,* signore! if you ever need a skin to make a drumhead, keep me in mind!" Then, with a loud laugh, he went on swimming.

After a little while, the puppet turned again and shouted even louder than before, "Don't forget, when you need some nice dry kindling wood, remember me!" Then, in the twinkling of an eye he had swum so far away you could hardly see him. In fact, all you could see was a little black dot on the sea when, once in a while as he swam, he raised an arm or a leg out of the water and leaped and cavorted like a happy dolphin who was having a very good time.

As Pinocchio swam along without a care in the world, he happened to look up, and there in the middle of the ocean, he saw a great towering rock that appeared to be made of white marble. Then—a strange thing—on the very top of that rock there stood a beautiful little goat that seemed to be calling to him with a most affectionate kind of bleat. Not only that, but the pretty little goat seemed to be making signs to the puppet to come to her.

But, the strangest thing of all! The little goat's hair was not white, or black, or a mixture of colors like other goats—it was *blue!* It was the very same blue as the good Fairy's hair!

Now, you can well imagine how hard Pinocchio's heart began to beat when he saw this. He began to swim as hard and as fast as he could toward that tall white rock where the pretty blue-haired goat stood. He was only halfway there when he looked back and saw, rising high out of the water and rushing toward him, the horrible head of a sea-monster! Its mouth was open wide like an enormous cave with three rows of huge, terrible fangs that would have scared anyone to death, even in a picture.

And just what do you suppose this sea-monster was? It was

Ciào: "So long." This Italian slang word can mean "Hello!" or "Hi!" as we might greet a friend on the street, and it can also mean "So long," "See you later," or simply "See you . . ." as Americans sometimes say. Also, this word is not pronounced "chow" as so many ignorant grownups seem to think. You can be one up on them if you say "chee-AH-oh" very fast but pronouncing each syllable clearly.

none other than that enormous Shark which has already been mentioned several times in this story. Because of its murderous rampages and its ravenous appetite, this awful Shark was known as the "Attila* of fish and fishermen."

Just imagine poor Pinocchio's fright when he saw the monster. He tried to dodge it by changing direction, and he tried to escape by swimming fast, but that huge cavernous mouth kept coming toward him with the speed of an arrow.

"Hurry, Pinocchio, for heaven's sake!" bleated the pretty little blue-haired goat. Pinocchio desperately thrashed in the water with all of the strength of his arms and legs.

"Quickly, Pinocchio, the monster's right behind you! Please hurry! Please, or you'll be swallowed up!" And Pinocchio swam faster than before, and he swam, and he swam, and he *swam*, until finally he was traveling through the water at the most incredible speed. He had almost reached the tall white rock and the little goat, leaning far out over the sea, reached out to try to pull him out of the water!

*Attila: The Shark was named after Attila, king of the Huns who, more than 1,500 years ago, became known for his cruel and savage invasions of European countries—including Italy.

But it was already too late. The huge Shark had caught up with him and, taking a deep breath, the monster sucked the poor puppet into his mouth as if he had been sucking in a strand of spaghetti. Then he swallowed him down so hard that, when Pinocchio finally dropped inside the shark, he came down so heavily that he was knocked unconscious for at least fifteen minutes.

When he finally came to, he had really no idea where he was. It was pitch-dark all around him and the darkness was so black that he felt as if he had fallen headfirst into a bottle of ink. He listened, but he could hear nothing. From time to time a great blast of wind blew in his face and, at first, he couldn't tell where the wind was coming from. Finally, however, he discovered that the gusts of wind were coming from the Shark's lungs* as he breathed. As a matter of fact, this Shark suffered badly from asthma, and when he breathed hard, it was as if the North Wind was blowing in great gusts.

At first, Pinocchio tried to be brave, but when he finally realized that he was actually shut up in the belly of the Shark, he began to cry and scream, "Help! Help! Oh, dear, won't anybody come and help me?"

"And just who do you think is going to help you in here, you poor fool?" came a voice out of the darkness that sounded like a guitar out of tune.

"Who's that?" asked Pinocchio, frozen with fear.

"It's me, just a poor Tuna fish who was swallowed up the same time you were. And how about you? What kind of fish are you?"

"I'm not any kind of fish at all, I'm a puppet!"

"Well then, if you're not a fish, how come you let this Shark swallow you up?"

"I didn't *let* him swallow me. It was all his own idea to chase me and swallow me! But now what do we do in this black hole?"

*. . . *the Shark's lungs:* You and I know that the shark is a kind of big fish, and that fish breathe with gills. Also, you can be sure that Mister Collodi knew this too, but the idea of an asthmatic shark breathing great gusts of wind seems much more exciting than a mere fish breathing calmly in and out through delicate, feathery gills.

"We just sit here and wait for the Shark to digest us!"[5]

"But I don't want to be digested!" howled Pinocchio and he began to cry again.

"Look, I don't want to be digested any more than you do," said the Tuna, "but I'm smart enough to know that when you're a fish, it's much more dignified to die under water than under hot oil in a frying pan!"

"That's silly!" said Pinocchio.

"Well, that's my opinion," replied the Tuna, "and according to all our great Tuna politicians, all opinions should be respected."

"That's all very nice, but I want to get out of here—I want to escape!"

"Well then, escape if you can."

"Tell me, is this Shark very big?"* asked the puppet.

*. . . *is this Shark very big:* You will recall that the Dolphin, in chapter 24, had already told Pinocchio how big the Shark was: ". . . he's as big as a five-story building, and he has a mouth so wide and deep that it could easily swallow a freight train. . . ."

"Is he big? His body is more than a mile long, and I'm not even counting his tail!"

While they were talking there in the dark, it seemed to Pinocchio that he could see a little light gleaming far, far away. He turned to the Tuna and asked, "What do you suppose that little light is that I can see so far off?"

"It's probably someone like us who's just waiting around to be digested."

"Well, I'm going to go and find out. It could just be that it's some old fish who could show us the way out of here."

"I certainly hope so with all my heart, dear boy."

"Goodbye then, *signor* Tuna."

"Goodbye, puppet, and good luck to you."

"Do you think we'll meet again?"

"Who knows? It's really better not to think about it."

· ❖ ·

Chapter 35

*What does Pinocchio discover
inside the huge Shark? Just read this
chapter and you'll find out.*

After Pinocchio said goodbye to his good friend the Tuna, he began to feel his way along in the dark, taking one step at a time through the huge belly of the Shark toward the light he saw shining in the distance. And as he walked, he felt his feet squish through puddles of greasy, slimy water that gave off such a strong smell of fish that he felt as if it was the middle of Lent. *1

The farther he went, the brighter the light became. He walked, and he walked, and he walked until he reached it at last.

. . . the middle of Lent: Lent is the period of forty weekdays before Easter. A hundred years ago, Roman Catholics were forbidden to eat meat during this perod, but they were allowed to eat as much fish as they liked. You can just imagine, then, how an Italian village must have smelled of frying fish in the middle of that long period of Lent!

And when he reached it, what do you suppose he found there? I'll give you a thousand guesses!

He found a nicely set little table on which there was a lighted candle with a green glass bottle for a candlestick. Seated at the table was a little old man with hair so white that his head looked as if it had been covered with snow, or even with whipped cream. This old man was hungrily eating a meal of live sardines, and those little fish were so lively that while he was eating, some of them actually jumped out of his mouth!

When he saw the old man, poor Pinocchio's heart was filled with such wild, uncontrollable joy that he felt as if he would go out of his mind. He felt like laughing and crying at the same time, and he wanted to say a thousand things, but he could only mumble a few broken and meaningless words. At last he was able to utter a loud, happy cry and, spreading his arms wide, he threw them around the old man's neck as he shouted, "Oh, Daddy—dear Daddy! I've found you at last! Now that I've found you, I'll never leave you again. Never, ever again!"

"I don't believe it!" cried the old man as he rubbed his eyes, "Can it really be my own dear Pinocchio?"

"Oh, yes, yes, it's me, really me! And you've already forgiven me, haven't you?[2] Oh, dear Daddy, what a good man you
are, and to think that I—oh, but if you only knew what I've
gone through and what terrible things have happened to me!
Just think, Daddy, the very day you sold your coat to buy me a
book so I could go to school, I ran off to see a puppet show, and
the puppetmaster wanted to throw me on the fire to roast his
mutton, and he was the same one who gave me five gold pieces
to take home to you, but then I met the Fox and the Cat who
took me to the Inn of the Red Lobster where they ate up all the
food like starving wolves and then left me all by myself, and
then when I went down the road in the dark, I met two robbers
who chased me when I ran away, and then when they caught me
they hanged me on a limb of The Great Oak, and then the
beautiful girl with the blue hair sent her carriage for me, and
then when the doctors looked at me they said, 'If he's not dead,
that proves he's still alive,' and then I told a big lie and my nose
grew so big I couldn't get through the bedroom door, and then I
went with the Fox and the Cat to plant my four gold pieces—I
had spent one of them at the Inn of the Red Lobster—and then
the parrot began to laugh at me, and instead of two thousand
gold pieces, I didn't find anything, and then when the judge
heard that I had been robbed, he put me in jail just to make the
robbers happy, and then when they let me out of jail, as I was
going down the road, I saw a lovely bunch of grapes in a field,
and then I was caught in a steel trap, and then the farmer—who
was absolutely right—put a big dog-collar on me and made me
guard his poultry yard, and then when he found out that I was
really innocent he let me go, and then the Snake with the smoking tail began to laugh and had a heart attack and died, and then
I went back to the house of the girl with the blue hair, but she
was dead, and then the Pigeon saw me crying and said, 'I saw
your Daddy building a boat to go to look for you,' and I said,
'Oh, if only I had wings like you!' and the Pigeon said, 'How
would you like to go to your Daddy?' and I said, 'Oh, I would
love to go, but who could take me?' and then the Pigeon said,
'I'll take you,' and I said, 'How?' and the Pigeon said, 'Just get
on my back,' and then we flew like that all night long, and then
the next morning all the fishermen who were looking out to sea

said to me, 'There's a poor old man out there in a little boat, and he's going to be drowned,' and, even at that distance, I recognized you immediately because my heart told me it was you, and I made signs to you to come back to the beach . . ."

"Yes, I recognized you, too," said Geppetto, "and I wanted so much to go back to the beach, but I just couldn't. The sea was so rough and a huge wave finally upset my little boat. Then a horrible Shark saw me in the water and swam toward me and he stuck out his long tongue, and licked me up and swallowed me like a strawberry tart."

"And how long have you been shut up in here?" asked Pinocchio.

"Since that day—it must be at least two years, Pinocchio, two long years that have seemed to me like two *hundred* years!"

"But, how were you able to live in here all this time? Where did you get the candle? and the matches to light it? who gave them to you?"

"Well, let me tell you the whole story. The fact is, in the same storm that upset my little boat, there was a big merchant ship that sank, too. All the sailors were saved, but the ship went to the bottom of the sea. Then, that same enormous Shark, who had a good appetite that day, swallowed up the ship the same way he swallowed me."

"You mean he swallowed up that ship in one mouthful?" asked Pinocchio in amazement.

"In one mouthful. And the only thing he spat out was the mainmast because it got stuck in his teeth like a fishbone. Lucky for me[3] the ship was laden with canned meat, biscuits, bottles of wine, raisins, cheese, coffee, sugar, wax candles, and boxes of matches. With this great bounty of the good Lord, I have been able to live these two years. But now my supply is gone. There's nothing left in the pantry, and that candle you see burning there—that's the very last candle I have."

'And then what. . . ?"

"And then, my dear boy, we'll be in the dark."

"All right then, Daddy," said Pinocchio, "there's no time to lose. We've got to find a way to get out of here right away. . . ."

"Get out of here? But how?"

"Well, we can escape through the Shark's mouth, jump into the sea and swim away."

"That's a great idea, Pinocchio, but the trouble is, I can't swim."'

"Oh, that's easy, I'm a good swimmer, and you can just get on my back and I'll carry you safely to shore."

"Ah, it won't work, my boy!" replied Geppetto as he shook his head and smiled sadly. "A puppet like you, a little more than three feet tall—you're just not strong enough to swim with a load like me on your back."

"Just try it and you'll see! Anyway, it's written in the stars that we all have to die sometime.[4] At least we'd have the consolation of dying in each other's arms."

Then, without saying another word, Pinocchio took the candle and walking ahead to light the way, he turned to his father and said, "Just follow me—and don't be afraid."[5]

They walked along for a long time in the huge belly of the Shark. Finally, when they came to the place where the monster's enormous throat began, they thought it best to stop and have a good look around and to wait for just the right moment to make their escape.

Meanwhile, it just so happens that this Shark was very, very old, and as you know, he suffered from a bad case of asthma, and because of this he had to sleep with his mouth wide open. So, when they reached his throat, Pinocchio found that he could look out through that huge, wide-open mouth, and see a broad strip of starry sky and a bright full moon.

"Now's the time," he whispered to his father, "the Shark is sleeping like a kitten, the sea is very calm, and it's bright as day outside. Come on, Daddy, in a few minutes we'll be free!"

Immediately the two—father and son—started walking up the Shark's long throat and, when they came to his cavernous mouth, they stole on tiptoe along his tongue which was as long and wide as any country road. Then, just as they were getting ready to jump out of the monster's mouth into the sea, he suddenly sneezed, and he sneezed so hard that it caused a regular earthquake that shook Pinocchio and Geppetto so hard that they were hurled right back into the Shark's belly. As they fell, their candle went out, and now father and son were in the dark.

"Well, now what do we do?" said Pinocchio in a worried tone.

"Now son, I'm afraid we're really lost."

"How can we be lost? Give me your hand, Daddy, and be careful not to slip."

"But where are you taking me?"

"We have to try again. Just come with me and don't be afraid."

Pinocchio took old Geppetto gently by the hand, and again walking on tiptoe, together they went once more up the monster's throat. Once again they stole down the long road of the Shark's tongue and at last climbed carefully over his three rows of sharp, savage teeth. Then, before they made the grand leap into the sea, the puppet said to his father, "Now, just climb on my back and hang on tight—just leave the rest to me!"

As soon as old Geppetto was settled firmly on his back, Pinocchio bravely jumped into the water and began to swim. The sea was as smooth as a pane of glass, the bright moon looked down in all its brilliance while the Shark went on sleeping a deep, deep sleep—he slept so soundly that not even a cannon could have waked him up.

Chapter 36

*At last! Pinocchio, the puppet,
becomes Pinocchio, the real boy!*

As Pinocchio swam with all his might toward the shore, he noticed that his father, who was riding on his shoulders with his legs trailing in the water, was trembling violently as if he had a terrible chill and fever. Was he trembling because he was cold, or because he was afraid? It was hard to tell; perhaps it was a little of both. But Pinocchio, thinking that the poor old man was shivering from fear, tried to comfort him: "Don't be afraid, Daddy! In just a few minutes we'll reach land all safe and sound."

"But, for heaven's sake, where *is* the land?" asked the old man, becoming even more nervous and squinting like an old tailor threading a needle. "I've been looking all around and all I can see is the sea and the sky!"

"But I can see land, too," said the puppet. "Don't forget, I have eyes like a cat. I can see better at night than I can in the daytime."

However, poor Pinocchio was only pretending to be cheerful, but instead . . . instead, he was beginning to be very discouraged. He became weaker and weaker and he had begun to gasp for breath. In fact, he just couldn't swim any farther, and the shore was still a long way off! At last he turned to Geppetto and stammered brokenly, "Oh, Daddy . . . ! help me . . . I'm dying!"

Father and son were about to drown when suddenly they heard a voice in the darkness that sounded like a guitar out of tune. "Who's dying?" said the voice.

"Me—me and my poor old father!"

"It seems to me I know that voice! Sure, you're Pinocchio!"

"That's right, but who are you?"

"Me? I'm the Tuna, your old friend from the belly of the Shark."

"But how did you ever get away from there?"

"Well, I did just what you did. You showed me the way out, so I followed you and escaped the same way."

"Dear old friend, you've come just in time! Now, for the love of all your own little Tuna children, please help us, or we'll drown!"

"Of course, I'll be glad to help! Just grab my tail and I'll tow the two of you behind me. In four minutes I'll put you on shore."

As you can easily guess, Pinocchio and Geppetto quickly accepted the big Tuna's invitation, but instead of holding onto his tail, they decided that it would be better if they climbed right up and sat on his back.

"Are we too heavy for you?" asked Pinocchio.

"Heavy—? Oh, no, you're light as a feather. It feels as if I have two empty snail shells on my back," answered the Tuna who was as big and strong as a two-year-old ox.

As soon as they reached land, Pinocchio jumped off the Tuna's back and then helped his father down. Then he turned to the Tuna and said in a voice filled with emotion, "Dear old friend, you have saved my Daddy's life and I just don't know how to thank you! At least, let me give you a big kiss as a token of my eternal gratitude."

The Tuna stuck his nose out of the water and Pinocchio, getting down on his knees, gave him an affectionate kiss right on the mouth. The poor Tuna, who was not really accustomed to such expression of warm affection, began to cry like a baby and, to hide his embarrassment, he suddenly plunged under the water and disappeared.[1]

By this time the sun had risen and it was no longer dark. Pinocchio put out his arm to Geppetto who, by now, was so weak he could hardly stand. "Here Daddy, lean on my arm and let's go. We'll walk along very, very slowly, and when we get tired, we'll just stop and rest ourselves along the way."

"But where can we go?" asked Geppetto.

"We'll look for a house or a cottage where we can ask for a little bread and some straw to sleep on."

They had hardly walked a hundred steps along the way when they saw a pair of ugly beggars sitting beside the road. And just who do you suppose those two beggars turned out to be? You're absolutely right! They were none other than the Fox and the Cat, but they had changed so much you would hardly have recognized them. Imagine! The Cat had pretended to be blind for so long that by now he was really blind. And the Fox—he had grown so old that his fur was completely moth-eaten on one side, and he no longer had a tail. In fact, that poor old thief had become so miserable that he had been forced to sell his tail to a peddler who used it for a whisk to keep the flies off him.

"Hey there, Pinocchio!" shouted the Fox with his voice full of tears, "Give a little something to two poor souls!"

". . . two poor souls!" repeated the Cat.

"Keep away from me, you thieves!" answered the puppet, "You stole my money once, but you'll never get anything from me again!"

"Oh, but believe us this time, Pinocchio! We're really poor and sick now!"

". . . really poor and sick now!" repeated the Cat.

"Well, if you're poor and sick, it serves you right. Just remember the old saying, 'Stolen money doesn't bear interest.'² So long, you thieves!"

"Please, have pity on us!"

". . . pity on us!"

"So long, you crooks. Remember the proverb, 'The devil's flour all turns to bran.' "

"Oh, don't abandon us!"

". . . abandon us!"

"Goodbye, robbers! Just remember the old saying, 'Whoever steals his neighbor's coat, usually dies without a shirt!' "

With this, Pinocchio and Geppetto went quietly on their way. But they had hardly gone another hundred steps, when at the end of a country lane, they saw a nice little cottage built of straw with a roof of red tile.

"Now, someone must be living in that cottage," said Pinocchio. "Let's knock at the door."

"Who's there?" asked a little voice from inside the cottage.

"It's only a poor old man and his son who have nothing to eat, and no roof over our heads," answered the puppet.

"Well, just turn the handle and the door'll open," said the same tiny voice.

Pinocchio turned the door handle and, sure enough, the door opened wide. They went into the cottage and they looked here, and they looked there, but they couldn't find anyone.

"Is there really anybody home?" asked Pinocchio in a loud voice.

"Here I am, up here!"

Father and son both quickly looked up toward the roof and there, sitting on a rafter, was—*Talking Cricket!*

"Oh, dear little Cricket!" cried Pinocchio with a deep bow.

"Aha! so now I'm your 'dear little Cricket,' am I? It seems to me I can remember a time when you wanted to get rid of me so bad you threw a wooden mallet at me to kill me!"

"Yes, you're right, Cricket! You should do the same to me—throw a wooden mallet at me! But, please have pity on my poor old father."

"Well, for that matter, I'll have pity on both of you—father and son—but I just wanted to remind you of the cruel and heartless way you treated me. I just wanted to teach you a very important lesson. I wanted you to learn finally that in this world you should treat everyone with as much kindness and compassion as you possibly can because, some day, you too may need that same sort of kindness and compassion from others."

"Yes, you're right about that, Talking Cricket! You've been right about that all along, and I've really learned my lesson at last. But, tell me, how do you happen to be living in a pretty little cottage like this?"

"Well, it happens that this cottage was given to me only yesterday by a lovely goat with blue hair."

'Really? And now what has happened to this pretty goat?" asked Pinocchio anxiously.

"I really don't know."

"Will she ever come back?"

"No, she'll never come back again. She went away yesterday bleating mournfully in a voice that seemed to say, 'Poor little Pinocchio, I'll never see him again, ever . . . by this time that terrible Shark must have swallowed him up, and he's gone forever'!"

"Did that little blue-haired goat really say that? Then—then it must have been—oh! it must surely have been—yes, it was—it was my dear little Fairy!" and Pinocchio began to cry and sob piteously.

After he had cried a long time, Pinocchio finally dried his eyes and went about making a warm bed of straw for old Geppetto to sleep in. Then he turned to Talking Cricket and asked, "Tell me, where can I find a cup of milk for my poor old Daddy?"

"Well, about three miles from here there's a farmer—Giangio is his name.* He keeps milk cows and you could try there if you want milk."

Pinocchio ran off at once to Giangio's farm and, when he got there, the farmer asked him, "How much milk do you want?"

"Oh, I only want a cupful," said Pinocchio.

"Well," said Giangio, "a cupful of milk'll cost you one *soldo*, so, first let's see your money. . . ."

"One soldo! Well, you see—I don't even have —I thought—" and Pinocchio lowered his eyes and stammered in embarrassment.

"Look, puppet," said Giangio, "if you don't even have one soldo, why should I give you any milk?"

"Yes, I guess you're right," said Pinocchio, and he turned sadly away.

"Now, just a minute," said Giangio. "Maybe we can make a little deal. How'd you like to turn my *bindolo*† for a while?"

"Turn your bindolo! What in the world is that?"

"That's a waterwheel that carries water up from the pond to water the fields."‡

"Well, I can try."

---

*. . . *Giangio is his name:* Pronounce his name Gee-AHN-gee-oh. Say it fast, but speak each syllable clearly.
†. . . *bindolo:* Pronounce this BEAN-do-loh.
‡*That's a waterwheel . . . to water the fields:* The bindolo that Giangio describes to Pinocchio is not exactly the kind of waterwheel that you may have seen in pictures of old-fashioned mills. It is really a large machine for drawing water and consists of a huge vertical wooden wheel fitted with water-buckets, and a smaller horizontal wheel fitted with wooden teeth which mesh with other teeth set in the hub of the big wheel. A donkey or an ox is harnessed to the shaft of the small drive-wheel and, by walking round and round, the animal drives the waterwheel which raises water from a stream or pond and empties it into a sluice or channel which carries it out to the fields. These primitive waterwheels may still be found in remote parts of Italy.

"All right, then, if you draw up a hundred buckets of water, I'll give you a cup of milk."

"I'll do it!"

Giangio led the puppet to the pond and harnessed him to the bindolo. Pinocchio went to work at once, but long before he was able to draw a hundred buckets of water, he found himself drenched with sweat from head to foot. He had never worked so hard before in his whole life!

"You understand," said Giangio, "that up to now, this work was done by my donkey. But now the poor animal is sick and dying."

"Oh, how awful!" said Pinocchio, "May I see him?"

"Of course."

When Pinocchio went into the farmer's stable, he saw a beautiful little donkey stretched out on a bed of straw. The poor little animal was worn out from hunger and ill-treatment.[3] The puppet took one look at him and said to himself, "I've seen that little donkey before—I'm sure I know that face!" Then, in donkey language, he said, "Who are you?"

At this, the poor dying donkey opened his eyes and said—also in donkey language—"I'm . . . I'm Lamp . . . I'm Lampwick!" and with this he closed his eyes and died.

"Oh, poor Lampwick!" murmured Pinocchio, and he took a bit of straw and wiped away the tears that were streaming down his face.

"It seems to me," said Giangio, "you feel awfully sorry for a donkey that didn't cost you anything! What about me? I paid a lot of money for him in hard cash!"

"Sorry about that, but he was my friend."

"What do you mean, your friend?"

"Well, you see, he happened to be a schoolmate of mine."

"A schoolmate!" shouted Giangio in a burst of laughter. "You mean you had a *jackass* for a schoolmate? Just what kind of a school did you go to?"

The poor puppet was so embarrassed by these questions that he didn't answer. Instead, he just took his cup of milk and walked sadly back to the little cottage.

Then, from that day, for more than five months, Pinocchio got up every morning before dawn to go to Giangio's farm to draw water for his fields just to earn that daily cup of milk for Geppetto. But he did't stop there. In his spare time he learned how to weave baskets of reeds and rushes, and with the money he earned by selling the baskets he made, he found that he could pay for all their daily needs. Also, he made a fine wheel chair in which he took his old Daddy for a ride now and then when the weather was fine and the air was fresh.

Then, every evening, he practiced reading and writing. In the city he bought a big second-hand book that had no title page and no index, but it helped him with his reading anyway. Since he had no pen, he made one from a reed which he sharpened with a penknife. And for an inkwell he used a little bottle filled with a mixture of cherry juice and blackberry juice.

But old Geppetto never really became well again, but through Pinocchio's cleverness and hard work, he was able to provide for himself and for the old man until they reached the point where they were living quite comfortably. The time even came when

Pinocchio discovered that he had been able to save up forty *soldi* to buy himself a new suit.

One morning, then, he announced to his father, "I'm off to the market! I'm going to buy myself a new jacket, a new cap, and a new pair of shoes. And, when I come back," he added with a happy laugh, "I'll be so fine you'll think I've changed into a regular *gran signore!*"

He left the house and sauntered down the road feeling very happy and satisfied with himself. All of a sudden, he heard someone call his name, and when he turned to see who it was, he saw a pretty little Snail coming out from under the hedge at the side of the road.

"Don't you remember me?" asked the Snail.

"Well, it seems to me I should, but then I'm not sure," answered Pinocchio.

"Do you mean to say that you don't remember the little Snail who was housekeeper for the Fairy with the blue hair? Don't you remember how I dashed downstairs to let you in, and I found you with your foot stuck through the door?"

"Of course! Now I remember everything! Oh, tell me quickly, dear little Snail, where is my good Fairy? What is she doing? Does she still remember me? Has she forgiven me? Does she still love me? Is she far away from here? Can I go and see her?"

Pinocchio asked all these questions as fast as he could talk, and without stopping even once to take a breath. But the Snail answered him in her usual slow, lazy way, "Ah, dear Pinocchio! I'm sorry to say that the poor Fairy is lying sick in a hospital!"

"In a hospital—!"

"Yes, unfortunately. She has had so many, many troubles, and she's so very, very ill, and she doesn't even have enough money to buy a little bit of bread!"

"Really? Oh, what terrible news this is! Oh, poor Fairy! poor Fairy! poor little Fairy! If only I had a million *lire*, I'd run and give them to her, but I only have forty soldi. Here they are. I was just going to buy a new suit, but take them, little Snail— take them quickly to my dear Fairy!"

"But what about your new suit?"

"Oh, the new suit doesn't matter anymore. I'd even sell these

175

old rags I'm wearing* if I thought it would help. Please go, little Snail, hurry! Come back in two days and I may be able to give you a little more money. Until now I have worked to keep my father. From now on, I'll just work five more hours every day to help my good little mother. Goodbye for now, little Snail. I'll expect you back two days from now!"

Surprisingly then, the Snail, contrary to her usual slow habits, scampered off like a lizard in the hot sun in August.

When Pinocchio returned home, Geppetto asked, "But what happened to the new suit?"

"Oh, I just couldn't find one the right size. It doesn't matter—I'll get it some other time."

That night, instead of working until ten o'clock, he went on working until the clock struck midnight. And instead of weaving eight baskets, he wove sixteen. Then he went to bed and fell sound asleep. And as he slept, he dreamed. And in his dreams he thought he saw his good Fairy, lovely and smiling.

She leaned over him and gave him a loving kiss, saying, "Bravo, Pinocchio! Bless your wonderful, good heart! I forgive you for all your past naughtiness. Boys and girls who really love their parents—as you do—and help them when they are poor and sickly, really deserve to be rewarded, even if they are not really the best-behaved and most obedient children. Just remember to be a good boy from now on, and you'll be a happy boy!"

At this point the dream ended, and Pinocchio came wide awake.

Just imagine his astonishment when he discovered that he was no longer a wooden puppet! Instead, during the night, he had turned into *a real boy!*

As he looked around him in amazement, he saw that the straw walls of the little cottage had disappeared, and he was now in a lovely bedroom furnished and decorated in elegant simplicity.

Leaping excitedly out of bed, Pinocchio found waiting for him a beautiful new suit of clothes, a new cap, and a brand-new pair of leather shoes.

*. . . *these old rags I'm wearing:* If you'll remember, in chapter 29 Pinocchio made himself a rude shirt out of a bean bag that an old man gave him. He must still be wearing that shirt.

As soon as he put on his new clothes, he naturally put his hands in his pockets and, to his surprise, he pulled out a handsome little purse trimmed with ivory on which was written, "The Fairy with the blue hair returns to her dear Pinocchio his forty soldi and thanks him with all her heart."

He opened the little purse and, instead of forty copper soldi, there were forty brand-new, shining gold pieces in it!

Then he ran to the mirror to look at himself, and as he did, he thought it was someone else he saw there. He no longer saw the reflection of a poor wooden puppet. Instead he saw the image of a bright-looking, lively boy with chestnut-brown hair and blue eyes who looked as happy and carefree as if he were enjoying an Easter holiday.[4]

In the midst of all these wonders that seemed to rush upon him one after another, Pinocchio was so confused that he could hardly tell whether he was really awake or just dreaming with his eyes wide open.

"But where can my Daddy be?" he cried suddenly. But when he rushed into the next room, there was old Geppetto, completely well again, and in a good humor just as always. He had once again taken up the art of woodcarving and now he was busy working on a handsome oak picture-frame all decorated with leaves and flowers and the pretty heads of rabbits and deer.

Lovingly, the new Pinocchio leaped toward the old man and covered him with kisses as he shouted excitedly, "Daddy! what's happened? Everything has suddenly changed! How? Why?"

"Well, dear boy," answered Geppetto, "it's really all because of you."

"Because of me? Why?"

"Why? Well, Pinocchio, it's this way—when a boy who has always been bad suddenly discovers that it's better to be good, he changes, and then everything around him changes. Suddenly he has the marvelous power of bringing happiness to his family, and he finds that he can put broad smiles of contentment on the faces of those who love him."

"But the old wooden Pinocchio—where is he now?"

"Ah, there he is, over there," answered old Geppetto as he pointed toward a chair standing in a corner. Hanging from the back of the chair was a marionette—a clumsy, wooden puppet—

with its wooden head hanging foolishly on one side, its arms dangling uselessly, and its legs bent awkwardly.

The new Pinocchio stood there looking at the silly wooden figure hanging from the chair. Then, after he had looked at it for a long time, he sighed and said softly to himself:

"Oh, what a great fool I was when I was a puppet! And now—now, how happy I am that I've become a real boy at last . . . !"

·❖·
Notes

These notes have been carefully prepared for those adults who would like to see what they have been deprived of for so long. They are intended to provide some common soil upon which English-speaking people can meet and comprehend the complex, and usually harsh and unfeeling, social system of Collodi's Italy of a hundred years ago. Also, they are intended for use by those who would like to read *Pinocchio* to their pre-school children and would wish to avoid the appearance of ignorance. Certainly such notes might have salvaged Uncle Charlie's reputation for savoir faire (see Introduction) had they been available to him that night 'way back in 1922.

Here and there you will find mentioned the names Murray, Della Chiesa, and Harden. These are the three earlier translators whose work I occasionally turned to for comparison. It was Mary Alice Murray, an Englishwoman who, in the 1890s, evidently made the first English translation of Collodi's masterwork and, stilted as her translation seemed to me at the time, it was she who introduced me, at a most tender age, to the delights and marvels of the *Adventures of Pinocchio*. As was the custom among female scholars and writers of her time, she signed her work "M.A. Murray" which led me to think that the work had been done by a man. (*Pinocchio: the story of a puppet* by C. Collodi. Translated by M. A. Murray with color illustrations by Charles Folkard. New York: E.P. Dutton & Co., 1919; *The Adventures of Pinocchio* by C. Collodi. Translated by Carol Della Chiesa with the reproduced illustrations of Attilio Mussino [1911]. New York: Macmillan Publishing Co., Inc., 1925 and 1969)

E. Harden was an Australian scholar and evidently a student of Italian folk-literature, although I have been able to learn very little else about him. His translation was published in 1944 and while I found it quite appealing, it lapsed from time to time into the quaint Australian idiom of his time, quite far removed from the 19th century Tuscan mode of expression. I found a dog-eared copy of Harden's *Pinocchio* in a bookstall in Naples in 1979, and at the time it was the only English translation available to me. (*Pinocchio* by Carlo Collodi. Translated by E. Harden. Melbourne, Victoria, Australia: Consolidated Press, 1944)

Meanwhile, this brief list of English translations of C. Collodi's *Pinocchio* must not be considered complete; there were many others, perhaps even scores more, to which I had not access at the time I decided to make my contribution.

Chapter 1

1. . . . Mastro *Cherry:* In the long catalogue of formal Italian titles of respect, *mastro,* derived from *maestro,* master, is still used to address artisans and tradesmen, although such masters of trades are becoming fewer and fewer. The title is usually used in combination with a first name (*Mastro* Peppino, *Mastro* Giorgio, etc.) and when it occurs before a name which begins with a vowel, it is elided as, for example, *Mastr'* Antonio. For more on the matter of formal Italian titles, see note 2, chapter 11.

2. *Could anybody be hiding inside it:* The folklore of practically any culture reflects the conviction that spirits of one kind and another, good and evil, benevolent and malevolent, inhabit living trees. It has been suggested that Collodi has drawn upon the Italian variety of this superstition by having *Mastro* Cherry wonder about his intractable piece of wood. However, as we go on, we find Collodi quite capable of inventing folklore to suit his own purposes, and it is sometimes difficult to distinguish tradition from invention. This fleeting thought of Cherry's, then, could just as well be the kind of foolishness which Collodi often put into the minds of his lesser characters for the sake of whimsy.

Chapter 2

1. *Geppetto:* As indicated in the footnote, "Geppetto" is the Tuscan diminutive of the name Giuseppe, which translates to something like "Little Old Joe," an appellation befitting old Geppetto's actual lowly station. It is, however, not appropriate to the Disney character who is represented as an apparently prosperous Tyrolean burgher (see note 1, chapter 12).

2. *Polendina:* Polendina is Tuscan dialect for *polenta,* a delicious corn meal pudding, and here is the recipe for it. It is especially good when served with grilled sausage or pork chops (Remember now! I promised your kids!):

1½   cups of yellow corn meal (polenta)
2   teaspoons (more or less, to taste) of coarse salt
6   cups of water

a. Bring the salted water to a full boil in a saucepan. Pour the corn meal into the pan so gradually that the water continues to boil. While pouring, be sure to stir the mixture gently but *constantly* with a wooden spoon.

b. When the mixture is complete, bring it to a simmer, still stirring, for about twenty minutes, or until it has reached the degree of thickness you think you will like.

The tomato sauce can be prepared thus:

2–3   tablespoons of olive oil
2   cloves of fresh garlic, thickly sliced
2–3   cups of undrained canned tomatoes, coarsely chopped
3–4   tablespoons of tomato paste
½   teaspoon (more or less, to taste) of coarse salt
1   pinch (more or less, to taste) of freshly ground black pepper

a. In a frying pan, sauté the garlic slices in the olive oil until they are lightly browned, taking care that they do not scorch.
b. Remove all of the garlic with a skimmer and discard it.
c. Transfer the oil to a saucepan or deep frying pan and to it add the chopped tomatoes and their liquid, the tomato paste, salt and pepper.
d. Simmer the mixture for forty-five minutes to an hour, stirring and tasting occasionally until you are satisfied with the flavor and consistency.
e. Make a shallow depression with a spoon in a serving of the piping hot polenta and pour a quantity of this simple tomato sauce into it.

Be cautious in your use of garlic in this recipe or, for that matter, any recipe that calls for garlic. Most Americans seem to suffer the illusion that Italians use garlic profusely in their cookery. It is indeed an illusion; garlic is used in Italy to be sure, but as a seasoning and not as a foodstuff. In the first rate *cucina*, it is used sparingly and to taste. If you prefer a lighter seasoning of the onion kind, substitute chopped onion or shallot and, if you choose, you can leave the onion or shallot in the oil after it is cooked.

Also, if a richer flavor is desired, you can add to the mixture while it is cooking such things as chopped fresh basil, parsley, or a little dried oregano or marjoram. Experiment with this basic tomato sauce and try adding varieties of seasonings such as fennel seed, capers, ground cayenne pepper, anchovy fillets, bayleaf, dried thyme, or rubbed sage. Remember, though, moderation is the byword for any seasoning you use and most particularly in your use of garlic. I think you'll be glad I told you.

3. . . . *one that could dance, fence with a wooden sword, and . . . I could travel all over and make him perform for people:* The puppet has been known since the earliest of times as a means of dramatizing mythological, historical, and religious events. During the Middle Ages, religious dramas performed by puppets became popular in Europe—especially in Italy—and became a useful medium through which the common people could be educated and entertained at the same time. The puppet show was essentially the theater of the masses and became

most instrumental in perpetuating ancient legends and traditions, while preserving old dramatic modes which had vanished from the live theater. The itinerant Italian puppet-showman himself was generally a simple, ignorant man who had learned his vocation from his father and, just as old Geppetto here proposes to do, eked out the most modest sort of livelihood by taking his portable theater, often upon his own shoulders, on donkeyback, or in a cart, to remote villages and to church-towns for their festivals and their street-fairs. When Geppetto speaks of a puppet "that could dance, fence with a little wooden sword and turn somersaults," he is, perhaps, innocently describing for us the chief activities in two forms of the Italian puppet theater: the genre of the *commedia dell' arte*, and the Sicilian tradition which is concerned with Ariosto's epic poem, *Orlando Furioso*. In the former mode, the dancing is associated with such characters as Harlequin and Columbine, while the somersaulting is one of the talents of the buffoon, Punchinello, and the various other *zanni* (see notes 1 and 2, chapter 10). In the latter, fencing is one of the main occupations of puppets dressed in the armor of Orlando and his Crusader knights and in the costumes of the sinister Saracen.

Chapter 3

1. *You wicked eyes:* This seems to suggest the glance of the notorious "evil eye" (*malocchio*), a superstition firmly established in the Italian peasant psyche from antiquity. The injury caused by such a look, as every knowing Italian understands, can be warded off only by a gesture which consists of pointing the index and little finger of the right hand at the offending eyes. Also, every knowing Italian understands the alternate significance of such a gesture directed at a husband whose wife has been unfaithful.

2. . . . *a big* carabiniere *appeared on the scene:* This carabiniere was a member of the national constabulary of Italy which was known in Collodi's time as *l'Arma de Carabinieri reali* (Royal Force of Carabineers). The Carabinieri actually originated in the island kingdom of Sardegna (Sardinia) as early as 1726 when their forces, then known as *i dragoni di Sardegna* (the Sardinian Dragoons), consisted of companies of cavalry the function of which was to protect the king and his court. We still find a similar body, of course, in the British cavalry regiment known as the Royal Life Guard—sometimes, the Royal Horse Guards, or Household Cavalry—whose task, while now largely ceremonial, is to protect the British royal family.

In 1859, at the outbreak of the Italian revolution known as *il Risorgimento* (the "Uprising"), the royal dragoons were reorganized as a single body of cavalry armed with the short musket or rifle called the *carabina*, or carbine, and were renamed *i carabinieri reali*, the Royal Carabineers. The Carabinieri then served as a dashing complement to the ragtag volunteer troops of the patriot, Giuseppe Garibaldi, and distinguished themselves in battle on the mainland of Italy as well as at the battles of Marsala and Palermo in Sicily.

In 1861, with the ultimate success of the Risorgimento under Garibaldi's fiery leadership, Italy was unified under a single ruler, Vittorio Emanuele II of the house of Savoy and former king of Sardinia. Almost immediately, the king recalled the Carabinieri as a kind of mounted national police force organized on military lines and charged with the protection of the public in the various provinces, particularly against the depredations of bands of robbers and cutthroats (*i briganti*) which terrorized outlying areas of the country. This military police force was invested with awesome power and authority over the districts they were supposed to protect and, for the most part, the briganti were brought under control. That power and authority, however, presently got out of hand and, inevitably, corruption appeared among the rank and file. The once proud and valiant military body became the arrogant, gaudily uniformed tool of the nobility and the propertied middle class which, in league with corrupt law courts and their unscrupulous magistrates and petty officials, often became the protector of criminals and the persecutor of the lower classes.

It was just this sort of abuse of authority that prompted Collodi, again and again throughout the story, to present the Carabinieri in an unfavorable light by representing them variously as puppets, as vicious dogs, and as pompous, domineering minions of the law (see note 3, chapter 3; note 1, chapter 11; note 5, chapter 19, and note 2, chapter 27).

3. . . . *took poor old Geppetto off to prison:* This is the first of a series of pathetic incidents which Collodi uses to illustrate the harsh social justice so prevalent in his Italy. In general, the law tended strongly to favor the aristocracy and the criminal "elite" to the detriment of the lower classes, as we shall see demonstrated in later episodes of the story (see also note 2 above).

4. *I'll tell you all about it in the next chapter:* As you know, the story of Pinocchio first appeared in serial form, and Collodi resorted to this conventional means of ending a current chapter of a serialized work.

Chapter 4

1. *Talking Cricket:* This, of course, is the very same cricket which Disney Studios, for cuteness' sake, felt compelled to rename "Jiminy Cricket" (which is about as Italian as Donald Duck), and to endow him with certain precious popular qualities which Collodi never intended him to have. For me, the Disney cricket seems too much a caricature of a dear old friend of mine, a wily and most adroit coin-machine salesman named George Glass, to make him credible as an "official conscience" to anyone.

Actually, the cricket is an Italian emblem of good fortune and in rural households it is not at all unusual to find crickets kept in cages made of osier or reeds and kept by the hearth.

It should be noted that all of Collodi's "good" animal characters lecture Pinocchio, in one way and another, on the subject of deportment and morality, and Talking Cricket is the most sententious of them all. But, unlike Jiminy Cricket, he was an abstract symbol, the dour familiar of the Fairy who, herself, is at once benevolent witch, guardian spirit, little Italian *mamma mia*, and fairy godmother.

You will discover that there is infrequent, and only incipient, evidence of conscience in Pinocchio until almost the story's resolution. Collodi's cricket, then, and all the other little preachers, were simply trying to teach the puppet what "conscience" means.

2. . . . *a little voice crying* . . . crì-crì-crì: It is a fact that Italian fauna make sounds which are different from those made by their Anglo-American counterparts, The difference, of course, is couched in phonetics. Italian is a purely phonetic language, whereas English has degenerated into a tongue which, for all its richness of expression, is anything but phonetic. For the Italian writer it is possible to represent the sounds of animals much more distinctly (to his own readers), as for example, the sound made by a cackling hen: *cò-cò-cò-deh!*

An Italian sheep, then, would bleat *bhé-é-é!* and a cat would cry *miàou*, while a donkey would bray *à-à! ih-à! ih-à! ih-à!*

The matinal Anglo-American rooster is conventionally represented as crowing *cock-a-doodle-doo!* but the naturally more lyrical Italian *gallo* sings *chì-chiri-chì!* in the same circumstances. My wife, until she was of college age, was reared and educated in Italy, and in the early days of our acquaintance, we carried on a running mock-argument about what roosters actually say. This continued until one day when she said, with no little chagrin, "You know, American roosters really do say 'Cock-a-doodle-doo!' "

Recently however, while spending an idyllic month or so on the rustic shores of Lago Maggiore in northern Italy, I was awakened regularly at five in the morning by not one but two Italian roosters neither of which crowed *chì-chiri-chì!* One of them, I am convinced, was calling to a friend in the next village, for his crow sounded exactly like *"Ehì! Donato!"* The other may well have been an immigrant Barred Plymouth Rock whose Yankee accent had deteriorated, for his shout was a listless, truncated *"Cock-a-doo. . . !"*

3. . . . *he remained dried up and flattened against the wall*: As terminal as Talking Cricket's condition seems to be here, we have not seen the last of him. He turns up as his own ghost in chapter 13, and again as one of the remarkable physicians summoned by the Fairy in chapter 16. Finally, he appears as the owner-by-legacy of the Fairy's cottage in chapter 36.

Chapter 5

1. . . . *the omelet flies out the window*: There is an inconsistency in that Collodi here refers to an "omelet," while in the text Pinocchio

decides against an omelet in favor of a poached egg. Incidentally, an omelet in Italian is *una frittata,* and to turn an omelet in its cooking is *girare la frittata* which, idiomatically, also means "to change one's mind." However, it would be reaching a bit to assume that Collodi really had this in mind when he made the apparent error.

2. *His nose . . . became even longer by at least three inches:* This reference to the growth of the nose from the effects of hunger is extraordinary when we discover later in the story that the growth of Pinocchio's nose is a sign that he is lying. Later, Collodi consistently uses the conventional Italian idiom "to yawn with hunger" in numerous passages. Since Pinocchio was composed piecemeal to serve the purposes of serialization, it is quite possible that Collodi thought of this device early on to describe the effects of hunger, and later decided that it was a far more dramatic way to demonstrate the effects of lying.

Chapter 6

1. *Pinocchio . . . still had no cap:* Many illustrators of various editions of *Pinocchio,* including the incomparable Attilio Mussino who illustrated the first large edition of 1911, overlook the fact that Geppetto had not yet provided his new puppet with a cap, and they depict him in this scene holding out a cap as he is directed to do by the old man.

Chapter 7

1. *. . . a sackful of wooden spoons . . . from a fifth-story window:* To their credit both Murray and Harden retain this great Collodi simile. Della Chiesa, however, unaccountably chooses to refer to a "sack of wood," thus destroying a nicely wrought image.

2. *The cat:* This short-lived, nameless cat was simply a bit of early Collodi local color. Very likely, however, its brief appearance in the original *Adventures of Pinocchio* inspired Disney Studios to describe old Geppetto as living alone "except for his black kitten, Figaro, and a pet goldfish he called Cleo."

The fact is, Geppetto was so dismally poor that he could scarcely keep his own body and soul together much less provide for two housepets. Collodi's playful cat serves its purpose here and is never mentioned again.

Chapter 8

1. *. . . I'll learn a trade:* This phrase seems to have vanished completely from the lexicon of youth. In my day, and within the memory of many of you, a boy whose parents couldn't afford to send him to college to prepare him for the professions as they were so reverently called, or at the very least, to put him au fait with the Liberal Arts, or the boy who was deemed intellectually incapable of such noble pursuits, was expected to "learn a trade." A trade, of course, was then

defined variously as a "vocation," a "gainful occupation," a "line of work" (or simply "a line"), and sometimes, jocularly, "a game." Whatever the designation, being a "tradesman" inevitably implied an occupation inferior to that of a "professional," *i.e.*, lawyer, teacher, physician, dentist, civil engineer, etc. The tradesman did have his level of distinction though, in that he was considered superior to the "day laborer" or the farmhand, and the unskilled factory drudge. Nevertheless, it was possible, even a hundred years ago and more, for a poor American (Honest Abe Lincoln?), by dint of hard work and unwavering pursuit of a goal, to distinguish himself in one or another of the professions.

Geppetto and Pinocchio, however, were in a far different situation: they were absolutely trammeled by a rigid class system—which still exists to a degree in Italy today—in which they occupied almost the lowest level. Geppetto was a peasant—an artisan, to be sure, but still a peasant—who could not by any means rise above his station. Pinocchio then, at the school he proposed to attend, would have learned only the three R's and a little geography and history, but little else to prepare him to face life. If he had decided to learn a trade, he would have had to apprentice himself to a tradesman such as a merchant, or to an artisan such as a mason, a cabinetmaker, or a blacksmith, for at least seven years during which time he would have had to toil and sweat with no recompense but food and lodging, both of the most miserable sort.

2. . . . *not beautiful clothes that make a gentleman but, rather, clean clothes:* As a matter of fact, in Geppetto's day, not even "clean clothes" could make one a gentleman because the *gran signore,* like his gentlemanly counterpart in Britain was a member of an established class and born to his station—of gentle birth—one cut below nobility, but still aristocratic. Later in the story we find Pinocchio dreaming of becoming *un gran signore* by increasing his hoard of gold pieces. This, however, was truly a dream because a member of a lower class could not, by means of wealth alone, raise himself above his station. He could attain the rank of *signore* only by order of his sovereign as a reward for some service to the crown. I feel compelled to add, however, that "service to the crown" could sometimes—especially in time of war or other moments of fiscal distress—have been as simple a matter as the contribution of a considerable number of gold pieces (*omaggio,* tribute) to the royal treasury.

3. . . . *a reading book:* This reading book is called an *Abbecedario* and is the Italian equivalent of our book of ABC's which serves as a primer from which first-grade Italian pupils first learn the alphabet and thus learn to read. When they have "learned their letters" the children then learn how to make syllables with them and then to combine the syllables to form words, then words to form phrases, and so on. The

Abbecedario, however, must not be confused with what we call a spelling book, or "speller." Italians are especially blessed in the fact that theirs is a phonetic language and, therefore, escape most of the childhood torture of learning to spell. Any Italian word is spelled the way it is pronounced, and pronounced the way it is spelled.

Chapter 9

1. *GRAND PUPPET THEATER:* The dramatic genre known as the *commedia del' arte* first appeared on the Italian stage in the sixteenth century and soon afterwards gave birth to a by-blow, the puppet theater, which followed the same improvisational dramatic pattern as its parent, except that instead of live actors and actresses playing the familiar roles of Harlequin, Punchinello (see notes 1 and 2, chapter 10), Columbine, Fiametta, et al., the characters were represented by marvelously wrought wooden marionettes, often dressed in magnificent costumes and presented on elaborately equipped stages in full-sized theaters as well appointed and well illuminated as any.

Puppet theaters were often permanent fixtures in the cities, but traveling puppet companies like this one held one- or two-week stands in the towns and villages in much the same manner as do the present-day traveling circuses, or the so-called carnivals. This particular puppet theater was one of the more elaborate of the traveling shows being housed as it was in "a building made of canvas and wood and painted in a thousand different bright colors" and, as we discover in chapter 10, provided with a full orchestra *cum* conductor, and a large auditorium complete with reserved seats.

2. *Pinocchio was on pins and needles:* Actually, in Italian, Pinocchio *era sulle spine;* that is, he "was on thorns."

Chapter 10

1. *Harlequin:* The character of Harlequin (*Arlecchino*) originated in the sixteenth century Italian theater with the form of improvised comedy known as the *commedia dell' arte* in which he was one of the comic servants called *zanni* (from which is derived the English word "zany," a buffoon or clown). From the commedia dell' arte, Harlequin drifted to the French stage where he became a character in what came to be known in France as the *arlequinade* and, in the late seventeenth century, he crossed over into England where he became the foolish, frustrated lover of Columbine in the wildly farcical "harlequinade."

In the meantime, Harlequin had been adopted as a marionette character in popular Italian puppet shows which still may be seen in Italy on certain occasions. Originally, as one of the *zanni,* Harlequin was dressed in a ragged suit covered with patches. Later, the rags and patches gave way to what is now easily recognized as the conventional Harlequin costume: a close-fitting suit consisting of bright, varicolored cloth diamonds sewn together. On his head he wears a huge cocked hat, and over his face he wears a small black mask which somewhat resembles a cat's face. Also, he carries a "slapstick," a bat made from two strips of wood fastened to a handle and which makes a loud noise when anyone or anything is struck by it.

2. *Punchinello:* Like Harlequin, Punchinello (*Pulcinella*) had his popular beginnings as one of the *zanni* of the commedia dell' arte, although he was apparently locally well known in Naples long before the development of that theatrical form. Tradition has it that the clownish Pulcinella was born (as *Policianelo*) in the Neapolitan village of Acerra in the early sixteenth century and appeared in street shows and pageants on festive occasions, often in large numbers, for scores of young men in Pulcinella costumes frequently went through the streets performing clownish antics and presenting ludicrous skits.

On the stage, Pulcinella was most often represented as a stupid, misshapen hunchback whose humor was sarcastic and usually vulgar. His costume consisted of wide, baggy white trousers, a voluminous white blouse or jacket (*giubba*), and either a stiff conical white cap, or a floppy white hat. Over his face he wore a grotesque black three-quarter mask which covered his forehead and most of his face, leaving only the mouth and lower jaw exposed, but giving the impression that it covered an enormous hooked nose. It is this clown's costume which the hunchback character, Canio, puts on in Leoncavallo's opera *i Pagliacci* (The Clowns) as he sings "*Vesti la giubba . . . la faccia in farina. . . .*" ("Put on your clown's jacket . . . whiten your face with flour. . . .")

It was as a marionette that the monstrous Pulcinella was most successful and, as the commedia dell' arte spread throughout Europe, the Italian puppet show followed close behind, and in Paris, Pulcinella became the sharp-witted Gallic *Polichinelle* who dominated the French marionette theater for more than a hundred years. In 1660 when the Stuart monarchy was restored to England, the theaters which had been closed by the Puritans in 1642 were reopened, and immediately Londoners were introduced to the Italian puppet show with the outrageous Pulcinella as its star. So popular did he become that England took him for her very own, first as "Polchinello," then as "Punchinello," and finally as the hook-nosed "Punch," the thoroughly English clown who became the very symbol of English humor and buffoonery.

3. *signora Rosaura:* This female character is impossible directly to identify by this name, although among the stock characters of the commedia dell' arte is one called Rosetta. Rosetta, Columbina (Columbine), Fiametta, and Pimpinella are comic serving girls who are the feminine counterparts of the *zanni* (see note 1 above). The name Rosaura may well have become, after some three hundred years, a popular Tuscan version of Rosetta.

4. *It's our brother Pinocchio:* This is another of Collodi's blithe

inconsistencies. Pinocchio had been carved from a billet of firewood only days before, yet Harlequin, who was born in the sixteenth century, recognizes him readily as "brother Pinocchio."

Chapter 11

1. . . . *two wooden policemen:* This is the first of the Collodi caricatures of the two *carabinieri* (see note 2, chapter 3).

2. . . . *signore . . . cavaliere . . . commendatore . . . eccellenza:* These are formal titles of respect with which Pinocchio politely addresses Fire Eater who, because of his occupation and social station, is worthy of none of them, although he might properly have been addressed as *Mastro* Fire Eater (see note 1, chapter 1). *Signore* is the equivalent of "sir"; *cavaliere,* a bit more courteous, might be expressed in English as "sir knight"; while *commendatore* is even more pompous and best translated perhaps as "knight commander." Finally, *eccellenza*—"your excellency"—is the most flattering title Pinocchio can think of offering—and, of course, it works!

Chapter 12

1. . . . *he's a pauper:* In this day and age of individual prosperity derived either from honest, hard work, or from the cornucopia of "public welfare," it is very hard to explain pauperism to a child—or, for that matter, to most grownups.

The American Heritage Dictionary defines a pauper first, as "one who is extremely poor," and second, as "one living on public charity." It is becoming more and more difficult to find anyone who fits the first definition unless one were to search among the rabble and rout of teachers and editors.

Collodi's Geppetto was plainly and simply a pauper (*povero*) whose actual occupation, woodcarving, was not even mentioned in the story until the very last page. On the other hand, the adapters of the Disney *Pinocchio* were so eager to please—and so loath to offend—that the Geppetto of their version was sweetly represented from the beginning as a comfortable, kindly, white-haired old wood-carver who "had spent his whole life creating happiness for others," rather than having spent his whole life struggling to avoid starvation.

In her translation, Miss Murray misses the point and has Pinocchio reply, "He is a beggar," although in her chapter 24, Pinocchio is ashamed to beg because "his father had always preached to him that no one had a right to beg . . ." Harden begs the issue (no pun intended) by referring to Geppetto as ". . . a very poor man," while Della Chiesa has, Disney-wise, "He's a wood-carver." Now that I think of it, the Disney *Pinocchio* was probably not an adaptation of Collodi's story at all, but must have been taken from the Della Chiesa translation.

2. . . . *here's five gold pieces:* Considering the value of the lira at

the time (see note 3, chapter 33) these five gold pieces represented a veritable fortune.

3. . . . *a shabby old Fox* . . . *a seedy old Cat:* In Italy, the fox (*volpe*) is, as it is in most cultures, a symbol of sly cunning with intent to cheat, while the male cat (*gatto*) is the symbol of sneakiness with intent to beguile. Oddly, Murray and Harden both refer to Collodi's "Cat" as *she* which is contradictory to the Anglo-American concept of the cuddly, motherly, and generally virtuous Tabby of nursery rhyme and story. Della Chiesa's "Cat," however, is allowed to remain sinisterly masculine.

4. . . . *a white blackbird:* In Italian, the blackbird is called *merlo*. However, ever so rarely, an albino of the species occurs and from this is derived the idiom, *un merlo bianco*, a white blackbird, which suggests something very rare or bizarre. The idiom suits Collodi's satire very well, and even better when translated.

5. *We have to go to Boobyland:* Collodi has *nel paese dei Barbagianni*, to the land of Owls. In Europe, the owl has generally been a symbol of stupidity since the early Middle Ages—and probably before—presumably because it is the only bird which is known to befoul its own nest. At some point in the Anglo-American cultural pattern, however, the owl turned respectable and came to symbolize great wisdom—perhaps by the influence of Edward Hersey Richards' jingle,

> A wise old owl sat on an oak,
> The more he saw the less he spoke;
> The less he spoke the more he heard;
> Why aren't we like that wise old bird?

In any case, "the land of Owls" simply would not properly express in English what Collodi intended.

Chapter 13

1. . . . *an inn called* The Red Lobster: Actually, Collodi called it *l'osteria del "Gambero Rosso"* (the inn of the Red Crayfish). However, like Della Chiesa, I have called it "The Red Lobster" for the sake of clarity. I doubt that a child, unless a native of Louisiana, would appreciate the crayfish as a table delicacy, or understand that, like the lobster, the crayfish turns bright red when it is cooked. Harden refers to the infamous inn as "The Red Crab," while Murray comes close to literal translation with the variant "Red Crawfish."

2. . . . *tripe in the Florentine style:* (*Trippa alla fiorentina*): I guess tripe is not as popular in America as it was when I was a boy when my mother used it, for one thing, in making a delicious pepperpot soup. It is a delicacy in Italy and elsewhere in the world where its proverbial toughness is mitigated, and its flavor enhanced, by thorough cooking and fine seasoning.

For anyone interested in reviving the taste for tripe, here is a good recipe to start with:

1 kilo (about 2 pounds) of tripe cut into pieces about ½-inch wide and 2 inches long
2 cups of beef or chicken stock
3–4 tablespoons of tomato paste
¼ cup of finely chopped onion or shallot
¼ cup of olive oil
½ teaspoon (more or less, to taste) of finely chopped fresh garlic (Please, don't use garlic powder!)
2 tablespoons of finely chopped parsley
½ teaspoon of dried oregano
½ teaspoon (more or less, to taste) of coarse salt
½ cup of grated Parmesan cheese

a. In a large saucepan, cook the celery and onion or shallot in the olive oil for about ten minutes and then stir in the tripe.
b. Heat the beef or chicken stock and mix the tomato paste with it. Pour this solution over the tripe and vegetables.
c. To the mixture, add the parsley, oregano, garlic, and salt.
d. Bring the whole to a boil, then cover the saucepan, reduce the heat, and simmer lightly for two to three hours, or until the tripe is tender enough to be pierced easily with a sharp fork.
e. Serve it piping hot and smothered with grated Parmesan.

 3. . . . *braised fat rabbit as it is cooked on the isle of Ischia:* (*Coniglia all' ischitana*): this is the recipe for a dish beloved of the people of Ischia, a sister-isle to Capri in the Tyrrhenian Sea:

1 kilo (about 2 pounds) of rabbit, skinned, dressed, washed, and cut into pieces
¼ cup of olive oil
2 tablespoons of minced onion or shallot
1 tablespoon of coarsely chopped parsley
2–3 crumbled bayleaves
 a pinch of dried thyme
 fresh lemon juice

a. Before cooking, marinate the meat by coating the pieces with a little of the oil mixed with a dash of the lemon juice. Lay the meat in a deep dish and sprinkle it with the minced onion or shallot, the chopped parsley, thyme, and bayleaves. Let it steep for about two hours at room temperature, turning the pieces frequently.

4—5 ripe tomatoes, peeled, seeded and coarsely chopped
1 stalk of fresh rosemary, or two teaspoons of dried rosemary needles
 a generous bunch of sweet fresh basil

½   teaspoon (more or less, to taste) of coarse salt
⅛   teaspoon (more or less, to taste) of freshly ground black
      pepper
1   cup of dry white wine

b. Sauté the pieces of rabbit in the rest of the olive oil.
c. Add the tomato, rosemary, basil, salt, pepper, and the wine, and
   cook the whole over low heat for about one hour, adding a few
   tablespoons of water, a little at a time.
d. When the rabbit appears to be well cooked, increase the heat to
   maximum for a minute or so.
e. Serve piping hot.
   4. . . . *breasts of chicken* alla bolognese: (*Petti di pollo alla bolognese*): here is an elegant savory reputed to have been created in the
kitchens of the ancient university city of Bologna. Whether it really
was or not is of little importance; the fact that it is sublimely delicious
is most important. The recipe:

4   half-pound chicken breasts, skinned and boned
      coarse salt and freshly ground black pepper
      flour
3   tablespoons of good butter
2–3   tablespoons of olive oil
8   thin slices of prosciutto
8   thin slices of natural Bel Paese cheese
      freshly grated Parmesan or Romano cheese
2–3   tablespoons of chicken stock

a. Carefully slice each chicken breast into two strips and flatten the
   strips between sheets of waxed paper with light blows of the flat of a
   broad cook's knife or a heavy spatula. Season the strips with a little
   salt and pepper, then flour each strip thoroughly.
b. Heat and mix the olive oil and butter in a large frying pan and sauté
   the chicken at moderate heat, a few strips at a time, until it is evenly
   browned.
c. Butter the inside of a shallow but ample casserole and place the
   strips of chicken breast in the bottom of it. On each strip place a
   slice of the prosciutto and a slice of the soft cheese. Sprinkle gener-
   ously with the grated cheese and moisten the lot with the chicken
   stock.
d. Put the uncovered casserole in an oven preheated to 350°F. and bake
   until the cheese has melted and is slightly browned.
e. Serve piping hot.
   5. . . . *forced to give the innkeeper one of his precious gold pieces:*
This indeed must have been a huge meal when one considers the kind
of restaurant dinner that could be had at the time for as little as 15
soldi (see note 3, chapter 33).

6. . . . *heaven protect you from the damp night air:* In practically every culture there is an age-old superstition that the dampness of night air is unhealthy. Indeed, the disease which we know as "malaria" derives its name from the Italian *mal aria* (bad air), and was once believed to be caused by breathing the air in marshy areas.

In fact, Italians in general seem to have a morbid fear of *la corrente*, or draft, which even the most sophisticated avoid as they might a blast of mustard gas. *La corrente*, it seems, is capable of causing any ailment from stiffness of the joints to liver disorder. A common admonition to guests in an Italian home on even the sultriest of summer days is *"Non stare nella corrente!"* ("Don't sit in a draft!") as the hostess scurries to close shutters or windows.

Chapter 14

1. *Pinocchio falls in with robbers:* In describing Pinocchio's adventures with that murderous pair of thieves, the Fox and the Cat, Collodi consistently uses the word *assassini*. However, the connotation of the term "assassin" is quite different from the Italian *assassino* which simply means "murderer." Therefore, I have used instead such words as *robbers, bandits,* and now and then, *murderers,* to convey the idea that Collodi intended.

2. *Your money or your life:* The Tuscan *brigante* of the time demanded *"O la borsa o la vita!"* ("Either your purse or your life!") The American or British equivalent of this was "Your money or your life!" or the more picturesque eighteenth-century "Stand and deliver!"

3. . . . *and Splash:* Unfortunately, the English *Splash!* does not convey the image of someone falling heavily and deeply into water as forcefully as does the Italian onomatopoea, *patapumfete!* which Collodi uses here very effectively. This wonderfully expressive word is pronounced—as nearly as I can express it—pah-tah-POOM-feh-teh! in measured tones with deep, dramatic emphasis on the *POOM!*

Chapter 15

1. *young girl with . . . hair the color of the blue sky:* This is our introduction to Pinocchio's Fairy (*Fata*). Her blue hair is not dictated by folkloric tradition; it was strictly Collodi's idea, and nowhere do we find her referred to as "the Blue Fairy" as we do in Disney and even in contemporary, inferior adaptations of Pinocchio.

2. *I am dead, too:* Collodi has made much effective use of the Dionysan death-and-resurrection theme in *Pinocchio:* Talking Cricket dies an ignominious death under Geppetto's mallet thrown by Pinocchio in chapter 4 only to appear again in later chapters. The blue-haired girl is dead in this episode although she is resurrected in a later chapter as a mature woman, while Pinocchio himself apparently dies by hanging and, later, by drowning.

Chapter 16

1. *. . . you should know . . . a beautiful Fairy who had lived . . . a thousand years:* You should also know that Tuscan fairies, especially those of the late nineteenth century, were renowned for their longevity.

2. *a Cricket . . . an Owl . . . a Crow:* This is a curious trinity of Collodi creatures used to represent physicians. The cricket, whom we later discover is Talking Cricket, is the emblem of good luck; the owl is the symbol of stupidity—even, perhaps, pretentious stupidity—while the crow is considered a harbinger of death. Can it be that Collodi uses them to represent the quality of Italian medical practice in his time?

3. *the careful physician . . . should keep his mouth shut:* Profound but generally unheeded advice, then as now.

Chapter 17

1. *It's bitter, but it'll help you:* Those were the days when most medicine for children was liquid and came in a small, square bottle with a little, evil-smelling cork. It was taken by the teaspoonful or, at best, mixed with a half-tumbler of tepid water. It was always extremely bitter and foul-tasting, for it was a superstition among physicians and parents that the efficacy of such medicine was measured directly in proportion to its nastiness. There was also a strong conviction among parents (that persisted, alas! well beyond my own childhood) that forcing children to take periodic doses of such fulsome confections as cascara, ipecac, Epsom salts, castor oil, sulfur and molasses, somehow contributed to their moral education as they purged the infant system of all manner of seasonal evils.

2. *jet-black rabbits . . . carried a little coffin on their shoulders:* Once again we find synthetic folklore! So far as I can discover, Italian rabbits have nothing to do with death—except, perhaps their own in providing many a dining-table delicacy. These black rabbit undertakers are another Collodi invention.

3. *lies that have short legs . . . lies that have long noses:* The Fairy here makes an observation which is half proverbial and half Collodi. As it turns out, there is an old Italian saying, *le bugie hanno le gambe corte,* "lies have short legs." It also turns out that there is an old English proverb dating from 1573, "lyes have short legges." The concept of the long-nosed lie, then, is Collodi invention.

Chapter 18

1. *Where can decent people . . . find a safe place to live:* Yes, they were saying it then, too.

2. *. . . a town called Fooltrap:* Collodi has *Acchiappa-citrulli,* "a trap for simpletons."

3. *. . . a Fox, a thieving Magpie:* Collodi uses these predatory creatures to symbolize the members of the upper classes of his time who, with the help of a corrupt police force and courts of law, preyed upon

the lower classes and kept them in a constant state of miserable poverty. The oppressed lower classes are symbolized, of course, by the "mangy dogs . . . sheep shorn of their wool . . . roosters who had lost their beautiful combs. . . ."

4. . . . *water the soil where you planted your money:* In Pinocchio's first encounter with the Fox and the Cat (chapter 12), the Fox not only recommended watering the soil where he planted his money, but also "sprinkling it with a little salt." The second phase of the technique seems to have slipped his mind here.

Chapter 19

1. *rosoli:* Rosoli, or *rosolio* as it is sometimes called, is a sweet, but strongly alcoholic cordial made in Italy and southern Europe from raisins and sugar. Other translators, apparently for fear of shocking the sensibilities of American parents, hedged and euphemized *rosoli* variously as "lemonade," "ice cream soda," and "root beer" although, mercifully, none of them went so far as "Coke" or "Pepsi."

Despite rumor and conviction to the contrary, well-bred Italians are not generally bibulous by nature. They drink wine more or less moderately with meals, and they serve whiskey, liqueurs, and cordials to visitors to be taken in only token amounts from tiny glasses (*bicchierini*) supplied by the host. On the other hand, Italian children, even in infancy, are given small amounts of wine—usually watered—as well as cordials which are savored as much for their sweet taste as anything, without the least suggestion or thought of immorality. It is not at all surprising, then, to find Pinocchio dreaming of having a "wine cellar filled with barrels of *rosoli*. . . ." any more than it would be surprising to find a little American boy dreaming of having a cellar full of cola drinks.

2. *alchermes:* In English, *alkermes,* derived from the French *kermes,* hence from Arabic, *al quirmiz,* and Persian *kerm,* a worm. Collodi here refers to a kind of exotic liqueur made from *kermes* which, for centuries, was thought to be a bright red berry that was harvested in enormous quantity from a species of evergreen oak in southern Europe and in northern Africa. Countless generations of Europeans smacked their lips over this delicious red brandylike drink until it was at last discovered that the pretty red berries—from which a brilliant red dye was also made—were actually the bodies of the pregnant female of the insect species, *Coccus illicis!*

3. . . . *those idiots:* Collodi has *quei barbagianni* (those owls). For a deeper insight into the true nature of the owl, see note 5, chapter 12, *We have to go to Boobyland.*

4. *the judge . . . turned out to be an ape of the gorilla family:* As it has already been observed, Collodi had slight respect for the local magistrate of his time. This one is an ape not by accident, but by design; he is doing in his own little court what his corrupt colleagues

were all doing in theirs. The gold-rimmed spectacles without lenses which he wore in a time when few could afford steel-rimmed glasses are a mark of opulent ostentation. The "eye trouble he had suffered for several years," of course, is the effect of his deliberate inability to see justice done in his court (see note 2, chapter 3).

5. . . . *two huge, ugly dogs . . . in the uniform of the* Carabinieri: Here the Carabinieri are represented in truly resentful Collodi style as "vicious dogs" (see note 2, chapter 3).

6. . . . *throw him in jail immediately:* Just as old Geppetto was marched off to jail (see note 2, chapter 3) for seeking to reclaim what rightfully belonged to him, *i.e.,* his puppet, poor Pinocchio is sent to prison for having denounced the criminals who stole his money.

7. *if you're a real criminal . . . that's the law:* Collodi continues to mock the outrageous legal process of his time in which the most reprehensible criminals were granted amnesty on the least pretext while those convicted of civil offenses were compelled to remain in prison. Now we find Pinocchio, "stir wise" from his four months in jail, summarily released for as absurd a reason as that for which he was committed in the first place.

Chapter 20

1. . . . *his legs were caught fast between two sharp irons:* This trap would seem to be a much larger and more powerful trap than would be needed to catch polecats. Collodi's description recalls the infamous "man-trap," a vicious contrivance used in Europe in the eighteenth and nineteenth centuries to trap poachers on private estates. Such a trap was capable of breaking a man's leg and holding him painfully and so securely that it would require the efforts of at least two strong men to release him.

2. *big polecats:* The reference is to the common polecat (*Mustela putorius*) which, because of its fetid odor, is also called the "foul marten." It is found generally in the woodlands of Eurasia and North Africa. It is a voracious animal which preys upon small mammals and any bird it can capture, especially poultry. It also eats eggs as well as lizards, snakes, fish, frogs, etc.

Chapter 21

1. *a little firefly:* The firefly or "lightning bug" is actually a small nocturnal beetle of the genus *Lampyridae* which emits a pale, intermittent light from the underside of its abdomen as it flies about, apparently aimlessly, on warm summer nights. As you might know, scientists have decided that this light has to do with sexual attraction when, all along, real people have known that its sole function is to attract five- and six-year-old children. Anyway, the luminescent creature known as the "glow-worm" is not a worm at all, but the wingless, and

more or less immobile, female of one species. The winged males of this species do not glow.

Chapter 22

1. *Melampo:* This may seem a strange name for a watchdog, even in Italian, and so it is. It is possible, however, that Collodi, as was often his way, had some oblique symbolism in mind, for *Melampo* is the Italian form of the Greek *Melampous.* In Greek mythology, Melampous was a great-grandson of Aeolus and a famous seer who, besides being able to predict the future, could understand and converse in the languages of all creatures. What Collodi may actually have had in mind, I shall not venture to guess. Knowing his love for the absurd, it is quite possible that he chose the name Melampo for the old dog for much the same reason that one might call a dog or a horse "Napoleon," or name a pet cat "Cleopatra."

2. *. . . serve you up for stewed rabbit:* In Pinocchio's time, just as now in rural America and Britain, thieving animals were punished even more harshly than thieving human beings. If this Tuscan farmer's punishment of the marauding polecats seems to you to be cruel and unfeeling, you are probably laboring under the conviction that none of God's creatures ever hurts any other creature: the "Bambi complex" visited upon generation after generation—yours included—by Walt Disney Studios. Make every effort to recover from this illusion in time to set your own kids straight on the fact that life is simply not all Bambi and Snow White.

3. *. . . we'll make you a present of a . . . young chicken:* Here, in spite of Pinocchio's pious reluctance to denounce the dead Melampo, he actually tips off the farmer as to what has really been going on.

Chapter 23

1. *Here lies the girl with the blue hair:* again the Collodi death-and-resurrection theme. The girl with the blue hair is patently dead and buried in this pathetic episode. Marvelously and happily she returns to Pinocchio and to us, as a mature woman in the next chapter.

2. *after he had slowly spelled out those terrible words:* You will recall—even if Collodi did not—that Pinocchio has not yet had a single day of schooling and not too long before this had to have the sign on the puppet theater read to him. On the other hand, it's quite possible that Collodi didn't really care about such a trivial matter; he had a story to tell. I recall noticing the evident discrepancy in my childhood experience of Pinocchio, but it certainly didn't upset me to the point of objecting.

3. *More than six hundred miles:* Like all Italian pigeons, this one exaggerates for dramatic effect! Taking the city of Poggibonsi as the approximate center of Tuscany, the shore of the Tyrrhenian Sea is only

fifty miles away, and the shore of the Adriatic Sea is not more than seventy miles off. Even a casual look at a map of Italy would indicate that it would be impossible in that peninsular country to be more than about 150 miles from a seashore.

Ah, but then one might argue that this Pigeon could have been referring to a flight from where they were in Tuscany to a shore point somewhere near, say, Bari, or even Otranto, to the southeast on the opposite coast. Even so, that would be a distance of a little more than 400 miles, and a journey to the southernmost beach in Italy, the Capo Isola di Correnti of Sicily, would be, as the Pigeon flies, about 500 miles.

4. . . . *fava beans:* These are a species of vetch, which genus has also provided a term which has vexed crossword puzzlers since about 1926. In any case, it is the "broad bean" or "horse bean" (*Vicia faba*) of Europe and Asia which has, since earliest times, been cultivated for animal fodder as well as for human consumption.

Also, surprisingly, since there are hundreds of varieties of edible beans to be found throughout the world today, the fava was the only edible bean known to the Old World before 1492.

5. *Hunger makes hard beans sweet:* Actually, Collodi had his Pigeon cite the Italian adage, *La fame non ha cappricci né ghiottonerie* (Hunger knows neither whim nor gluttony). This seemed a little ponderous, so I took the liberty of substituting a Middle English proverb which dates to about 1350, "Hungur makyth harde benes swete."

Chapter 24

1. *A Dolphin:* The common dolphin which often grows to a length of 8 feet (2.45 meters) is found in large numbers in the Mediterranean region. It is known in fact and in legend for its affinity for man, and the many tales of drowning sailors being rescued by friendly dolphins no doubt find their origin in the Greek myth of the poet Arion whose singing charmed a school of dolphins into carrying him safely to land after he had been thrown into the sea by a band of pirates who robbed him of his treasure.

2. . . . *too bad for them if they go hungry:* This sentiment, perhaps, will be as difficult to explain to your children as the idea of pauperism (see note 1, chapter 12). In the Italy of the nineteenth century and, indeed, much of the twentieth century, there was no such thing as "welfare," or "relief" as it was called in America during the Great Depression, nor was there unemployment compensation, food stamps, and the like. Poverty was a part of life among the Italian lower classes, and those who were "too old or sick" to work were forced into beggary to avoid destitution and, at last, starvation.

3. . . . *a lovely big plate of spaghetti with tomato sauce and grated cheese:* Collodi's "pretty young lady" promised Pinocchio *un bel piatto di cavolfiore condito coll'olio e coll'aceto* (a lovely dish of cauliflower

dressed with oil and vinegar)! Would your kid wash the car or mow the lawn for such a reward, even in the face of starvation?

Chapter 25

1. *. . . my great love . . . told me:* And besides, it is very unlikely that there were many nice little ladies in Tuscany at that time whose hair was blue.

Chapter 26

1. *. . . as he was walking to school:* I am sure you will have some explaining to do here. Children in Pinocchio's day actually *walked* to school . . . no school buses, and no mommies running the school shuttle with the wagon!

2. *I wonder if it could be the same shark:* This is also what Collodi wanted his young audience to wonder. Just as he has other key figures—Talking Cricket, Fox and Cat, the *Carabinieri*—appear intermittently and significantly throughout the story, so does he have the shark do the same; the first and second times by rumor and report and, at last in chapter 34, in the very flesh.

Chapter 27

1. *. . . like the Seven Deadly Sins:* (*Sette come i peccati mortali*) These sins, traditionally catalogued by the Christian Church as Pride, Covetousness, Lust, Envy, Gluttony, Anger (Ire), and Sloth ("Accidie," or spiritual torpor), are also referred to as the "capital" or "cardinal" sins.

The list is not of Biblical origin, but stems from the spiritual writings and prescriptions of such early Christian monastics and churchmen as the fourth century monk, John Cassian, the fifth century hermit of Monte Cassino, St. Benedict, and the sixth century "father of the medieval Papacy," St. Gregory the Great. The concept of the Seven Deadly Sins was then carried forth into the Middle Ages where it was at last forged into doctrine in the thirteenth century by St. Thomas Aquinas in his monumental *Summa Theologica*.

In the didactic appendix to a mid-twentieth century Douay Bible I discovered what would seem to be the modern Roman Catholic attitude toward the fatal catalogue. In his commentary, the editor observes that the "Seven Capital Sins" are not properly sins at all, "but rather *tendencies* in man's nature to sins of pride, covetousness, lust, etc. They are called *capital* because they are the fountainhead or source of other sins. The Christian life is always a struggle against these seven leanings or tendencies or inclinations to sinful acts. . . ." (Rev. John P. O'Connell, ed. *The Bible*. Chicago: The Catholic Press, Inc., 1950). In light of this definition, then, Pinocchio's epithet for his evil companions seems most apt.

2. *He . . . saw two* carabinieri *coming toward him:* Once again Pinocchio has a run-in with the Carabinieri. Note that they arrest him summarily on purely circumstantial evidence; they are trundling him off to jail simply because he did the humane thing by staying with his stricken schoolmate while the others, the truly guilty ones, ran off.

Chapter 28

1. *Alidoro:* This is another fanciful name for a domesticated animal (cf. *Melampo,* note 1, chapter 22). For what the information is worth, the name is derived from the Italian *ali d'oro,* literally "wings of gold" which, as a proper name, might be expressed as Goldenwings. Now that I think of it, this name for a dog is no more far-fetched than "Silverheels" which was the name of a Morgan mare I once knew.

2. *The Green Fisherman:* This bizarre character is certainly Collodi's invention, but he is also a caricature of the primitive *pescatori* of Italy who lived, from earliest times—until fairly recently—in caves and huts along the coast of the peninsula. Their sole occupation was fishing and, just as is the case with the Green Fisherman, they subsisted almost totally upon what they took from the sea.

In the fifteenth century, the delightful Neapolitan poet, Jacopo Sannazaro celebrated the lives, the loves, and the longings of those strange, lonely people in his "piscatory" eclogues, just as fifteen hundred years earlier, Virgil, a fellow Neapolitan (by choice) sang of the Italian shepherd and husbandman in his *Eclogues.*

3. *. . . it's always a comfort to get fried with friends:* Collodi has "*L'essere fritto in compagnia é sempre una consolazione*" (To be fried in company is always a consolation). However, I couldn't resist the license of translating this to a more raffish sense.

Chapter 29

1. *. . . they took all my clothes, too:* Of course you will have noted here that Pinocchio tells two more barefaced lies, but his nose doesn't grow longer again. This is the sort of Collodi oversight that seems greatly to disturb grownups but which upsets children not at all—or so they would have us believe.

2. *. . . the iron knocker suddenly turned into a live slippery eel:* Many doorknockers have this strange mutational faculty. Remember the one in *A Christmas Carol* that changed into the death-mask of Jacob Marley and frightened the Dickens out of Ebenezer Scrooge?

3. *hot chocolate with whipped cream:* Collodi has *caffé e latte* (coffee with milk). However, I was not allowed to drink coffee when I was Pinocchio's age. Naturally, then, when this was read to me, I was deeply shocked. However, I said nothing about the matter in the hope that the reference might educate my parents enough to repeal the prohibition. Needless to say, it did not.

Chapter 30

1. *Pinocchio sneaks off to Toyland:* Collodi himself called this enchanting country *paese dei Balocchi*, literally, land of Toys. Harden called it Playland, while Della Chiesa translated it directly as Land of Toys. Meanwhile, Murray called it the Land of Boobies which name I unconsciously adopted to describe the *paese dei Barbagianni* of chapter 12 (see note 5). I felt that Toyland had been done to death by everyone from Victor Herbert to Walt Disney, although to my surprise, I found that Disney actually called the place "Pleasure Island." Briefly I considered calling it "Funland." This, however, carried too much suggestion of carnivals and amusement parks and I ended up right where Collodi would have wanted me to and called it Toyland.

Chapter 31

1. *The boys all loved this jolly little coachman:* The jolly coachman is truly a Mephistophelian little devil. Lampwick and Pinocchio, in the spirit of Faustian self-indulgence, mortgage their souls to him in return for a life of indolent pleasure. As we discover in chapter 33, he is right there with his "jolly laugh" to foreclose.

2. *Lampwick snored like a dormouse:* The dormouse is a small squirrel-like animal of the Old World. Earlier, it was made famous by Lewis Carroll in his *Alice's Adventures in Wonderland* which was first published in 1865, twenty-five years before Pinocchio's birth. The dormouse is a nocturnal rodent, and it hibernates from fall to spring; therefore, it has earned its reputation for sleepiness from the fact that it has been most often discovered fast asleep! During a recent sojourn in the hills of Piedmont, my niece, Carla, whose English is generally flawless, told of having seen two "cute little *logs*" crossing the road the day before I arrived. It seems that in Italy, when one sleeps soundly, he sleeps like a dormouse (*dorme come un ghiro*) just as Lampwick does here. Italian–English dictionaries, however, translate *dormire come un ghiro* to its Anglo-American idiomatic equivalent, "to sleep like a *log*." Hence the amusing but understandable mistake.

3. *. . . the poor little animal was crying:* This is readily understandable for, it seems to me, having half of both one's ears bitten off would make anyone cry bitterly.

4. *He'll laugh on his wedding night:* I have asked questions and searched endlessly for a proverbial source of this expression and can conclude only that it is simply the kind of very Swiftian phrase of which Collodi was quite capable. It is possible, too, that it was a Tuscan regionalism of Collodi's time.

5. *Some were playing marbles:* Actually, the boys were playing *castelli di noci* (nut castles), an ancient Italian childhood game played in late summer and in autumn with *filberti* (filberts, or hazel nuts) in which sets of four nuts are topped with a single nut, thereby represent-

ing castles. An antagonist then tries to demolish each castle by throwing single nuts at it.

6. . . . *some were playing ducks and drakes:* An allusion to a child's game beloved of most adults in which flat stones are made to skip along the surface of a body of water. The resultant series of annular ripples is reminiscent of a drake followed in single file by a seraglio of ducks.

7. . . . *tricycles and bicycles:* Although the first practical bicycles (known also as velocipedes and "dandy horses") were developed in the early nineteenth century, it was not until 1865 that the first crank-driven bicycle was perfected. It was known in England as the "bone-shaker" or the "penny-farthing" and was equipped with a front wheel of huge diameter and a relatively tiny rear wheel. By the 1880s—Pinocchio's time—the front wheel of the bicycle had attained a diameter of well over five feet making it necessary for its rider to have quite long legs. The tricycle, then, constructed along the same general lines but considered safer, came to be preferred by women and by men of shorter stature.

8. . . . *riding wooden hobbyhorses . . . and marched up and down with squads of cardboard soldiers:* For an even more graphic overview of this riotous scene in Toyland, look up a print of *The Games of Childhood*, a wonderful work of the sixteenth-century Flemish painter, Pieter Brueghel the Elder (?1525–1569).

Chapter 32

1. . . . *his ears had grown:* You will recall from chapter 3 that Geppetto tried to pull Pinocchio's ears to punish him, but he "couldn't find any ears to pull" because he had forgotten to carve them. No matter! See Collodi's facile explanation of this phenomenon in the following paragraph.

Chapter 33

1. *Whatever happened to poor Lampwick, I can't say:* But he does say in chapter 36 when he describes his demise as an exhausted farm donkey driven to death on the *bindolo,* a kind of treadmill waterwheel.

2. *He was brilliantly decked out for the occasion:* Considering the fact that the donkey has been the animal drudge in Italy, the Levant, and in what we now know as the Middle East since time beyond recall, Pinocchio as a donkey had to be spectacularly brilliant and clever enough to appeal to a circus audience to whom the ordinary donkey was a commonplace sight on any country road or city street.

3. *Twenty* lire . . . *twenty* soldi *for him:* The basic Italian monetary unit is the *lira* (plural, *lire*) which is equal to 100 *centesimi*. A second coin division of the lira is the *soldo* (plural, *soldi*), equal to five centesimi, or one-twentieth of a lira, just as the United States nickel is one-twentieth of a dollar. Both the *centesimo* and the soldo have,

except in theory, long since disappeared with the gross inflation of the lira since World War II.

It has been very difficult to determine the relative value of lire and soldi in the 1880s, but it may help to know that, in Pinocchio's time, a graduate engineer began his career with a salary of slightly less than 100 lire a month, and an annual salary of 1,800 lire was considered a princely income. A full-course dinner at a restaurant—and you know those Italian dinners!—could be had for about ten soldi including service; a liter of good wine was perhaps two soldi extra.

Reckoned by the present purchasing power of the lira, the twenty lire the ringmaster asked for his lame donkey would amount to something like 100,000 lire today, and the twenty soldi for which Pinocchio was finally sold to the donkey trader would therefore amount to about 5,000 lire. It need hardly be mentioned that, in the Italy of today, not a single thing can be purchased for one lira.

4. . . . *I only want him for his skin:* Collodi did not represent this man as particularly reprehensible or cruel. He was the honest practitioner of a trade in which superannuated or disabled work animals were bought, slaughtered, and their remains converted to other practical use. In fact, in the next chapter when the tables are turned on Pinocchio's buyer, Collodi refers to him variously as *il povero uomo* (the poor man), *quel buon pasticcione* (that poor bungler), and finally *il povero compratore* (the poor buyer). The vocation of this nineteenth-century donkey buyer was surely no less admirable than that of his Anglo-American counterpart, the knacker, who buys up aged draft horses—and even old race horses—to send them to what is cynically called the "glue factory." Nor could he have held a candle to the marauders of the American southwest who ruthlessly hunt down mustangs to be slaughtered and ground into "pet food."

Chapter 34

1. . . . *he is swallowed up by a terrible Shark:* According to Collodi, this enormous fish which swallowed Pinocchio, as well as old Geppetto and other things of considerable size, was in fact a shark (*Pesce-cane*, which literally means "dog-fish," but which is the generic Italian name for the shark). Murray saw fit to translate *Pesce-cane* directly as "Dog-fish," while Della Chiesa and Harden have it simply as "the terrible shark," and it is the example of these last which I have followed here. The Disney adapters, for reasons all their own, chose to represent their sea-monster as a whale which they even endowed with an engaging name: "Monstro." I think, however, that all children—and even some grownups—know by this time that whales are the real heroes and heroines of the deep, and that the shark is the true monster.

2. . . . *the good Saint Anthony:* No mention of St. Anthony was made by Della Chiesa, Murray, or Harden in their translations. It may

be reasonably assumed that the Collodi reference is to St. Anthony of Padua to whom devout Italians appeal for help in finding lost articles. However, there is nothing in the history of that good man to suggest that he ever wrought punishment upon sinners by turning them into donkeys. Once again, Collodi appears to have been indulging in whimsy.

3. . . . *the good Fairy . . . sent a huge school of fish . . . and they began to eat me:* This seems to have been the good Fairy's favorite means of metamorphosis. You may recall the remarkable but similar method she employed to restore Pinocchio's nose to its original size after he had lied it to elephantine length (chapter 18).

4. . . . *gusts of wind were coming from the shark's lungs:* The image here certainly suits Collodi's whimsical purpose, but any alumnus of Rutgers Preparatory School (Established 1766), class of 1937, knows full well that the shark does not have lungs. In his biology course at that hallowed academy Mr. Rudy, for some reason now lost to memory, required us to submit detailed drawings of the shark and his inwards which specifically drew attention to the fact that this sinister fish has gills—rudimentary, to be sure, but gills they are—and not the lungs of the dolphin or the whale. Moreover, Mr. Rudy drummed into our reluctant brains that the shark is an *elasmobranch* [<New Latin, "plate-gilled ones" <*elasmo*, plate + -*branchia*, gills].

5. . . . *wait for the Shark to digest us:* It would certainly have been a slow digestive process for we find Pinocchio, in the next chapter, discovering old Geppetto in the shark's belly. Geppetto has been there for two years by his own accounting with, as yet, no sign of having been digested and assimilated (this last is a Rudy-taught term).

Chapter 35

1. . . . *he felt as if it was the middle of Lent:* (omitted by Murray and Harden). The observance of the Lenten fast was particularly strict in Italy in Pinocchio's day. Lent, of course, begins on Ash Wednesday (*Mercoledi delle Ceneri*), forty weekdays before Easter Sunday (*Pasqua*), and formerly, during those eight weeks, the eating of meat was forbidden. Consequently, extraordinary quantities of fish were prepared and consumed, and the odor of fish, cooked and uncooked, pervaded every Italian village at the height of the Lenten season, making this figure a very apt one.

2. . . . *you've already forgiven me, haven't you:* Ah, the innocent presumption of childhood! If your own child's wanton behavior had reduced you to a miserable, candle-lit existence in the smelly belly of a shark for two years would your forgiveness be so spontaneous?

3. *Lucky for me . . . :* Lucky indeed! "With this great bounty of the good Lord," old Geppetto has enjoyed two years of luxury the like of which he had never experienced in his whole miserable, impoverished life.

4. . . . *we all have to die sometime:* Murray and Harden both carefully circumvented this reference to death, apparently to avoid what they considered a subject possibly offensive to children. But what do kids know about—or care about—such an abstraction as death? Such grim concern is left to adulthood, which province, however, you unfortunately now occupy.

5. . . . *follow me . . . and don't be afraid:* Note here that Pinocchio has finally come to manhood. From this point to the end of the story, he is in charge of all matters.

Chapter 36

1. *The poor Tuna . . . to hide his embarrassment . . . plunged under the water and disappeared:* Compare the behavior of the embarrassed Tuna with that of the obliging Pigeon (chapter 23) which, after having borne Pinocchio "six hundred miles" to the seashore to find his father, shyly "flew away and disappeared into the clouds" to avoid being thanked.

2. *Stolen money doesn't bear interest:* Pinocchio here begins to cite a series of three proverbs in his bitter revilement of his old enemies, the Fox and the Cat. The first of these is *I quattrini rubati non fanno mai frutto* (stolen money never bears fruit, i.e., never brings a profit). The closest English parallel to this dates to the early seventeenth century: "Stolen goods never thrive."

The second proverb Pinocchio cites is "The Devil's flour all turns to bran." This is a literal translation of *La farina del diavolo va tutta in crusca.* A similar proverb occurs in English as early as 1592 as "The Devil's meal is all (half) bran." This has been interpreted by a somewhat righteous nineteenth-century editor to mean ". . . unrighteous gains are sure to disappoint the getter."

The third and last proverb Pinocchio cites is "Whoever steals his neighbor's coat, usually dies without a shirt," which may be read in Italian as *Chi ruba il mantello al suo prossimo, per il solito muore senza camicia.* There appears to be no direct equivalent of this proverb in English, although one can be sure that the moment this statement is published, a veritable horde of readers with sententious ancestors will report having heard grandparents recite the very same adage, word for word.

3. . . . *the poor little animal was worn out from hunger and ill-treatment:* Sad to say, this poor little animal was only one of countless donkeys, mules, and oxen that were driven to death not only on the *bindolo* but on other similar contrivances designed for grinding grain or for crushing olives for their oil. Most often these torturous engines were located in dark cellars or caves where the animal was unable to see that he was being driven in an endless circle. Where the machine was located out-of-doors, the animal's sight was cut off by means of a blindfold or, more barbarously, by outright blinding. In any case, these

miserable beasts were goaded, beaten, and driven day in and day out at this cruel labor until finally, like this little donkey, they dropped in their tracks.

4. . . . *an Easter holiday*: Actually, Collodi has *una pasqua di rose*, "Rose" Easter or, perhaps, "Rose Sunday." This corresponds with Whitsunday, or Pentecost, the seventh Sunday after Easter, which in Italy is as festive as Easter itself.